DEEP SAHARA

Not your typical Zombie
Apocalypse

by
Mike Maykin

Published by Mike Maykin

DEEP SAHARA

Published by Mike Maykin, Brisbane, Australia
mikemaykin@outlook.com

Other books by Mike Maykin

The Dark Earth series -
> Book 1 'Nightfall'
> Book 2 'The Rise of Sol'
> Book 3 'Emissaries'
> Book 4 'Almost Human' (coming soon)

> Ophelia Series -
> Book 1 'Lavender Cottage'
> Book 2 'The Land of Frankincense'

CONTENTS

CHAPTER 1

"Scorpions", he said as he shook and then patted down the sleeping bag.

"Have you checked for scorpions?" Rudy asked.

"Yes. I'm good, for now," she said.

"The little buggers get into everything. There were two in my boots this morning, death stalkers, I almost put my foot in and got stung," he grumbled.

"Yeah, gotta be careful, although it's snakes that give me the creeps, vipers especially; they hide in the sand and they're just so fast, by the time you see them, it's too late," she said.

"Have you ever been bitten?" he asked.

"Yeah, I have actually," Danielle said as she looked into the distance. "One time when I was in Morocco, in the Atlas Mountains. I got bitten on the leg and was lucky they got me out and back to a clinic in time. That was a painful few hours. So yes, you can keep the snakes. I'd rather have the scorpions and just go through the shake-down routine each morning and night."

"What were you doing in the Atlas Mountains?" he enquired.

"We were doing vaccinations. It was my first mission in North Africa, so I was a bit green and foolish," she said with a chuckle. Then she said, "Later," and left him to organize his own bedding as she wandered back to the campfire.

The dinner of fresh baked flatbread, dunked in goat and tomato stew, was finished and cleared away. The tour operators were very efficient as they silently went about their business, wearing their indigo and black robes, and mumbling to each other through their veils in Tamasheq, their Tuareg Berber language. She sat on the rug and reclined back on her elbows looking up at the impossible clarity of the Saharan night sky. The aptly crescent moon looked so close. She felt that if she climbed a nearby rocky pillar, she could touch it. However, before she could fully lose herself in the moment, one of the other tourists sat down next to her.

"Hi, sorry to bother you, but can I get you to have a look at something, if that is OK?"

"Sure, what's up?" Danielle asked.

The lady pulled up the bottom of her cargo pants to reveal a rather nasty abrasion.

Danielle got out her torch and shone it on the wound, and then she said, "Oh dear, how did you do that?"

The lady, whose name was Sophie, said, "I tripped over this morning and grazed it on a rock. I didn't think much of it at the time, but then after riding the camel all day, it must have rubbed and got worse. Do you think you could clean it up and put bandages on it? I figure if I don't get it sorted now, it's going to get worse."

"Yes, it needs to be addressed," Danielle said. "Don't worry, I should be able to patch it up. I'll just go to my tent and get the medical pack."

She went over to her small tent. She was the only tourist who did not share, which was fine by her. She grabbed the pack, returned to the light of the fire, and performed her modern magic. As she dabbed at the wound she said, "Don't worry, it'll just feel like a scratch." It is what she always said to patients, be it a tiny needle, a huge canular, or re-setting a broken bone.

Danielle had recently graduated as a medical doctor in the UK. After a couple of years internship, she volunteered with Médecins Sans Frontières (MSF) in North Africa. With her commission now finished, she was doing a camel trek deep into the Sahara. It was the last chance to experience the wonders of the desert before tying herself to the UK National Health Service, and a grey domestic life in Northeast England.

Of course, she was doing this travel completely in the face of the UK Foreign, Commonwealth & Development Office (FCDO) travel warning advice; especially pertinent for remote and border regions where there was the risk of terrorism and kidnapping. Indeed Djanet, in Southeast Algeria, the town they had just left, was listed as a kidnapping hotspot. But she had done it before, travelling to Wadi Sura in Libya and seeing the Cave of Swimmers. Although, that trip was done with vehicles during the winter months, this was now camels in the summer.

It was around 40°C during the day, and 25°C at night, and it was extremely dry. The caravan consisted of five tourists, two guides, and twelve camels. It was small compared to other expeditions, but being summer, the tourist numbers had dropped right off, with only the most rugged and foolhardy up for the challenge. For Danielle it was more a case of fitting it in when she could. She was not what you would call a thrill seeker or glutton for punishment, despite outward appearances.

She had flown from Algiers to the UNESCO listed city of Ghadames; where Libya, Tunisia, and Algeria meet. She had explored the old part of Ghadames, with its under-house enclosed streets, its Roman, Arabic, and Ottoman architecture, and its revitalizing springs and ancient bathing pools. It was a place where one could experience life going back to the 4th millennium BC and explore the nearby ruins of the Roman garrison of Cydemus. It was in Ghadames that she had met Rudy as he admired the stone and mud-crafted multi-story buildings.

Rudy was a recent graduate in architecture from Germany. He was taking a gap year before starting work for a large consulting firm in Amsterdam. Rudy was a couple of years younger than Danielle but had buddied up with her as they travelled. There was no romantic interest, at least for her part. He was a fun and free spirit who had travelled extensively and was full of stories. But in other ways he was quite regimented and inflexible in his behavior, bordering on OCD, a trait sometimes attributed to Northern Europeans. That part of his character would drive her insane. So as attractive as he was, with his deep blue Nordic eyes, and tousled blonde hair, she recognized he wasn't the man for her. There was another, however, that piqued her interest, although so far he had kept to himself. Not that she was really looking for someone, not yet anyway.

From Ghadames, Danielle and Rudy took a 12-hour bus journey to Djanet, 900km South, and deeper into the furnace and desiccation of the Sahara. The scale of everything was just mind blowing. Algeria was ten time the size of the United Kingdom. Heck, the whole of the United States could fit inside the Sahara, with a push and a squeeze. One does not think of the Sahara as mountainous and rocky; it is the sand that gets all of the publicity, even though it accounts for less than a quarter of the land surface. However, even where it's rocky and mountainous, the sand and dust still get into every crack and crevasse.

They travelled through the Tassili N'Ajjer rocky plateau and stopped briefly at the prehistoric Tin Taghirt rock art galleries and shelters. Fortunately, the road was paved, but still they arrived in Djanet exhausted and well after dark. The bus had air conditioning, but it barely worked. It was not quite as hot inside the bus as it was outside, but it was still too hot to be pleasant, and due to sweat, everyone smelled and was brittle with dust by the end of the journey.

Djanet was situated in a valley within the Tassili N'Ajjer mountain range. It was a mystical and romantic city of 15,000 people, founded by the Tuareg some 500 years ago, now with ruined hill forts and tranquil oasis. From some angles, and in some courtyards, it seemed that time had stood still. A stop for caravans in the past, it was now a staging post for exploring the rock art and engravings left by the far more ancient inhabitants of the region; those ancient people who live here back in the Neolithic, some ten thousand years ago when that land was wet and lush.

From Djanet they travelled in pickup trucks a further 140km Southeast to Panneau d'entrée de la Tadrart. Then it was a further two days camel trek through the scorching Sahara lowlands, and then over mountain passes, canyons, and hidden valleys, to reach their current site in the Tadrart

Rouge, the red desert. As at previous sites, the art documented the wet and dry phases of the Sahara, and the progress of humans from hunter gatherers to herders and then farmers. This was a continuous story in pictures of climatic, geographic, and human evolution that covered the past ten thousand years. It was something she just had to see before returning to cold wet of England.

They had just finished their second day and were camped amongst the bright red sand, punctured by dark stone pillars. The deep brown through to black mountains that surrounded them, shaped by wind into impossible spires and stacks, stored the heat during the day and radiated it back at them through the night. Sure, the Sahara got freezing at night, but not here during these few months. One was never cool or refreshed unless diving into the waters of an oasis, the sustainers of life.

They all had sleeping bags just in case, but really, they were only used as mattresses over the rugs. Hence, home was sand, rug, sleeping bag, then tent, in that order. Danielle really wished she had packed a light-weight stretcher, like others had thought to do. It would have kept her off the ground and away from the scorpions and creepy crawlies, although it still would not be high enough to avoid snakes.

They would spend tomorrow exploring and then continue on a two-day circuit that would bring them back to the road, to their vehicles, and then ultimately to civilization. And never a truer reference to Djanet could be made. For once they left the buildings, services, and the roads, there was absolutely nothing to suggest that humans inhabited this planet. So barren and lifeless was the landscape that it was hard to imagine anything able to live out here, and yet it did. It was hidden away in the cracks and crevasses of the mountains. Some deep valleys harbored pools of water supporting marooned stands of palms, remnants of climates and ecosystems of times long past.

Throughout the night most of the tourists had disturbed sleep, including Danielle. Camels were kept close to the camp, and they were noisy. But one cannot reason with a camel, although maybe the Tuareg could and did. They were too valuable, and essential for survival, to be tethered too far away. The Tuareg were used to it, and probably they slept because of the noise of the camels, rather than despite it. If there was no noise, then that would mean the camels had escaped or had been stolen. That would mean death to the travelers of the sands.

Dawn was short, given they were on the Tropic of Cancer, and at its zenith the midday sun was directly overhead. Before the sun had broken the horizon Danielle had gone to the nearby seep, with its reeds and mosquitoes, to wash the best she could in her shorts and singlet. The Tuareg were very respectful toward the women, and presumably also the other two men on the trek. She met the other two women at the seep; the men had designated a 15-minute window for the women to use the small canyon for washing and toilet.

Sophie's leg was looking better, and after being washed, Danielle disinfected and bandaged it again. The other woman was called Bernie, a forty-something journalist. She was working on a writing project, but even she wasn't quite sure what it was. She said that she needed to experience the Sahara, and its people, to write a series of articles relating to the politics of North Africa. It was a complex topic, and with the nomadic Tuareg woven into the tapestry of several countries, and with all of those countries experiencing internal and external conflict, as well as Western and corporate meddling, no one's future was clear.

When their time was up, they returned to the camp. They would be staying at this site for the full day and then ride the camels tomorrow along a scenic route back to the main road. Breakfast for the Tuareg was typically sweet tea, however, for their Western guests, they provided bread and oil left over from the night before. There was also a selection of muesli bars that had been bulk purchased in Algiers and freighted to Djanet. It was rather odd to see the plastic packaged modern food in such an ancient and natural setting.

The final member of the tour group was Sebastian. When Danielle first met him, he introduced himself as a French Canadian from Quebec. He was fluent in Québécois, being a region-specific Canadian French, but was still able to communicate with the guides better than anyone else in the party. He also spoke perfect Canadian English, which sometimes made Danielle giggle to herself when she reckoned it against her aplomb, albeit Yorkshire, English.

She could see him sitting in the distance, where he had climbed up onto a rocky outcrop. He had with him his camera and sketch pad. She remembered him saying he was some kind of artist, visual artist she assumed, and he took a lot of pictures. Presumably, they would be as a reference for when he got back to his studio and put brush to canvas. Sophie had instantly taken a shine to him, but from what Danielle could see, although he was friendly, he kept Sophie at a physical and emotional distance.

Sophie was ready to settle down. She was in her early thirties, and like Danielle she was from the UK, a Londoner that worked in something to do with accounting. She was short and stocky with a bit of a friendly pudding face and homely bottom. She would make someone a good wife, being cheerful and dependable, but to imagine her and Sebastian together was to imagine mixing oil and water. Yet still Sophie tried, and you had to give her credit for her optimism and persistence. Rudy would have probably been a better fit, although the age difference and his supposed 'master race' looks and attitude, probably made her a non-starter.

Bernie, being divorced, had nudged Danielle on the first day when Sebastian was lifting something heavy, and glistened with sweat on muscles, saying, "I wouldn't mind a bit of that."

So given the chance Bernie would probably take the opportunity if it presented itself, but yet neither was Bernie the type of person to openly fawn and promenade. She was too proud, and self-assured, for that. Instead, like the good witch, she would stir the pot and see who or what the brew affected.

They were about thirty minutes away from the first hike of the morning, so Danielle decided she would go for a stroll, and a climb, to experience what Sebastian saw and recorded. She had walked about twenty meters before Sophie called out, "Wait, wait for me, I'll come with you."

Danielle slowed her pace whilst Sophie jogged up to her. For a stout person she was surprisingly fleet of foot, injury and all, perhaps more the gymnast than the ballerina. She was also a very in-your space and tactile person. As she walked alongside Danielle, she linked arms and began to tell her of how she slept and the dreams that she had. It was a less common behavior amongst the British, outside of the family and especially between almost strangers, than it may have been for those closer to the Mediterranean. Maybe the overt bonding served dual purposes, like keeping your friends close and your enemies, or rivals, closer.

CHAPTER 2

It was a short climb to where Sebastian had positioned himself. As the sunlight slowly crept down the nearby walls, it made for a lovely view of the camp and the valley. The sirocco wind had not yet started, so it was still, and probably 25°C. As the sunlight hit them, they could feel its power, and within an hour or two the air would be into the high thirties.

His professional SLR camera was next to him on a small tripod, and in his hands were a sketchpad and pencil. He looked over at the women as they approached, and then back at the landscape.

"Good morning," he said, whilst continuing with his work.

"Good morning," they said in unison, then Sophie continued, "What are you doing?"

Sometimes when people are trying to be sociable they ask the most ridiculous questions. Then again, maybe it was rhetorical, because it was obvious to all concerned that he was sketching the hidden valley. Perhaps it would form the basis of a watercolor, and he would use photographs to remind him of the colors once he was back in his studio. Something that would transport him back to this moment even when it was the dead of night, or a busy Monday morning in Montreal, or wherever it was that he lived.

"Just sketching," he said, "Trying to get my eyes and hands in. I'm a bit out of practice with landscapes."

"Oh...," said Sophie, "what, do you normally do, portraits?"

"Sometimes," he said, still not looking over at them. "Most of the time it is still life and abstract city structures, like part of a bridge, or a bird on the pavement. It's a bit hard to describe. It's whatever takes my fancy in the moment."

"Are we disturbing you. Would you like us to keep walking so you can finish your work?" Danielle asked.

"No, it's fine. I'm almost finished. I wanted to capture the contrasts of the sunrise, and I think I have done that."

"Can I see?" Sophie asked enthusiastically.

"Sure," he said as he almost tossed the pad to her, as if it was something of little value, like the sports section of the newspaper. She greedily caught it and neatly arranged the pages whilst making noises and expressions to show her approval and express her wonder at his skill.

She held them up as if she owned them, showing them to Danielle, but not allowing her to take possession of the sketchpad. She then leafed through other pages and in turn held them up so that Danielle could see them.

"These are very good," Danielle said. "Do you display or sell your work?"

"Sometimes," he said rather wistfully, "but not for enough money to make a living from it."

"I'm surprised to hear that, but then I don't know much about the art business," she said.

Not to recede into the background Sophie said, "They are fantastic, I'd buy one. Do you have a website, and like sell your pictures online?"

Of course, there was no phone reception where they were, so there was no way to peruse or stalk. That would have to wait until they got back to Djanet, and even then it would be limited, intermittent, and expensive.

"Yeah, I've got an agent who does all of that." Then he chuckled to himself and said, "And it makes just about enough money to pay his fees."

"So how do you get by then, if that is not too personal to ask?" Danielle asked.

"Oh, you know, barista and waiting work, some odd jobs and commissions. So, I thought I would save up to pay for this trip. Get out here to photograph and paint new scenes; I'm hoping there is a market back home. Especially with people wanting to escape the Canadian winter."

A struggling artist. That really wasn't very high on Danielle's list of traits she was looking for in a man. All the same, he *was* physically attractive. He had dark wavey hair, the beginnings of a beard from just the past few days, and the most gorgeous smile. Unfortunately, he didn't smile anywhere near enough. So not only was he a struggling artist, but he was also probably one of those tormented ones. Oh, how so Van Gough of him; he probably wrote songs and poetry is spare time.

But how perfect that would be for Sophie. With her business and accounting skills, she could probably support and even promote him. She would adore him and soak up his ambience, and the excitement of the circles he moved within. If only he could love her. But from what Danielle could see, that was not likely to happen. He showed little interest in Sophie, and to be honest, very little interest in anyone else. Maybe there was some dark mystery in his life. A wounded heart that may or may not heal with time. Sophie was probably the best medicine for that, but then once he had recovered, he would fly away like a majestic eagle with a mended wing.

Sebastian packed his materials into an elegant leather satchel; something befitting a serious artist, and then they headed back to the camp. The climb back down the outcrop was awkward, and he surprise both of the women by being unexpectedly gentlemen-like, assisting each of them, one after the other. Holding their hands as they stretched from one step-down to the next. Some people can have characteristics that surprise you. Maybe he had gone to a fine arts school, the Sorbonne in Paris perhaps, and maybe he had degrees in philosophy or literature; one could only fantasize, and Danielle did.

The camels would be resting today. Not that they had been overworked or anything like that. It's just that it wasn't worth the effort of loading and attempting to drive them to some of the more difficult to reach places they would see today. So instead, the tourists would be hiking and carrying upon their person that which would have been on the camels, such as water and food.

One of the Tuareg would remain with the camels whilst the other would be their guide for the day. Although Danielle had put her trust in these guides, indeed all of their lives depended upon them, she was still apprehensive to be separating from the camels and the rest of their luggage. It would be all too easy for their hosts to desert them. The only consolation was that the tourists, especially the women, were worth far more alive as hostages, slaves, or brides, than they would be as desiccated corpses buried by the shifting sands.

It was a long hot day, but fortunately there was shade, and small seeps and springs amongst the overhangs and deep canyons. The rock art was extraordinary, and rather special due to its remoteness and inaccessibility. Very few people ventured this far into the Sahara, and into bandit territory, to see such things. It was certainly a feather in her cap, and a collection of memories that would stay with her when cold and housebound during winter.

Rudy stayed close to Danielle. It seemed he was always there when she turned around. In contrast Bernie was happy to wander off by herself, not needing to be sociable. In that way she was like Sebastian, self-sufficient and content with her own company. And then there was Sophie, always around someone, and always talking. It was as if her existence depended on her interactions with others, and especially with Sebastian. He neither seemed bothered nor content with her presence. Instead, he just took pictures, and every now and then that would include one or more of the group. Perhaps for scale, and perhaps for the juxtaposition of the ancient and the contemporary, the living and the long dead. Digital photography was wonderful, with thousands of pictures stored on tiny little cards. He would have enough high-quality pictures for prints and coffee table books, if that is what he chose to do. These would be things that she just might purchase if she saw them in a bookshop or gallery.

They returned to the camp relieved to find it as they had left it. In the immediate vicinity there was very little wood to be found, even though some thorny shrubs grew in the dry river course. The area must have been picked clean over the decades and centuries. Who knew how old these stunted trees were. For this reason, the Tuareg made only small fires, in stone bounded pits, using bags of 21st century compressed charcoal briquettes, and only now and then throw a small dry piece of wood on top to produce a flame for light. There were also a couple of battery powered LED lights over by the tents, so people didn't lose their way in the dark.

Their guides did not often speak in a soft and friendly way, even to the women. They seemed to be hard men. Instead, it would either be camel riding instructions, or it would be to point out, but without explanation, the artwork they had been contracted to show the tourists. But on this evening, they were more friendly and talkative; for what reason Danielle did not know. There the group sat in a circle around the coals. The Tuareg sat cross-legged on the rug, with their ceremonial, and probably very functional, daggers at their waists, they also sported amulets and sacred objects that held verses from the Quran. A couple of large plates of goat and rice were shared around, with each person being sure to eat with their right hand, followed by burps of satisfaction.

The Tuareg lit up their pipes and began to recount stories of ancient battles, feats of great bravery, and of the interventions, and sometimes wickedness, of the many djinns. These spirits were an indispensable part of Sahara lore, lurking in the dark, the isolation, and traveling on the wind. Modern technology usually protects people from the dark and the fear of the other. But naked and alone in the Sahara, one could not help but develop a rapport and profound regard for the imagined, or real spirits, that were all around, both day and night. Like traditional Inuit on the ice, with their rich tradition of supernatural beings, so too were the Tuareg on the desert sand.

There was movement this night. Although they were somewhat sheltered in the valley, the dry wind caused the tents to flap, and it kept the camels on edge. The tiny sparks from the fire were mesmerizing; little fireflies that flew into the dark and then disappeared. The Tuareg slept on the ground between the fire and the camels. Sophie and Bernie shared a tent, and normally Sebastion and Rudy shared a tent, although on this night Sebastian remained alone by the fire, and Danielle had her own tent to herself.

She retired when the others did, and as she lay in her tent, she could see through the flaps Sebastian sitting and looking into the coals. Was he enjoying his alone time, or was he ruminating on troubles that robbed him of sleep? She figured it probably wouldn't be long before Sophie saw him sitting there and miraculously found that sleep also alluded her. However, she reckoned that Sophie would have better luck if she just went into Rudy's tent and said she wanted someone to cuddle up with. He'd likely oblige with no strings attached and no guilt in the morning. He was the type of guy that would share a sauna or spa, in the buff, with any gender, so proud he probably was of his body.

Danielle fell asleep not knowing the answers to the comings and goings of the night, be they the djinns on the wind, or the frail passions of the wicked and wanting humans. She woke at 2AM from an exceptional gust that carried with it dust and sand that peppered her face. They hoped that they would not encounter a sandstorm. Although in the valley it wouldn't be as bad as being caught out in the open lowlands. Still, it would be an inconvenience and may trap them for a couple of days.

She got up, and after shaking them, put on her boots. The waxing crescent moon was still in the sky, and a few glowing coals revealed there was still life in the fire. She turned on her small lamp. It wasn't much more than a book light and did not throw a beam. However, even with that feeble light she could see that Sebastian had fallen asleep on the rug near the fire, that the Tuareg slept near the camels, and the others were in their respective tents. Needing constant hydration, she had drunk several glasses of tea during the evening. Now she needed to go to the toilet, somewhere down wind and out of sight if she wanted to keep the light on.

She walked toward the opposite side of the camp from the camels and Tuareg, not wanting to stir them. Occasionally a spark from the fire whizzed past and then blinked out. She remembered a rocky outcrop not far away and figured she could just squat in its lee. The sand was alive with movement. It seemed that night revealed the real Sahara. Not the baked brightness of the day, but the cooler night when life sprang forth from the sand. In just the short distance she had travelled she saw scorpions and spiders. There were also the tracks left by small mammals and even a snake. She hoped that nothing would surprise her when her pants were around her ankles.

From her hide behind the rocks she could hear the wind blowing though the stone peaks to the side and above her. At times it howled and was frightening. She felt extremely vulnerable, like there were spirits that watched her. She felt she had to be ever vigil, or they would enter through her mouth, and take over her soul. She wouldn't see them coming, she couldn't see how close they were getting. All around she was surrounded by the noisy stirring dark, so she kept her mouth closed tightly. She understood now why the Tuareg men wore their veils.

Having finished her pee, she began to walk back to the camp, very briskly. Yet she walked in such a way that if she were observed, it wouldn't look like she was panicked, but instead like an Olympic walker. How peculiar was that to maintain one's composure even though one was in the dark and completely alone. Perhaps she did it to fool the spirits, so they were not emboldened by her fear, so that they kept their distance because this one was a lively one and not ready to be taken.

She got back to her tent and felt strangely comforted to have a piece of flimsy cloth between herself and the night. It was too hot to get into the sleeping bag, or to hide under a sheet even if she had one. So, she lay there, taking comfort in the fact that the beasts, and spirits, and scorpions, would go for the easy pickings first, like those sleeping outside. The only salvation from her imagination was to fall back to sleep. Somehow those that slept were protected from the dangers of the night.

CHAPTER 3

Danielle was woken by Sophie and Bernie peering in through the entrance to her tent. It was girl time down at the small pool, or puddle to be more precises, and they were telling her to get a move on lest she miss out. The group would be breaking camp early for the two-day trek back to the vehicles. As she walked with them, she spied the rock outcrop that she had visited in the early hours of the morning. It was not as far away from the camp as she had remembered; it seemed so much further in the dark. However, she noticed that her footprints had been swept away by the wind during the night. It was as if she was never there. Now it was only a moment that existed in her memory, so significant to her at the time, and yet so insignificant in the vastness of the desert and in time.

Apparently, Sophie and Bernie had slept solid throughout the night, unaware of the windstorm that blew through. Hence, Danielle also surmised that Sebastian would have slept undisturbed, at least not by the women. And Rudy, he always seemed to sleep well, like a light that switched off at the same time every night.

The guides had prepared a light breakfast as

was their adapted custom for dealing with the Westerners. This morning there was a choice between sweet tea and coffee, and then a muesli bar. Obviously, they had been holding out on them, if she had only known they had coffee in the supplies earlier, she would have asked for it.

Sophie was already sitting next to Sebastion, being the best flower that she could be in the morning sun, but it seemed that Sebastion was a bee that just wouldn't land. It was one wish too far for her. Danielle sat in the circle of people, and looking at Sebastion she said, "I noticed you stayed out by the fire last night. I got up at 2AM and you were still there, but you were sleeping."

"Yes, it was so peaceful, and the coals so mesmerizing, that I just lay there until I fell asleep. If it is good enough for the Tuareg, then it's good enough for me," he said in a matter-of-fact way.

Sophie chimed in, "Were you deep in thought? I do that sometimes when I've got lots on my mind."

"Yeah, maybe," he said. "There is always something to think about. When I came out here, I was supposed to be leaving all that behind and getting a fresh perspective on things...," he tapered off and took a bite of his bread.

"Did you notice the wind last night?" Danielle asked.

"Yes, it was enchanting, like magic was carried

on it," he said.

One of the Tuareg spoke up, "Like the dust it brings, it also stirs the spirits of the desert. They watch and they tempt the traveler who wanders too far from the fire."

"That is how it felt to me," Danielle said wide eyed.

"I saw you last night," Sebastian said, as if it was something insignificant.

"Really! I thought you said you were asleep," she said with surprise.

"Apparently not at that time. It was actually more like a dream. I remember your light, and it disappeared into the night and then returned a bit later," he said.

She was a bit embarrassed and said, "Oh, I just went over there for a pee," as she pointed vaguely toward the rocks.

The Tuareg mumbled to each other and then one said, "That was very brave to go alone. Maybe next time you should wake someone so they can watch over you."

She smiled and said, "Well apparently I didn't need to, I had Sebastion watching over me," and they both laughed.

It seemed that Rudy, not wanting to be redundant, said, "You can wake me next time. I am happy to stand guard. I am a light sleeper." A statement that Danielle knew from the past week of travelling with him to be completely inaccurate, but at least it was a nice gesture, and she thanked him.

Bernie watched and took note, as someone who stands back to see the bigger picture, in the manner of a silent witness.

They broke camp leaving nothing more than a ring of stones and some ash. Even the unburned charcoal was collected and bagged for the next fire. Nothing was wasted; it was how the Tuareg survived out here when no one else could. The camels were refreshed, and the goatskin water bags had been filled. Even though the route would take them past a few more springs, they still carried enough water to make the 100km rendezvous with the vehicles.

They made good time, driving the caravans though the brilliant red dunes of the Tadrart Rouge and then climbing to the top of the rocky plateau. They made camp that night in a valley between the black rock massifs. The rugs were placed on the few depressions that were filled with sand, being slightly cooler than the surrounding bedrock. At least in this more exposed location there was a breeze. A breeze so dry that every ounce of sweat cooled the skin. There would be no cooling seeps or puddles tonight though. The last one that they passed was perhaps two kilometers back down in the last valley.

After pitching tents, the campfire was lit. It would likely be their last night out in the open. By the end of tomorrow they would have met up with the vehicles and driven back to Djanet. There they would stay in their comfortable motel rooms. It would be sad to leave the life they were becoming accustomed to, but it would also be very pleasant to have a shower, air conditioning, and other modern comforts. They would be back where they could communicate with the outside world, check in with loved ones, and upload all those selfies.

Their Tuareg hosts prepared a larger meal than the previous nights. No doubt they were using up the remaining supplies to lighten the load, and to consume items before they spoiled. It also seemed that there was an increased vigor on the part of some to socialize and perhaps consummate fantasies. Sophie presented herself around the campfire in a style unbefitting a woman within a Muslim country. That is not to say that in the West she would be considered exposed or salacious, but much more of the pudding was on display, and seemingly directed toward Sebastian. Yet still he did not care for a slice.

Bernie was tough, tight, and well presented for someone between thirty-five and forty-five years of age. No doubt she frequented the gym, yoga, or Pilates, and her work had kept her active. It seemed that she had decided to seduce Rudy, and he appeared to be an easy mark. Once they made it back to civilization, they would probably go their separate ways, thus it was to be a discrete desert fling.

Danielle noticed them exchange gestures, then one got up and left the firelight, followed shortly by the other. Somewhere in the shadows they reunited for silent pleasures. It would not be a stretch to say the age difference was ten to fifteen years, but they were both consenting adults, the breeze was warm, and the stars and moon were bright. When Bernie left, her hair was up in a scraggly bun, and when she returned it was down and long past her shoulders.

If Sophie wanted some, she should have gone for Rudy, but now that chance was gone, probably. Instead, she continued like the moth fluttering against the closed window and chasing the unobtainable light. But it wouldn't destroy her. It was probably a modus operandi that had a long history around the office, amongst friends, and unrequited chance meetings in coffee shops and bookstores. She would settle down, and probably soon. There would be a similar moth or pudding with which she would eventually connect. And their lives would be fantastically happy, albeit perhaps mediocre, and slightly below current expectations. Danielle had to check herself for being so judgmental. Love is love, regardless of the chocolate box it comes in.

Long after the others had gone to their respective beds, Danielle, Sophie and Sebastian reclined on the rug by the fire. Sophie remained as close to Sebastion as she dared, whilst Danielle sat across on the other side of the fire. It was she who met his eyes when he spoke, and it was she that was aloof and unobtainable. This was perhaps a more potent aphrodisiacs than being within easy reach, especially to someone who may be both confident and complicated, like him. It wasn't that she was looking for anything, and yet the nights out here were so naked, bold, and exposed the very soul to the elements. It was easy to connect with those people of ten thousand years ago and their primality. On a night like tonight, they probably painted themselves, danced around the fire, and then made children in the dark.

It got to the point where amorous thoughts invaded her mind and triggered chemicals in her brain and body. It would be best to avoid complications and excuse herself for the night. She should return to the safety of the flimsy fabric tent, with its door flaps that fluttered in the breeze. The privacy and security were only symbolic, nothing more. As she lay atop her sleeping bag, she could see them sitting by the fire. It was evident that Sophie was tired and was fighting to stay awake in the hope that there may be progress, if not before, then maybe now. But he was immovable and stoic, staring like the Sphinx even as she lay there as an offering to the God.

It was around 2AM when Danielle woke up again. Something had crawled across her arm. On most nights she would wear long sleeves of linen to protect herself from the insects. Tonight, she only wore a singlet but had applied plenty of insect repellent along with the usual healthy dose of moisturizer. She was a peaches and cream blonde; therefore, long sleeves and hats during the day, as well as plenty of sunscreen and moisturizer. Since being in Africa, she was conditioned to look before swatting at insects. It is far better to just brush off a wayward scorpion than to provoke it into stinging you. She reached over and turned on her small light, the one that just illuminated like a glowing ball about her.

Sure, enough a scorpion was continuing on its nightly journey prowling for food. There was nothing for it than to let it continue as she guided it back out the front of the tent. The sides and the back of the tent were buried in the sand, so critters could only enter from the front. If she wanted to be really diligent, she could have buried the bottoms of the door flaps, like she had on previous nights, but her fear of the desert, and living on the ground, was subsiding with each camp.

She had to pee again. She rummaged through her luggage and found a proper flashlight. It still wasn't very powerful, unlike some of the other campers that had military grade equipment, but it did direct a beam several meters which would be more than adequate. She shook and slipped on her boots, then silently climbed out of her tent. Without shining the flashlight directly on them she could see two bodies remaining in front of the fire. They were close but not together. It would appear that Sophie had fallen asleep by the fire next to Sebastian, however, his body pointed away from her. Danielle felt a little sad for Sophie, but she had to give her points for trying. It takes a lot of guts to put yourself out there and exposed to rejection.

As she walked past with her flashlight scanning the beyond, she was startled by a voice, "Hey, Danni. Are you off to relieve yourself?"

She turned quickly and shone the light at Sebastian. He squinted and put his hand up to his eyes. Only her family called her Danni; that was rather familiar of him.

"Sorry, I wasn't thinking," she said as she redirected the light so not to dazzle him, "I thought you were sleeping," she said.

"Yeah, I was but I woke up about ten minutes ago. The camels were making some noise. I think there is something prowling around the edge of the camp."

"Oh my God, what do you think it is?" she asked with dread in her voice.

"I would imagine it's just a big lizard, hyrax, or fox," he said with a shrug.

"Yeah, but what if it's something else, like a lion, cheetah, or hyena?" she exclaimed.

"The Barbary Lion is extinct, the Saharan Cheetah is critically endangered, as too are the Stripped Hyena. Regardless, I don't think they are found in this area anyway. And if it were hyena or painted dogs, we would have heard them calling."

"You're pretty sure of yourself," she said.

"I did my research, just in case we spotted something that would make for a good picture," he said as he stood up and stretched. After riding a camel all day, and then sleeping on the hard sand at night, one felt aches and pains in all of the usual places.

He began to walk over to her, and she asked, "What are you doing?"

"I presume you are going for a pee. I'm coming with you, like the Tuareg suggested. Don't worry, I won't look."

She actually appreciated the offer, but she didn't want to appear too pleased. She said, "Ahh..., OK... I think there are some rocks over this way," as she gestured with the flashlight.

The air was still and there seemed to be noises all about them. And as they stepped up from the sand onto the bedrock, gravel crunched under their feet. The walking distance was quite a bit further than the previous night, so she was thankful not to be alone. Finally, she said, "You just wait here whilst I go around the other side of those boulders."

"Fine, I'm just going to go here," he said as he turned, and she heard him unzip his pants. Oh, how convenient it was for the boys she thought. Not having to get down with the scorpions and spiders and whatever.

She was as quick as she could be. It wasn't frightening like it was the previous night. Just knowing someone was there settled the nerves. And although she could hear animals and insects, there wasn't the whispering and moaning wind like before. This time she strolled back to camp, talking softly so not to disturb people and camels. She was tempted to sit next to him around the fire. And probably would have if he asked, and maybe even let him in her tent if he had asked. But neither she nor he did any asking, and so they went back to sleep on their respective bedding.

It was another early start for their final day. They would wind their way through the gorges and then out onto the dry flood plain. Back onto the scorching white lowlands and then finally reach the main road to Djanet.

It was late afternoon by the time they could see the road from a vantage point. A back strip that shimmered like a mirage. As they left the shelter of the canyons, the temperature rose to 42°C. It must have been much warmer at midday, perhaps topping out at 45°C. They were thankful that soon they would be driving in air-conditioned vehicles, and tonight have cool showers, and sleep in air-conditioned rooms on comfortable beds. There was even some beer at the motel, but strictly to be consumed in the privacy of one's room. A shower and a cold beer made her salivate like Pavlov's dog, even hours before the event.

CHAPTER 4

They set up camp a few hundred meters back from the road. There was no shade but thankfully there was only a couple of hours of sunlight left. The camels were unloaded, and in typical Tuareg style, a fire was made to boil water for tea. The Tuareg would be spending the night here and then head North, or maybe West. It would depend on the information they received when the vehicles arrived.

Everyone was surprised that the vehicles were not already there waiting for them. It was what had been arranged, but it wasn't like they could just call them up and find out how far away they were. There was no phone reception this far from Djanet. Thus, there was nothing more they could do than just wait for the vehicles to arrive. And it wouldn't have been the case that they had arrived in the wrong spot, with the two groups waiting for each other kilometers apart. Firstly, there was nothing around for miles, so it wasn't like anyone, or thing, could be obscured from view. But secondly, the Tuareg were experts at navigation. Their lives depended on it almost every day they were in the desert. No there wasn't a misunderstanding or a mistake, as one of the

Tuareg said, there must be something wrong. And by that they implied that possibly it was an attack from bandits or rival political factions. It was possible that the vehicles had been shot up, or hijacked, and that they may never come.

Before sunset the group had pitched the tents and the Tuareg made dinner with what was left of the rations. They would wait out the night and see if the vehicles arrived in the morning. If they still did not come, then the caravan would head North to a small town called Irh Arrikine where they could get water, supplies, and access to the phone and Internet. If the vehicles were still not coming, the caravan could cut through the mountains, along the dry valley of the Oued Arrikine river, and get them back to the main road about 30km South of Djanet.

Everything in the Sahara worked at a different pace. When sandstorms happened, or the very rare rainstorms, then everything would stop. Likewise, if something like a fuel delivery was delayed, or there was a power outage, then once again everything would be delayed. And then finally there was the potential for conflict. An armed incursion or terrorist incident would cause everything to be rerouted or delayed.

The Tuareg were concerned; Bernie and Danielle could detect this. Perhaps those two women were more attuned to subtle behaviors and the increased mumbling between the two guides. Of course it was hard to read their expressions, for they always wore their veils. But voice and posture could be read, and based on interpretation of these, they believed the Tuareg were worried.

It was a hot and windy night, and no one stayed out late by the fire. The Tuareg slept behind a screen that sheltered both them and the camels. Wrapped in their blue robes, they were afforded extra protection from the wind and the stinging sand. Bernie had moved into Rudy's tent, given that Sebastian had not slept in there for the past two nights. She went into the tent before Sebastian retired, and when he did go there to get out of the wind, he was surprised to find the two of them enjoying each other's company. Of course that left Sebastion, well actually the remaining three of them, in a predicament. It is possible that Sophie had orchestrated the whole switch or at least suggested it. Sebastian now had to choose between the camels, the fireside, Sophie's tent or Danielle's tent.

Of course, the bidding was opened by an offer from Sophie for him to join her in her tent. It all sounded above board and reasonable, but it was not. Sebastian had suggested that perhaps the girls should sleep together and that he use the free tent by himself. That did not go down well. After some back and forth a solution was found, being probably the most impractical and childish of all possibilities. They merged Danielle's and Sophie's tents and then they lay down three wide with Sebastian in the middle. It's not that Danielle was hankering for any particular advantage, but it just irked her to let Sophie win. Thus, this was the compromise as they lay in the dark, the wind pushing and tugging at the fabric. It seemed also that there was a general drift of bodies toward Danielle's side of the tent. Presumably Sophie would push up against Sebastian, and he in turn would retreat further toward Danielle. She did not mind. It made her feel better protected from the spirits that came on the wind.

Like clockwork she woke up at 2AM. This was becoming a habit. It must have been the diuretic properties of the tea and the amount that she was drinking to offset dehydration. She turned on her soft light, Sebastian was facing her, and he was inside her comfort zone, although it wasn't uncomfortable. He must have sensed that he was being watched, as people sometimes do when asleep, and he woke to find her looking at him with the soft light between them. She got a bit embarrassed and spluttered, "I need to go to the toilet."

He said, "Sure, I'll come with you. I need to go as well."

Quietly they slipped out of the tent and were immediately hit by the hot wind. It was very dry and gritty, and tasted dusty. There was very little to allow the wind to make its noise, beside the tents, the ruffling of their clothes, and the way the air raced across their ears. They got their bearings and headed away from both the fire and the camels. Other than their camp, they were on a flat featureless plain. Perhaps if it rained it may turn into a boggy claypan, but there was little chance of that happening tonight.

They only walked about ten paces and then Danielle said, "OK, here will do. Please turn around."

He held the light against his chest, and as he did, she found herself plunged back into darkness, with the saltating sand peppering her behind. She was as quick as she could be, not even worrying about doing up her belt properly before rushing back to his side and holding up her pants. Even being just a few meters away from the light felt like she was on the edge of a great black abys. As if one could fall horizontally into the desert and keep falling forever. He hadn't quite finished doing his business and there was a moment of embarrassment when she surprised him. It turned to a laugh, quite a hearty laugh by both of them. Perhaps on her part it was the release of nervous energy, and the relief at being back in the light.

They sneaked back into the tent without disturbing Sophie and resumed their positions.

As Danielle turned off the light, she thought to herself that she and Sebastian had had a moment. Something kind of personal and special to just the two of them. She would have liked to have slid a bit closer, so she was touching him, but did not dare. This was for three reasons. Firstly, because she felt it would be a betrayal to Sophie, which was ridiculous, but she felt it all the same. Secondly, she did not know what Sebastion would think of it. Would he begin to slide away from her as he had done with Sophie? How would that make her feel? And finally, she was better than that. She shouldn't need to be touching him to feel secure, and she reminded herself, he was a struggling artist who lives in Canada. Not really the type of relationship she should be looking for. She wasn't like Bernie who could turn it on and off. She was not fleeting or pragmatic like that. If she was in for a penny, then she was in for a pound. She believed in love and fell into it easily and deeply; thus, her sometimes distant demeanor was also her armor.

No one woke her in the morning, and she found herself in the tent alone. There was no refreshing natural pool to wash in this morning, and as she emerged into the bright sun, she saw the others sitting about the campfire drinking their tea. She felt dry, stiff, and brittle. Her hair was starting to stand by itself, at angles that defied gravity. But she was not alone. They all looked emaciated and disheveled, that is except for the Tuareg, they looked as they did when the journey started. The common sense of their clothing, and ways, was starting to show through. They could have continued for weeks like this, but the Westerners needed to touch civilization soon lest they start to turn into wild beasts of the desert.

They remained at the camp until midday, all the time exposed to the full force of the sun and the withering wind. Finally, a sign was left with rocks on the ground saying they had moved on. They mounted the camels and headed for the small town to their North. They arrived there late in the afternoon. The air was hazy with dust, and for the most part the settlement looked abandoned. Fortunately, it was not, and there was a barracks that they were able to use, and a fenced yard next to it that had water for the camels.

The person who had attended to them kept his distance from the group. Even as the Tuareg approached him he backed away. However, he showed great interest in where the Westerners had come from, how long they had been in the country, and whether anyone was feeling sick. His strange questions were answered, and then for the most part forgotten, as everyone wanted to get out of the sun and the wind, and to get under a cold shower.

Only one room in the large building was air

conditioned, being an office. There was also only one shower, so they had to take turns, and they were instructed to limit the time in the shower to around five minutes due to a shortage of water. Regardless, the experience was very welcome, and most of them still had a reserve of clean clothes they could wear after washing.

Food was brought to them, but once again people kept their distance. It was home-cooked and left in pots just inside the door, and then those doing the delivery would disappear. Was it possible that they were scared of the Tuareg, or maybe the Westerners, or even the veil-less women? Surely not. These towns folk did not appear to be traditional ultra-conservative people living a tribal life. No, it must be something else.

They were disappointed to find that there was no cell phone reception in the town. There was an Internet connection, but its operation was intermittent, and they were told that currently it was not working. It was decided by all concerned that they would rest up for the night and then make further enquiries the following morning.

It was quite a treat to have electric lighting after six nights illuminated by firelight and flashlights. They stayed up later than they normally would have, sitting around the table talking. Strangely, or perhaps not so strangely, after the Tuareg had bathed and eaten, they returned outside to the yard and spent the night with their camels. Perhaps they found it more comfortable, or normal, and maybe they were wary that the animals may get stolen during the night.

The Westerners bunked in a dorm room that had rows of beds, as if used for soldiers or company workers. It was impeccably clean, including being free of sand and dust, which was exceptional and welcome in the middle of the Sahara. The wind blew throughout the night making the structure creak, and the exposed angles and gaps howl and whistle with each gust. It was a reminder of the vast blackness outside and the djinns that inhabited it. Danielle was relieved to be inside, surrounded by flimsy yet reassuring civilization. The light from the office spilled into the dorm though the partially opened door, keeping the darkness at bay.

Like clockwork, at 2AM she got up to go to the toilet. Everyone else was asleep and there was no need to wake anyone, so she slipped out and went to the bathroom. The wind was still up, and the voices called. After using the bathroom, she thought she would take a look outside. To just quickly poke her head out into the yard where the Tuareg and the camels were sleeping. The door was in the lee of the wind, so no rush hit her or pulled at the door. She was relieved to see the camels and Tuareg still in the yard, with its wire fence and locked gate.

There were two streetlights in the whole town, one at each end of the 'main street'. All they revealed was blowing dust and abandonment. She wondered how many people lived here. Perhaps forty or fifty in the whole town; but then there was a school across the other side of the road, so maybe there was more life and future than suggested by current appearances. She would have liked to go for a stroll down the empty street, just to take in the experience, but it would have been too dangerous, especially for a woman alone. She closed the door and went back to bed. It was slightly cooler tonight, but this had little effect inside the closed-up corrugated iron building. They could not open the windows, or it would fill with sand and dust. So being closed it retained the heat that had built up during the day. She laid back on the bed, draped a thin cotton sheet over herself and fell back to sleep.

CHAPTER 5

Danielle was woken by Rudy quietly calling her name. It was morning yet still quite dark in the room due to the heavy shades that were drawn over the windows.

"Danielle, wake up," he said.

She woke with a startle, "What is it?" she asked with concern, immediately thinking that he was going to tell her that the Tuareg had disappeared leaving them stranded.

"We've been locked in, all of us," he said.

"What… what does that mean?" she said with confusion.

"I just went to go for a walk through the town but found a chain and lock had been put on the yard gate. Then I tried the front door out to the road and that was also locked. I know it wasn't locked last night, because I tried it, and it opened."

"So does that mean we can't get out?" she asked just for clarification.

"Well, I mean we could get out. It's not like anything is very secure. We could climb the fence, force the door, or break a window. But who wants to do that, and what kind of trouble might we get into? But really the question is why we have been locked up, and by whom?"

"Have you asked the Tuareg? Maybe they know something," she said.

"No, I haven't. Not yet. They are still sitting in their camp making tea. I'm not sure if they even realize. But they don't seem to be getting the camels ready for leaving. Perhaps it is still too early? I'm just not sure," he said.

She looked around and the others were still sleeping. This could be a serious development; therefore she figured it would be best to wake and inform them. It's what she would want them to do for her because anything could be about to happen. They may find they are being held hostage, and that a militia or bandits could be on their way. She told Rudy to wake everyone up, but not to alarm them.

As a group they went outside and over to the Tuareg encampment where the latter remained seated and relaxed. With Sebastien being the person best able to communicate with them, he asked if they were aware of the situation. As it turned out, they were not. However, they did not seem overly concerned, saying that they would just break down the fence when they were ready to leave.

Then one of them said, "We are Tuareg, we cannot be locked in. Our people are fearless warriors, they will not dare to provoke our people. The Tuareg will ride across the sands and take these people away, never to be seen again. This they know."

It was a rather frightening side of their hosts that up until this point had been concealed.

Not wanting to provoke a conflict, or rash actions, Sebastian said, "Maybe we should ask someone first before we jump to conclusions. It could be something very simple and innocent. Perhaps it was done for our own protection, like if there are bandits in the area or something."

As they were talking a man called out from the road beyond the fence. They all walked over to the boundary, and one of the Tuareg spoke to the man in what seemed a fast and agitated voice. The conversation was conducted in a Berger language that none of the Westerners understood. They thought better than to interrupt whilst the exchange was going on, but it seemed like the man on the road was being apologetic and almost pleading with the Tuareg. After a few minutes of this the Tuareg turned to the group and said in broken English, "We are free to leave if we wish. Now we must decide what is the best thing to do."

Sebastian then spoke to the Tuareg in French. None of the others were fluent on French, but they could pick up some of the words and meanings. After a back-and-forth conversation between himself and the two Tuareg, he turned to the tourists and gave the following report.

"There has been another global pandemic, and everything has been shut down, apparently everywhere. It is said to be much worse than COVID; it is a different type of disease. From what the Tuareg were told, it is like rabies for people, but it is not rabies."

"How is it transmitted?" Danielle asked.

"They believe it is airborne, and the people that have it have been infected for a long time. They have no symptoms for weeks, and then they go rabid as if they are a wild animal, and then they die from dehydration and hunger. It sounds like PCP; you know Angel Dust. People get high, hallucinate, get violent and go crazy; very dangerous," he said.

"It sounds extremely bad," Danielle said, "Their brains are getting locked into that state until they die. So, I am assuming it is too early for a vaccine or cure?"

"From what I understand, there is nothing to treat it yet. It took the World months to develop something for COVID, and this seems like a completely new type of disease, so who knows how long it will take," Sebastian said.

Then Danielle continued, "And if it is airborne and has a long gestation, then God knows who has been infected. We may all be infected and don't know it. We travelled here by aeroplane and bus, so we've had lots of exposure over the past few weeks."

"Exactly," Sebastian said, "That is why they locked us in here. They didn't want us to be wandering around their town and possibly infecting them."

"So, what about communications?" Bernie asked, "Why don't we have phone reception, and on that matter, what has been the impact on global communications?"

"The phone has not worked here for a few weeks, so that outage pre-dates the pandemic. They do, however, have Internet here. There is an Internet café down the street. They are prepared to let us use that for a short time today, provided we don't go anywhere else or interact with anyone. As you can appreciate, they are scared that we may be infected, so they are just following government instructions and trying to protect themselves," he said.

"How will we know when we can use the Internet?" Bernie asked.

Sebastian turned to the Tuareg and spoke to them, afterward he said to Bernie and the others, "Someone from the village will come back around noon. They will bring us some food and after we have eaten, they will let us walk down to the café and use the Internet."

There was nothing else they could do but just sit about in the shade or go inside to the air-conditioned office. Despite now having creature comforts, the boredom made it more tiresome than if they were heading somewhere on a camel. All of them wanted to get back to

Djanet. They all had motel rooms where they had stored luggage they didn't take on the camel trek. Danielle and Ruby maintained the rent on one room between them, but the others had single rooms that presumably they were still being charged for. Also, they all would have felt safer in Djanet because there were police and government offices, as well as travel agencies and transport terminals. But then again, depending on how far the pandemic had spread, maybe Djanet was no longer safe.

Around noon someone arrived with food. The tourists were told to step back from the door as the delivery was placed just inside the entrance. The door was then closed and once again locked. After eating, the man from the town returned and unlocked the door. Even the Tuareg came out. Apparently, they were Internet savvy and maybe they even had email accounts for contacting distant friends and relatives. The Sahara held such contradictions between the ancient and the modern, especially when it came to useful and appropriate technologies like phones, trucks, and guns.

As they walked down the main street, they saw no one apart from the man they followed. It seemed that everyone had hidden themselves away, such was the fear of this new disease. Perhaps they viewed it more like the bubonic plague, or some kind of flesh-eating disease. Ignorance can make people very wary, as it should. If it was as lethal as the plague, the Black Death, then maybe half of the world's population was doomed to a horrible death. Danielle was keen to get onto the World Health Organization (WHO) website and read the latest updates and warnings.

There was only a single computer in what was basically a small convenience store. And even though they had spent the past few days in close proximity with each other, they decided that only one person would enter the establishment at a time, spend around 5 minutes online, and then let the next person go in. If someone needed longer, then they would have to wait until everyone had a turn before they could go back in and have more time online.

They let the Tuareg go first because they just wanted to send and receive emails and said they would be quick. The others waited in a shady courtyard at the side of the café. It had a small water feature that was decorated with blue and white tiles. The Tuareg thoughtfully brought out crisps and soft drinks for them to enjoy whilst they waited for their turns. It was the least healthy food they had eaten for a week. But hey, if the world was ending, then why not engage in a little bit of sin.

They decided to let Danielle follow the Tuareg

because she was going to look up the specifics regarding the disease and its implications. She went in and found the café was air conditioned, which was a welcome relief after the 42°C outside. She firstly logged into her email account, there were several from family and friends asking if she was OK, but there was less than she had expected. Without spending much time on the replies, she wrote that she was alive and well, still deep in the Sahara, and was unsure about travel but would update them when she could. That same message was cut and pasted to everyone on her contact list and done in about 1 minute.

Now she went to the WHO website; thankfully it was still working. She had been expecting lots of traffic, and the possibility that it could be down. The warnings were stark and the details grim and frightening. The disease had spread across the world undetected, with up to half the global population infected. It was airborne, long-lived, and resistant to everything. So far there was no vaccine or cure, and one may be years away. It took up to three weeks to know if a person had contracted the disease, therefore also if they were in the clear. Over those three weeks the person could also be infectious without knowing it.

The symptoms came on quickly and it was always fatal; all hospitals and medical facilities were overwhelmed. Within hours of showing symptoms, people would become deranged and violent, wandering the streets until they collapsed from exhaustion. The infected apparently did not have the wherewithal to eat, drink, or seek medical attention; they were highly infectious, and like anthrax they were still infectious after death. It was a zombie apocalypse, but without the supernatural. Its impact was very much like the Black Death that spread across the globe in the 14th century. And in a similar way, this event would change the course of human history. The past had warned the World many times over of the potential for such events, but very little heed had been taken.

All transport had been halted. In the rich countries martial law had been declared, with food and services delivered via air drops, or soldiers wearing biohazard suits. In less developed or politically unstable countries, it was presumed to be absolute chaos, however, there were no reliable reports, just rumors and speculation. Algeria, and its North African neighbors, had all declared martial law, and all travel had been restricted. Danielle printed off some bulletins and technical papers, to be read later and to be shared with the others, and then her time was up. At least now the others didn't have to waste time on the specifics of the pandemic, but instead focus on their loved ones, or news that was closer to their home.

Each of them in turn did their time on the

computer and then returned to the courtyard with a sunken look and little to say. Within the hour they were escorted back to the compound and were once again locked in. At least they were safe, for now. That is, assuming none of them had the disease and sat amongst them like a ticking timebomb. So provided the food continued to come, and the water still flowed, then they were perhaps in one of the safest places on Earth.

Danielle sat and read the reports. She noticed that the disease's ability to survive, outside of a host, was limited in hot dry conditions. This suggested that their current location afforded some protection, even if the medical facilities, or the control over movement, may not be as strict as it was in their home countries.

CHAPTER 6

The Tuareg were keen to return to their families in a settlement just beyond Djanet. That was convenient for the others because they also wanted to return to Djanet. The remainder of their luggage was there, and being a regional center, there were more resources available, and maybe the opportunity to travel. In their current situation the tourist remained completely reliant on the Tuareg, their camels, and their navigation skills, to cross the almost 100km back to Djanet.

There were cars in the small settlement, but none of the owners were prepared to give them to the tourist, or to drive them, even if they sat outside in the tray bed. They were also afraid that they may get into trouble with the authorities if they were caught driving. The country was under martial law, and the driver was risking prison or even being shot on sight. Also, with the world turning upside down, the value of money and resources had changed. Presently no amount of money could have bought a car or a camel.

Danielle sat with Sebastian and the Tuareg. She used him to interpret as she discussed the implications of the disease and how it related to their predicament. She said, "Tell them that the best thing they can do for their families and themselves is to stay here for a couple of weeks. At the end of that time we will know if any of us have been infected. Please tell them that it would be very sad if their families had survived, only for them to return home and infect them."

He explained this to the Tuareg and then after further discussion said to her, "They agree. They said that we should all stay here for a few weeks and then they can take us through the mountains to Djanet."

"Yes, this is a good plan," she said.

Sebastian and the Tuareg spoke some more and then he said to Danielle, "They need to feed the camels. They will take them to some of the valleys and seeps near the town and let them graze, but they will come back each night. They have already discussed this with the people of the town, and they have agreed. So, they say to us, don't be alarmed when we see them leaving, they will return before the sun goes down each night."

There was little the tourists could do but agree to this. They could not control what the Tuareg did, only the desert could do that.

The first week passed with no one getting sick, either amongst the tour group, or within the town. Furthermore, the locals were getting used to their presence and showed less fear toward them. Yet despite this they were still locked in each night and were kept at a safe distance.

It seemed the phone service was never going to get fixed, especially not with the lockdown. So, every second day they were allowed to use the Internet café. It would be the same routine, after their lunch, and with the streets and café empty. No doubt they were watched from the rooftop terraces and gaps in the stone walls. Who knows, maybe they even had guns train on them. Their only protection, and probably legitimacy, was the respect afforded their guides. Whilst they remained under the protection of the Tuareg, and not just the two guides, but the whole loose affiliation that spanned the Sahara, they would be safe.

Each time Danielle logged in the news got worse. Only a third of her contacts now responded to her emails. They all relayed the same story of being locked down and scared. Everywhere was coming under martial law, even in the UK, although she was told it was better there than in Europe with its more porous borders. So many people were dying, estimates were putting the figure at around one quarter of the global population in just the first week. Was it propaganda, or sensationalism, it was very difficult to say. It was indiscriminate, everyone from politicians to news anchors were just disappearing and presumed dead. Everything was breaking down. Conspiracy theories were all across the Internet. Increasingly authority and trust were dissolving, and sometimes the stories were so sensational and incendiary it was hard to know who or what to believe. Was it a biological weapon, a human made disease? Or maybe it was alien, a result of the Earth passing through some comet debris.

Surprisingly, given that their small group was effectively all getting the same information, the beliefs and responses within their band were also quite different. It showed how different people's upbringings, and minds, can interpret and respond differently to the exact same information. Regardless of who they believed was responsible, and how the authorities should respond, they all acknowledged that where they found themselves was actually their good fortune, and that for now they were as safe as anyone could be.

It was late afternoon, and some trees now shaded the yard. The Tuareg had just returned with the camels, and they settled them down near the water trough. They were all sitting outside, sick of being confined in the building, when they heard the sound of motor vehicles. They looked to the road and saw two 4WD pickup trucks drive down the dusty street and stop near the Internet café. Ten people unloaded from the vehicles, including women and children. Some of the men were brandishing automatic rifles and acting as if on guard duty.

The Tuareg watched and then said, "They are Arab Berbers; they are from this region, maybe a nearby town."

The Tuareg were multi-lingual and could understand what was being said, if not perfectly, then at least sufficiently. A local called out from the café, although remained behind the locked door, then another local appeared from a building on the other side of the street. He carried a gun, and he signaled to several roof tops and walls where other men had appeared and were carrying guns. It seemed that this group was going to be received in the same many as their own group, that is, put into quarantine, and the Tuareg relayed as much.

"This won't do," Danielle said, "It will mess up our time in quarantine. We only have one more week before we can declare ourselves disease free. If we mix with these people, then we will have to wait another three weeks."

Sebastian explained this to the Tuareg, and at this they produced guns from their otherwise innocuous cloth camel packs and stood over by the fence. Two men from the new arrivals, and another man from the locals, came over to the fence. Based on the stance and language of all concerned it appear there was going to be a stand-off. The Tuareg became very loud and animated, and the Westerners were concerned that the situation may get out of hand and shots would be fired.

After negotiations the Tuareg talked to Sebastian, and then he in turn spoke to the rest of them, "It seems that we do not have a choice, the new people will also be put in with us. However, they will be separated by a line in the sand. They will stay outside in the yard on their side and only come into the building to use the facilities at agreed times. The locals will let us out of here in a week when we have completed our quarantine, and then the new arrivals can take over the whole compound."

Although no one was happy with the compromise, they all agreed to it. What choice did they have? Then Danielle asked, "Do you know if they are all healthy, or if they have any signs of the illness?"

Sebastian asked the Tuareg, who in turn ask the group on the other side of the fence. The message came back through the chain that a mother and a child were sick with something unknown. Given her time with MSF, Danielle knew this could be any number of illnesses apart from the pandemic. And these other diseases could also be highly transmissible such as Cholera and Tuberculosis, or if they had travelled from sub-Saharan Africa, then possibly one of the hemorrhagic viruses like Ebola or Marburg.

She said to Sebastian, "Tell them that I am a doctor, and I have worked in countries across North Africa. Ask if I can have access to their medical supplies so I may get masks, the equipment to diagnose, and hopefully treat the sick people."

They agreed to this, and as Danielle, with Sebastian as interpreter, was let out of the compound, the new arrivals drove their vehicles inside and made camp opposite the camels and the Tuareg. Danielle and Sebastian followed the man from the town, being sure to keep a respectable distance, to a clinic. It was surprisingly clean, professional, and well stocked with supplies and equipment with which she was familiar. Yes, this would do nicely she thought; and it was even air conditioned.

Through Sebastian she asked the man, "Where is the doctor who works in this clinic?"

Sebastian relayed, "They had a doctor that visited each week, but they have not seen him for the past week, and given the current lockdown, they do not believe anyone will be coming. He also said that they have a woman who is a nurse here in the village, who assists the doctor and performs basic medical procedures when the doctor is away."

She said, "Tell him it is good that I am here. I can work with the nurse and treat the people. Tell him I will wear a mask and monitor myself for any symptoms."

Sebastian relayed her message, and the local man seemed to smile, and then said in English, "Thank you," he then bowed and finished with a prayer.

Whilst preparing the clinic, Danielle sent Sebastian to get the sick woman and child. It was essential that she identify what was wrong with them, given their close proximity to everyone, and the resources that were being shared. When they returned, she donned a mask and gloves and began to inspect the patients. From what she could understand they had spent time further South in the humid southern boundary region of the Sahara, and she had a strong suspicion they both had malaria.

Fortunately, she had the facilities to test for this straight away, being a microscope capable of identifying parasites in the blood. She took samples and then confirmed it was malaria. It was a common, although serious condition, and the clinic had stocks of the drug needed to treat the patients. She put them on a course of chloroquine phosphate, hoping that the strain was not resistant. Ideally, she would have sent samples away for more comprehensive testing, but that just wasn't going to happen now. So, she had to go with her gut instinct and change the treatment if necessary. She would know within two weeks if the drugs were effective.

Whilst she had them in the clinic, she also performed other tests and procedures including vaccinations. She then asked if they could send each of the new arrivals, one by one, to get assessed and receive any necessary treatment. This gesture went a long way to allaying the hostilities and fears between the groups.

The nurse arrived to assist Danielle. Her name was Samia, she was around the same age as Danielle, and she spoke English, French, as well as several Arab-Berber dialects. This would be extremely handy and negated the need for Sebastian to be present, which cannot be overstated in a Muslim country when treating women. Over the following week people from the local village also began to attend the clinic, meaning that Danielle was effectively there all day, every day. She felt fortunate that she could get out of the confines of the compound, could be in air conditioning, and most importantly, feel useful and rescued from the otherwise soul-destroying boredom.

Danielle's tour group had two days left of their quarantine. They had been diligent at keeping their distance from the locals, the new arrivals, and also from each other. The sun had set and there was a gentle breeze outside, so all of them sat with the Tuareg and ate the evening meal. A small campfire was burning and the Tuareg were making tea. Bernie came over to Danielle and said, "Can I speak to you in private for a minute."

"Sure," she said, and got up to followed Bernie to the far side of the compound.

"I didn't want to alarm anyone, but I've been having what seems like an ocular migraine. I've got squiggly lines in my eyes and blurred vision. I know about them because I've had them before, but usually they only last about fifteen minutes, and I don't normally get a headache at the same time. But this time it is different. I've had it for hours and it seems to be getting worse. I've got a splitting headache, and I feel dizzy."

Danielle was concerned but didn't want to alarm her, so she said, "It could be getting triggered by any number of things. I suppose my first question would be, have you had enough water to drink today? As you know it is very easy to get dehydrated in this heat. And secondly, how well have you been sleeping?"

"I've had plenty to drink, the same amount as I normally do, and as far as I recall I slept well last night, again the same as usual," she said.

Danielle noticed that Bernie kept leaning on the wall. She would push off of it and stand upright but then fall back against the wall. It was very subtle, but it seemed like she was having trouble maintaining balance. The medical clinic had a computer with an Internet connection. She had used it between patients to do research on cases related to the pandemic. The symptoms that Bernie described were included on a list issued by WHO as indicators of infection.

Danielle said to Bernie, "I'm sorry but as a precaution I'm going to ask you to isolate. We can move your bed outside over by the wall, and I want you to wear a mask all the time."

"You don't think I've got R24 do you?" Bernie said with a look of horror.

R24 was the name given to the pandemic, although in the medical literature it was a longer combination of letters and numbers. It was called this because it was a rabies like disease that was first identified in 2024.

"I'll be honest with you; I just don't know. We will have a better idea by tomorrow morning." Thinking that there could be a chance it was normal rabies, Danielle asked, "Did you get bitten, scratched, or possibly come into contact with animal saliva in the last two to three months? Did you get vaccinated against rabies? Because you can be asymptomatic for up to three months before it starts to show."

"I had my rabies shots before I travelled, along with all of the other vaccinations, and no I haven't had any contact with animals that may have been infected," Bernie said.

Regardless of whether it was normal rabies or R24, it both cased now that she was symptomatic, it would be fatal. However, with R24 there was a far greater risk of her infecting everyone else; and there would also be the risk of her attacking them, like a raging zombie.

Danielle then said, "Rudy is not going to like this, but I'm going to tell him to isolate as well. The two of you were in close contact whilst you may have been contagious."

CHAPTER 7

Rudy did not take it well. He said he felt fine and could not see any reason to further isolate within the already quarantined group. Yet neither did he want to be in close contact with Bernie for fear of catching what she had; the irony escaped him. It seemed that as soon as there was a chance that she was infected with something, which could have been anything, then all comradery and romance went out the window.

Was he being unreasonable? It was difficult to say. The consequences of contracting R24 were to face a descent into madness, and then an excruciating death. It was unknow if people where conscious of their actions once the symptoms began, but it seemed that the most humane thing to do was to kill them as soon as the crazies and violence started. Maybe some people were inadvertently killed when they just had delirium induced by a fever, or some other sickness. Maybe people could recover if they were restrained and cared for. But there were no resources or confidence left to do this, not here, not anywhere in the world.

Reluctantly Rudy isolated and wore a mask, both of them ostracized by the others in the compound, including the Tuareg. The level of paranoia was palpable. Danielle had been completely transparent with everyone about the WHO reports, and this included evidence that R24 also effected animals, specifically mammals. Therefore, there was a chance that the camels could contract the disease or even spread it. So far there was no suggestion that they had been infected, but the Tuareg were concerned and guarded them as if they were their own children.

It was the early hours of the morning when Danielle was woken by one of the Tuareg. He said, "You must come, the lady is saying things. Many bad things, like the djinn has gotten her."

Danielle got up, put on her face mask, and quietly followed him outside as everyone else in the dormitory slept. The lights from the road shone into the compound and Danielle could see Bernie sitting up on her bed. Rudy had left his and was several meters away watching. As she approached, she could hear Bernie mumbling, her head moved from side to side and then there would be the occasional full body spasm. It was not looking good. She halted a few meters away, squatted down, and shone a flashlight onto Bernie's face.

There was dribble coming from her mouth and nose, her eyes were red as if almost ready to bleed, and there was a blank expression on her face. It was as the Tuareg had said, she looked like she was possessed. The flashlight seemed to agitate her, or was she now just an it? Bernie thrust her hands out as if to grab at the beam of light, even though the flashlight was out of reach. Danielle immediately turned the light off for fear she would get to her feet and start to chase it, and then she carefully backed away until she was level with the Tuareg. One of them stood with a rifle at his side. He asked Danielle, "Does she have the R24?"

Danielle thought for a moment, worried that he may take matters into his own hands and shoot Bernie right there and then. Yet based on everything she had read in the medical literature, there was no doubt in her mind that Bernie had entered the final stage of R24. It would be too dangerous to approach and restrain her, yet without such restraint she would begin to attack every living thing in the compound. There had been reports of first responders placing hoods over the heads of the infected, but this just caused them to flail about. To move her they would have to put numerous ropes about her, and restrain her from different directions, a dangerous act in itself. And finally, they did not have the equipment to further confine her, as in putting up an additional fence or some kind of barrier, and the town's folk certainly wouldn't let them take her out of the compound.

Danielle wracked her brain and tried to assess the situation, but she could not see a solution, but one. She was angry at herself for not thinking this through more thoroughly over the previous days. Instead, she had cushioned her thoughts with delusions that no one would get sick, and if they did, then it would be slow to progress, and they could work to find a solution. But none of that was available now. The reality was that all of them were locked inside the compound with a rabid and highly infectious beast that once was a human. Someone that she considered a friend and had confided in her, had trusted her.

She gestured for the Tuareg to slowly back up and return to their camp. She then said, "Just watch her but don't make any rapid moves or loud noises. I will go inside and get the others. I think we all need to be a part of what happens next."

She went inside and woke Sebastian and Sophie, telling them to come outside slowly and quietly. When they were outside, they called Rudy over but made sure he stayed at a downwind distance from them.

In a soft voice she addressed the group.

"I am convinced that Bernie is in the final stage of R24. None of the literature, and certainly none of the facilities at our disposal, indicate that there is anything we can do for her. We can't even be sure if she is really in her body anymore. It is like she is the walking dead, a zombie. I hate to say this, but I believe the only option we have is to put her down. It would be the humane thing to do and would be the best for everyone else's safety."

"What is this 'put her down'?" asked one of the Tuareg.

"It means that you would shoot her in the head," Sebastian said very bluntly.

"You can't do that, it would be murder," Rudy said, "You don't have the authority, no one has the authority. We have to fence her in somehow. Maybe we could put her inside, like lock her in the office or something. They should have a building here we can put her in, some place that is secure."

"We are the authority now," Sebastian said. "There is no longer any police or functioning government. There is no one coming to save us. There is just us and our collective decision."

"Yeah, well I don't recognize your authority or your decision. We are not animals, this is not how civilized people behave," Rudy pleaded.

"Maybe we are being civilized," Sophie said, "and maybe, like Danielle said, Bernie isn't in there anymore. What if she is just a zombie and we are doing her a favor."

"You can't know that!" Rudy said.

"If she didn't have R24, but instead started to go around and kill everyone, like a homicidal maniac, then wouldn't we have the right to defend ourselves, and even go as far as to use deadly force? Of course we would," Sophie said.

"Yeah, but it's not her fault, Rudy pleaded. "If she were to attack us in this state, it's because she doesn't know what she is doing."

"Exactly," said Danielle. "This is my whole point. I don't think she will know what she is doing, and she will never know anything again. She will just become more and more agitated, and dangerous, until she dies. And even then, her body will be a source of infection and dangerous to us. We really don't have any choice but to shoot her now whilst she is calm and then drag her body and bedding out and away from the town. We would also need to bury everything, so it doesn't get scavenged by animals and spread the infection."

"I can't let you do this; it has to be a unanimous decision, and I do not consent," Rudy said forcefully.

"Well, no, it is a majority decision," Sebastian said as he looked at the Tuareg and then realized that it wasn't even that. It was a decision for those that held the guns.

Then Sophie said what was on everyone else's minds, "Rudy, we all know why you are protesting so much, it's because you think that you will be next."

He stood up straight, and with bluster said, "I'm fine, perfectly healthy."

"So was Bernie yesterday," she retorted.

"Well, that isn't exactly true," Danielle said.

"She told me she was having problems seeing, had a headache, and was starting to get dizzy. Rudy, you have to tell us if you start to have these symptoms."

"What, so you can shoot me like a rabid dog?" he shouted back at her.

All of them had been getting louder and more animated. Then Sophie screamed and they turned to find Bernie had silently walked toward them, being now only a few meters away. They all backed up against the wall. Obviously, Bernie's eyes were still working, and she quickly scanned each of them as they moved, like a wild beast picking its prey. The Tuareg raised his rife and then slid the bolt to load a round. Bernie stopped and looked intensely at him. Everyone watched her dripping distorted face. Did she recognize the gun and what was about to happen? Was she really conscious but just not able to communicate? Had a djinn possessed her one night when she was alone in the dark desert?

Rudy said, "See, see, she is in there, she knows he is going to shoot her. She knows it's us." Then he called out, "Bernie, Bernie, go and sit back down. Just turn around and walk back or they are going to shoot you."

She redirected her focus onto Rudy, obviously her hearing was also functional. Then she started to walk towards him, as he backed away toward the camp of the still sleeping new arrivals. No doubt if they were awake, they would have already put a bullet into Bernie, and maybe even Rudy at the same time.

The Tuareg aimed his rife and said to Danielle, "Tell me what to do doctor. You must tell me now," he said forcefully.

Danielle looked at Sebastian and Sophie, then she looked at Bernie and called out to her, but she did not respond or stop. It seemed that she had become fixated on Rudy's movement. She called out again, and maybe, just maybe Bernie hesitated, and maybe she tried to look around at her, but it was not enough. Softly Danielle said, "I'm sorry Bernie, I truly am," and then she looked at the Tuareg and said, "Shoot her in the head. Make it a good shot."

He fired the rife. It was a good shot. Perhaps the result of many years practicing out in the desert, shooting animals for food, rocks off of the tops of pillars, and maybe even shooting at bandits and rivals. Bernie's body fell instantly and quietly, sprawling across the sand that greedily soaked up the blood.

The new arrivals instantly awoke and grabbed for their guns. Fortunately, no further shots were fired. People from the settlement were also awakened and soon line the fence to see what had happened. After such an event no one would be going back to sleep. Thus, it was decided to place Bernie's body, and possessions, on a makeshift sled to be towed out into the desert for burial. Several vehicles and lots of people formed the funeral procession. Many were simply there to ensure she was buried deep, like people in the Middle Ages ensuring a vampire did not return from the grave.

It was a sad and bizarre funeral, conducted more like work on a construction site, than a poignant farewell. Danielle was the only person who cried. She had liked Bernie and listened to stories about her children and extended family. She was a talented writer and very much a modern woman of the world. Now she would just disappear, like so many others had in just the past few weeks. Her children and her friends would not know what happened to her, there would be no flowers or goodbyes. Indeed, only those present during this pre-dawn service even knew where she was buried.

When the last shovel of sand was thrown over the body, Danielle began to collect up some rocks to mark the grave. Upon seeing this Sebastian started to help her, and then others joined in until there was a large pile. At least there was now something to show that Bernie had existed and had been buried with a modicum of respect and ritual. Prayers were said in different languages and faiths, and then even before the sun had risen, everything went back to how it was before.

CHAPTER 8

Everyone kept their distance from each other. R24 had just become very real and confronting. They could only imagine what it must have been like in the major cities of the world. Death would have been ruthless, from Chicago to Lagos. It would have gone through populations like the Back Death, indiscriminately infecting loved ones and turning them into soulless zombies, where parents had to kill children and vice versa. And no one knew who was infected until the symptoms showed, and apparently only giving a few hours' notice. The paranoia must have been as debilitating, and even destructive, as the death rate.

Everything, absolutely everything had, or would, breakdown. Food production, delivery systems, energy supply, industry, medical, and civil services. Absolutely everything. Humans had lived close to the land when previous plagues hit, but now, with technology and sophistication, humans were so much more removed from the means of production, and thus so much more vulnerable. There would be as many people dying from starvation, preventable disease, or from violence, as there would be from R24. Overnight the world was cast into a new dark age. What was owned and owed was wiped clean. There would be new rulers and systems. Crops would grow where houses and carparks once stood, and after R24 had run its course, only a tenth of the population may remain. Not unlike the destruction wrought on the Americas after first contact with Europeans. In that regard it really wasn't anything new. Yet with all the 'modern' world's knowledge, and access to the chronicles of history, still no one saw it coming.

Rudy was sullen as he sat alone eating his lunch. Wearing a mask, Danielle came over to talk to him. She was the only person to approach him since the funeral. Even travelling to the funeral, he had to ride alone in the tray of a pickup. Everyone feared he was contagious without knowing, and that he would be the next to turn into a zombie.

"How are you feeling?" she asked.

"I feel just fine," he said.

"So, no blurry vision, headaches or dizziness?" she asked.

"No, nothing. I feel just fine," he said defiantly.

She believed him. Based on her calculations she figured that Bernie probably got infected in the few days before they started the camel trek, probably on a flight or shuttle bus. If she had given it to Rudy when they hooked up in the desert, then his symptoms wouldn't show for another couple of days. Bernie had felt fine right up until she didn't. Also, based on her reckoning, if the rest of them didn't show symptoms within the next few days, then they would all be in the clear. It would be an excruciating wait.

With each person's visit to the clinic, Danielle documented their past movements and interactions. In this way she was able to put people into risk categories and have some idea of the minimum time they needed to spend in quarantine. The analysis showed that the new arrivals were a low risk, but they maintained the strict quarantine regardless.

Over the following two days she kept a close watch on Rudy. If he had been infected, then he would become symptomatic in the next few hours. He was already showing signs of being agitated, but still he was lucid and steady on his feet. It was now the morning of the day that she expected he may start to show symptoms. She walked over to him as he ate breakfast and asked, "How are you feeling this morning?"

"I'm OK, but I'm finding the sun a bit bright. It makes my eyes hurt and blurry."

This was not a good sign. Bernie's eyes were also the first symptom.

"Is there anything else?" she asked.

"No, that's all," he said, and then he dry

retched, but stopped short of vomiting.

She was alarmed and asked, "Do you feel like you are going to vomit?"

"No, I'm OK. It's this bowl of something that the other group gave me," as he gestured toward the new arrivals sitting in their separate camp. "It tastes absolutely awful and makes me want to throw up."

"What is it?" she asked.

"I've got absolutely no idea. They said it was medicine from the desert. It's supposed to be a mix of special plants. Rare plants that they only know about. They said that it fights off the evil spirits and they take it when someone is sick from something unknown."

"Do you think it is having any effect on you, either good or bad?" she asked.

"Well, I can't say if it is having a good effect on me, I feel the same as I did before. But as you can see its pretty difficult to swallow. It tastes bitter and foul. They said that it needed to be awful to drive out the demons. I figured there was no harm in taking it, if it works then great, if it doesn't then I'm probably going to die anyway," he said with a defeated tone.

Since Bernie's death the local people had stopped locking the compound. They saw that those in quarantine were as conscientious as the locals to isolate and stop the spread of the disease. Thus, Danielle was free to go to the clinic anytime and work with Samia. This morning before she left, she gathered together the Tuareg, Sebastian, and Sophie, and told them to keep an eye on Rudy. She explained that if he had the disease then he would become symptomatic within the next 6-12 hours. If he did begin to show symptoms, she wanted them to get her, rather than do anything themselves. Then she reinforced to the Tuareg that they were not to shoot him unless someone was in imminent danger. She also asked the Tuareg to relay the same message to the other group that quarantined with them. She didn't want anyone taking matters into their own hands.

It was a short walk to the clinic; in fact, it was actually an enjoyable walk. Some of the buildings that she passed were very attractive. They were two-story mud homes, with stone and tile facades. Most of them had courtyards shaded by palms, figs, and olive trees. One house had a grapevine growing across a rail with bunches of black muscatel grapes hanging down. She picked a few as she walked past, hoping that she was not committing any offence that may get her hands cut off. They were sweet, juicy, and very ripe, with a hint of raisin. Further back in the yard was an apricot tree heavy with fruit. It was out of reach but made her think to ask Samia if they would be able to get some fresh fruit for those in quarantine, especially for Rudy. She felt so sorry for him and the hell he was going through. Even if he were going to die, at least he could enjoy the fruits of the Earth in his last hours.

When she entered the clinic Samia was attending to a child with a cut on their foot. She had bathed and cleaned the wound and was now putting on a dressing. She was a good nurse and no doubt very competent when the doctor was away in other towns. She had told tales of how she had done all manner of procedures, from tooth extractions to delivering babies.

If Danielle didn't have a life and plans back in the UK, she could see herself working here for an extended period, maybe several years. And if she were to meet a romantic partner, then maybe she could even settle down somewhere in Algeria. Then the reality struck her, maybe there was no life to go back to in the UK. Maybe she was one of the fortunate few who by sheer luck was in the right place at the right time. Maybe this was where she would be staying, this was now her clinic, and this was her lot in a post-apocalyptic neo-medieval world.

She looked at the supply room and wondered how long the essentials were going to last. Would someone ever be coming to restock them? Perhaps they would have to start relying on some of the traditional medicines, like the one the desert people made for Rudy. Roots and berries that had been tried and tested over thousands of years. Maybe that was the future rather than the past.

It was mid-afternoon when Sebastian and Sophie knocked on the door of the clinic. They were forbidden to enter due to their quarantine status, so they stood beyond the threshold and waited patiently. When Danielle finished the injection, she was giving someone, she opened the door.

"It's Rudy. He has gotten worse. I think you need to come as soon as you can," Sebastian said.

She turned to Samia and said, "Do you think you can finish up here, I need to go back to the compound and check on Rudy?"

"Sure, you go. I'll be fine. If there is a problem I will send for you," Samia said.

In a tiny town, nobody was more than 5 minutes away from anyone else. When they arrived back at the camp Rudy was sitting on his bedding. Through bloodshot eyes he stared into the distance with a blank expression and rocked side to side. Wearing as much protection as she could find, and as she could bear in the heat, Danielle approached Rudy. Would he be a zombie, a dangerous animal that would grab at her? It was not the same as with Bernie, who was overcome in her sleep, and with no knowledge of the impending doom. This time Rudy was fully aware of the horror that would take him over.

Would this result in a different kind of zombie? One that was more aggressive. Most of the media stories, typically coming from cities, reported aggressive zombies that chased anything that got their attention. They would lurk in the shadows, wanting to stay out of the light, or they would come out at night, and attack any unfortunate person that wandered into range.

She edged closer and said softly, "Rudy, can you hear me?"

His gaze didn't shift as he just sat there swaying like a metronome. She knelt down and moved her hand slowly in front of his field of vision and again said, "Rudy, are you there? Please say something."

Gradually the swaying reduced, but did not stop altogether, and his eyes seemed to come back into focus as he looked at her."

In a slurred voice, as if his lips were numb, he said, "It's happening, isn't it. It's taking over."

She took the opportunity whilst he was lucid to ask questions.

"Can you still think straight?"

"Yes, I'm still me," he said. Then with a tear in his eye and a breaking voice he said, "Don't kill me…, please don't kill me. I can fight this."

"Rudy, you are not alone. We will work through this together. Do you know what is happening around you? Can you describe where you are?"

"I'm in the compound…, I'm sitting outside on my bed. The bright light is hurting my eyes, but I can't close them. They feel dry and sore."

"OK, and does it hurt anywhere else, can you move your body?"

"Everything is numb, like I'm in a dream. My head hurts. A headache, a very bad headache that is taking over everything," he said with a blank expression.

Danielle looked across to her side. A few meters back, and out of Rudy's line of sight an old woman from the new arrivals camp stood with stretched out arms holding a cup. Silently she gestured to Danielle to take it and give it to Rudy. What could it hurt, she thought? At this stage in the disease's development there was nothing that she could do for Rudy, short of tie him up and watch him slide into madness.

She slowly stood up and Rudy said, "No, don't go. Stay… stay."

She said, "I'm not going, I'm just getting you something to drink. You stay still, it's just here, I'll only be a few seconds."

She took the dark tea-like brew, softly thanked the lady, and then returned, crouching down in front of him. She remained on her feet, ready to spring out of his reach should he try to grab her.

"Do you think you will be able to hold this cup?" she said as she showed it to him. "Please try to reach for it."

He extended his arms and managed to put his hands each side of the cup. They were shaking as if he had Parkinson's disease, but she could see that he was concentrating with all of his will to hold the cup and get it to his mouth. Slowly he got it there and tipped it up. Due to his lips being numb lots of if dribbled out of the sides, but still a significant amount was going in.

"Can you swallow?" she asked.

He did not respond but there was movement in his throat suggesting he had gulped.

"Now swallow again," she said, "and keep doing it."

It took a few minutes but eventually he had emptied the cup. She didn't know how it would impact the progression of his condition, but at least he would be hydrated, and that may keep him lucid.

She asked him, "How did that taste?"

Given that when he had drunk it previously it was making him want to vomit, but this time there was no reaction. He responded by saying that he couldn't taste anything. It seemed that the disease was having a significant impact on the nervous and sensory systems in his brain. Yet the medical literature did not identify the disease as causing encephalitis, as in a swelling of the brain and surrounding tissue. Instead, it was more like an attack deep within the brain, like something caused by chemicals and hormones. Perhaps the disease released a potent neurotoxin, or in some way caused the brain and nervous system to turn on itself, like an autoimmune response.

Danielle managed to get Rudy to lay down on his bedding, which was in the shade, and then she rigged up a cover to reduce the light. She also tried to get him to close his eyes, and after considerable effort he did. His condition remained serious but stable for the next few days. Every few hours she would get him up to drink the potion prepared by the old woman, keeping him hydrated, and perhaps was responsible for arresting his decline. It would have been a miracle if there was something in the drink, overlooked or unknown to modern medicine, which helped the human body resist and even fight back against R24.

CHAPTER 9

The Internet was breaking down. The data farms, power supplies, and the human support were all crashing. The cascade of collapse was rapid, especially at end of line locations like central Sahara. Modern technology required constant finesse to keep it running properly, and even if it didn't fail completely, it operated intermittently and sub-optimally. As a result, their small town was becoming cut off from the rest of the world.

It was unknow if they would even be able to get supplies of fuel. There was enough in the town to last a few weeks under normal conditions, and thus if travel were dramatically reduced, it could maybe last 6 months or more. Fortunately, the electricity was generated using solar power so they would always be able to keep the lights on, at least for the next few decades. After that it was unknown if there would be a solar panel or electronics industry. Maybe the world would be healthier, safer, and more efficient after half or even three quarters of the people were gone. The past hundred or so years may have been just a blip in the greater history of humanity, and maybe things were settling back to normal.

Over the following week Rudy's condition remained unchanged. He was extremely ill, but he was lucid and intelligible. And although he had not turned into a zombie, they still built a fence around him. Thus like a wild animal he was caged outside in the shade. Most of the time he would lay on his bed, but then he would go through bouts of angry pacing up and down in his enclosure. He continued to drink the potion and was also able to eat some food. It had to be mashed into a slurry and then poured into his mouth using a funnel. He had lost a lot of weight and looked thoroughly emaciated, but he was alive. And from what Danielle had gleaned off the Internet, he was probably the world's longest-surviving patient of R24.

She tried to find out all she could regarding the potion. It was a very old recipe passed down to the old woman from her mother, and her mother's mother before that. There was not enough equipment in the clinic to analyze the ingredients, and she could not get the scientific names of the plants that were used, so she could not search them up on the Internet. Obviously, the woman did not know their formal botanical names, and either their local names had not been documented in the scientific literature, or perhaps they were not even known to science.

Regardless, Danielle had a suspicion, and a hope, that it was the potion stopping Rudy from slipping further, and just maybe he could recover. Perhaps it would keep the effects of R24 at bay long enough for his body to manufacture a defense, and then a counterattack. Would he fully recover, or would he suffer side effects? There was no way to know.

It had also been a week since the calculated date for symptoms to appear for her, the other tourists, and the Tuareg. Thus, it was assumed that they had not been infected. Also, it was coming up on the date for the new arrivals, and so far, none of them had shown symptoms.

They were running low on ingredients, so a decision was made to travel back into the Tassili N'Ajjer mountains to gather plants to make more potion. Presently they only had enough to support Rudy, so if anyone else got sick, they would run out. Also, Danielle wanted to experiment, if that is what it could be called, by giving people the potion in advance, as if it were a vaccine. Perhaps it would work, it would be a case of trial and error. This was how humans had developed medicines over the past tens of thousands of years; mixing potions and repeating what seemed to work. It had kept the species from going extinct in the face of innumerable pathogens and parasites.

There were no roads where they were going. Sure, they could drive across the plains and the sand dunes, but they could not drive through the rugged mountains and into the canyons where the plants grew. Thus, the logical solution was to go by camel, and this meant being led by the Tuareg. The party would consist of the two Tuareg, the old Arab-Berber woman and her male escort, Danielle, and Sebastian who insisted to go as her escort. She thought that was very chivalrous of him; perhaps that was how things were going to be in these new and dangerous times.

Sophie would stay behind to look after Rudy, and to also help Samia in the clinic. Sophie had stepped up since Bernie's death. She had also lost a lot of weight, likely due to the healthy rationed diet, and probably stress. Also, the hot weather drained both the fluids and the appetite. It was too uncomfortable to be chubby in the Saharan heat. And of course, their diet contained virtually no processed carbohydrates or refined sugar; not since the Tuareg had run out, thus the only sweet things she ate were dried dates, as well as dried and fresh fruit. It made her look several years younger and even increased the spring in her step.

When they loaded up for the journey, the Arab-Berbers handed over some of their guns and ammunition. Now everyone had a rifle apart from the old potion woman. Danielle was not sure if she refused to take a gun, or if her male escort had forbidden it. Despite the massive upheaval to the world, many aspects of culture survived.

Neither Sebastian nor Danielle had any experience with guns, but they understood the importance of having one and knowing how to use it. Animals could carry R24 and would attack as if they had rabies. And of course, they did not know if they would be coming across zombies, or uninfected but still dangerous bandits. Thus, they were given instruction and practice with their rifles before they left. Not that they could fire many rounds, given that it may prove impossible to replace the bullets in the future. The guns were strictly for emergencies, and only as a last resort.

There was a wind blowing from the East and the humidity had risen ever so slightly.

The Tuareg pointed to the hazy horizon and said, "There might be a storm. It is rare, maybe one every year of two, but they do come sometimes. We will not camp in the rivers or canyons. They may have a flood."

"That would be a rare and refreshing sight," she said, "to see water in the desert and then to see the plants grow and the flowers bloom for weeks afterward."

"Yes, I'd like to see that," Sebastian said, "It

would make for some excellent pictures and paintings."

They were travelling to the North, higher up onto the mountain plateau, and would reach around 1,500m above sea level. When they crossed the exposed areas, the wind was stronger and there was a lot of dust in the air. The only thing that would settle the dust was a sprinkle of rain, but then it would also turn everything dusty into mud.

It wasn't until late afternoon when the buildup of clouds finally blocked the sun. It felt eerie to be in the shade, especially when the temperature was still over 40°C. The old woman said that there may be some of the plants in the area, so it was decided to make camp whilst they searched the spaces between the rocks and deep in the canyons. There were three distinct plants they were looking for. None of them were normal food plants, and they would be ignored unless one were foraging specifically for medicine. These plants were as plain and invisible as those that produced frankincense and myrrh. Desert shrubs that only yielded their secrets through knowledge only known to the healer, Sharman, or witch.

They pitched the tents before dark and the Tuareg attended to the camels and campfire. The other four set out on foot, carrying packs on their backs with water, space for collected plants, and rifles over their shoulders. They probably had an hour of light left, so they did not venture too far. What they couldn't get done tonight they would pick up again in the morning. The sky continued to darken, and flashes of lightning could be seen in the distance. It was still too far away to hear the thunder, but the storm was slowly drifting toward them. They would be in for a blustery night regardless of whether it rained or not.

They had not progressed very far down a small valley when the old woman began to speak in her language. Her escort then relayed it in French to Sebastian, who in turn relayed it to Danielle in English.

"She says that there are two of the plants we are looking for growing in here," Sebastian said as the woman pointed to a small patch of spindly bushes. They went over and inspected them, and then the woman showed them which parts to pick; so, they did and began to fill their packs.

Then, through the series of interpreters she said, "The other plant is found higher up in the rock crevasses. It has small seeds that we need to collect. We will not find them today, there is not enough light to continue."

They stripped the bushes. The old woman said they would grow back, but it didn't really amount to very much. She assured them that it was very potent, but still Danielle couldn't see it lasting very long. Especially if they got another case of

R24, or if she were to try and vaccinate everyone.

Sunset was shrouded behind the clouds and there wasn't even the usual orange glow. Instead, it was all silver and grey, and quickly coming in dark. The Tuareg had prepared the evening meal using supplies brought from the town. It was spiced lentils on rice, accompanied by camel milk yogurt that was infused with dried fruits. Dinner was followed by dates and tea. They were not travelling on a well-known route, or staying in a regularly frequented area, so there was dead wood around them. Thus, tonight's fire was larger than normal, and the flames lit up the nearby rock walls. One could imagine the ancient people carving and painting, as the flames and shadows flickered on the walls and made those images come to life.

They had only pitched two tents, and initially the old woman's escort had said that he wanted Danielle to sleep with her, and he would sleep with Sebastian. However, Danielle explained that they couldn't do that because the woman and the escort were both still under quarantine. They did not want to compromise themselves for the sake of his customs, regardless of how strongly he believed in them. Thus, the escort elected to sleep out with the Tuareg.

Sebastian then turned to Danielle and said, "Do you want me to sleep outside as well. I am happy to do that if it makes you feel more comfortable."

She replied, "Don't be silly, you can sleep in the tent with me. Actually, I'd probably prefer if you did. I get jumpy when its windy, with all the noises in the dark. And anyway, it might rain."

"The Tuareg have a wax cloth they put over themselves when it rains, so I wouldn't get wet if that's really what is worrying you," Sebastian said.

"No, I won't hear of it, you will sleep in here with me and that is the end of it," she said with a laugh.

Of all of the people Danielle had met since beginning her journey from Algiers, Sebastian was the person she had the closest affinity with. They were quite different personalities, but they were closely aligned where she thought it was important. If the world had gone to hell in a handbasket, and partners were hard to find, then she would be a fool to let him slip through her fingers. Sure, it sounded pragmatic, but then isn't marrying for love just a modern concept. In the past people partnered for far more practical reasons, and that could be how it would be in the future.

But Sebastian had never made a pass at her, or ever really flirted with her. He had just always been there for her, always ready to help, and always on her side. These were important things. Of course, it didn't hurt that he was the right age, and that she found him physically attractive. Yes, a relationship was probably something she'd be forced to cultivate, lest she lose him to Sophie, or someone else. Then again, what if they had to repopulate the world and polygamy became acceptable or the norm? No, she didn't want to think about that; in that regard she was very conservative.

By the time everyone was ready to turn in, the lightning was putting on quite the show in the otherwise pitch-black night. The storm was now close enough that they could hear the rumbling thunder and at times it boomed off the stone mountains surrounding them. Sebastian followed her back to the tent where she had her trusty little lamp aglow. She wondered if she would ever be able to get batteries for it again. Surely the world had ten years' worth of AA batteries in shops and warehouses. But having them transported out into the middle of the Sahara, well that was a whole other question.

Despite the wind and the approaching storm, it was still around 25°C, and it felt warmer due to the elevated humidity. They lay on top of their sleeping rolls as the mosquitoes buzzed about. They must have come in on the wind, or perhaps there were some pools nearby. Fortunately, they put on insect repellent several times a day, so they weren't bothered. Still, it was amazing how ubiquitous mosquitos were, ranging from the desert to the jungle, and then all the way to the tundra. One of nature's great survivors; she just hoped they weren't capable of transmitting R24, like they were with malaria and so many other diseases that threatened humans.

CHAPTER 10

Danielle was awoken by a loud clap of thunder. The wind was blowing hard, and it was raining. They were big drops of rain, like tropical rain, and every now and then the wind would push them in through the front flaps of the tent and wet her feet. She felt for the trusty lamp that she kept next to her head. She turned it on and then rolled over to find Sebastian awake and looking at her. He blinked as his eyes got used to the light and then propped himself up on his elbow and smiled.

She asked, "I didn't wake you, did I?"

"No, the storm woke me up," he said.

"Yes, I think it woke me as well. And hey, it's raining. You'll get to take some good pictures, and then if we're still out here, I mean in Irh Arrikine, you'll be able to paint the desert as it blooms," she said.

He looked at his watched.

"It's 2AM, isn't this your go to the toilet time?" he said with a smirk.

She got embarrassed and said, "No... not always. Why have you been taking notes or something?"

He laughed and said, "I could set my clock by you, that's how regular you are."

She couldn't think of a good comeback, so just hit him with the rolled-up towel she used as a pillow.

Then she said, "Well as it happens, I actually could go to the toilet right now, but that doesn't prove anything. I just don't want to go out in the rain though. Do you know how long it has been raining? Surely this heavy rain won't last too much longer."

"It was raining heavy when I first woke up, so it's been going for about 15 minutes. I expect that it will ease off soon. You know, this may be the only rain they get this year, or even for the next few years. All the life out here, and the plants we are looking for, they all depend on this one shower of rain," he said.

"Yes. They are living in the crevasses and holes far above the springs and groundwater seeps. This is all they are going to get. I suppose it's what makes them so hardy, and maybe so packed with chemicals, helping them to resist heat, dry, grazing, and insects."

They continued to talk for another 15 minutes until the rain seemed to just stop. One minute it was raining heavy, and then there was no rain at all.

Sebastian said, "I think this is your opportunity. Better rush out and do your business in case it starts up again. I suppose you want me to come with you?"

"Yes please," she said.

They put their boots on. The ground would be crawling with insects and wildlife after the rain and then pushed out of the tent into the cool moist air. The wind had died right down, now that the gust front had past, and deeper in the valley they could hear frogs. It was amazing that they had remained buried for months, and then with the first sprinkle of rain they were at the surface ready to breed. Flying insects immediately began to buzz around the light. She held it at a distance so they would not land on her clothes or get tangled in her hair.

The petrichor, that damp earth fragrance, was rich in the air. It was as invigorating as any incense, calling all life to attention and signaling time to reproduce. Maybe it was also an aphrodisiac for humans, it would kind of make sense out here; it was working on Danielle. They walked to the edge of camp, which had been strategically chosen because there was a boulder outcrop nearby for shelter from the wind, and for going to the toilet. Sebastian waited on one side, and she carefully made her way around to the other.

Just when she was most vulnerable, she heard a stomping sound, like something stamping its foot. It was close and alarmed her. She could not see anything beyond the small ball of light that surrounded her. It stomped again, and as loudly as she dared, she called out to Sebastian, "Did you hear that?"

He replied, "Yeah," and then turned on the flashlight he was carrying. He headed toward her side of the rocks, but shining the beam further afield, careful not to embarrass her. They saw numerous white figures standing still and looking at them. They were uncomfortably close and thus presented danger. He recognized them as Oryx, a herd of about twenty, and the male with his long sharp horns was stomping the ground as a warning to Danielle to back away.

Sebastian said in a soft voice, "I think it's time to head back to camp. Slowly walk towards me whilst I keep the light on them."

As carefully as she could, she raised herself into a stoop and crept back toward him, careful not to give the large antelope a reason to charge at her. Just when you think the desert is barren and lifeless, such wonders appear. It was likely the herd had followed the rain, and would in turn be shadowed by cheetah, hyena, and African painted dogs. All of these would view Danielle as prey, especially if she were alone in the dark. Perhaps the cave paintings were more than just the animals the ancient's hunted, but also a warning about the animals that hunted them. It seemed almost everything out here, where life is tenuous, was dangerous.

They returned safely to the tent, and the guns

that lay next to their bedding. In retrospect, next time they went out into the dark, it would be wise to take them also. A second bout of rain started, but this time without the wind. Again, it was heavy and lasted about 15 minutes. That was all that fell, there was no more. Sebastian fell back to sleep almost instantly; even though it was pitch-dark she could tell because his breathing changed. She lay there thinking of the morning, hoping to see a transformed world with running streams and pools of fresh water.

The morning was bright sunshine with a brilliant blue sky. No clouds remained, having moved further to the West. The haze that had persisted ever since she travelled inland from the Mediterranean Coast was washed from the atmosphere, and when one climbed to a vantage point, it was clear like a photograph all the way to the horizon.

Indeed, from the moment he got up Sebastian began taking pictures, from landscapes all the way down to twigs and beetles. Many plants had already responded to the water, unfurling otherwise dead leaves, and beginning to change color. There were also more small animals around, including all types of birds that they had not noticed before, as well as reptiles and mammals. Everything in nature was energized, and would be for the next few weeks, until the waters either evaporated or seeped beneath the sand.

After breakfast they set off again to find the elusive plants. They needed more of what they had gathered yesterday, requiring a new stand because they had picked the previous one bare, but more importantly the seeds from the third plant which they were yet to find.

Heading off on foot they squished through damp sand, mud, and sometimes small streams. Whilst it was still relatively cool, they begin to climb higher up the rocky slopes, stopping at each pothole and crevasse. The old woman had described what they were looking for as a small rounded spiky bush that had what looked like pea pods on it. Danielle assumed that it was some kind of legume. It wasn't till they had reached almost the top strata of rock, that then opened onto a deeply weathered stone plateau, that the old woman alerted them to one of the plants.

They hurried over to where she stood as she pointed down into a depression. Inside was what looked like a tumbleweed but still rooted to the ground. There were dried pods hanging from what looked like a dead bush no larger than a basketball. As he had done before, Sebastian took several photographs of the plant, to document its location in the landscape, and also the particulars of its appearance and physiology. It was important that they recorded how to find and process the plants, should they not survive.

The old woman picked off the pods and then peeled them open to reveal several small black seeds, similar in size and appearance to peppercorns. She collected about twenty individual seeds from the plant and then tossed five of them back into nearby depressions. She said that if they did not do that, then there would be no pants next time they came through this area. It was a sensible conservation and sustainable practice. One could imagine people going crazy and harvesting every seed that they found, only to find that they had sent the plant extinct within a few years. This especially being the case with desert plants that are often clinging on at the edge of survival.

The collected seeds were treated like little nuggets of gold. As the party spread out across the plateau, each person in turn discovered a plant and called out with excitement. They carefully gathered the seeds, being sure to return a quarter back to the earth. It took them all day to gather around 1kg of the seeds. It was a bit like harvesting spice, being a slow and painstaking process that could only be done by hand. Maybe in the future someone would invent a way to cultivate them. But then again, hopefully after the pandemic had run its course, they wouldn't need the potion in such large amounts.

When they returned to camp in the

late afternoon, their backpacks were full of ingredients for the potion. It was carefully packed into bundles that would be loaded onto the camels for the trip back to Irh Arrikine. It was reminiscent of the ancient caravans that had plied the Sahara. Traveling from oasis-to-oasis carrying precious goods like gems, salt, spices, and fragrances to trade in the markets, and grace the temples, of ancient Egypt, Arabia, Carthage, and Mesopotamia. The only difference now was that the traders had sunglasses, flashlights, and guns. Other than that, they were living as if it were two millennia ago.

Not far from the camp was a small waterfall fed by an ephemeral spring that had been activated by the recent rain. Its clear water poured into a deep sandy bottomed pool. The camels had been kept away from the little oasis and instead were led to drink further downstream. This kept the water crystal-clear for the party to swim and bath in. It was the first time the Tuareg had remove their indigo robes, but even then it was brief, and the woman were not allowed to watch. Then, as the old woman's escort stood guard, she bathed in the water, briefly and modestly. When she had finished, he also bathed, stripping right down to a loincloth.

Finally, at sunset the natural pool was available for Danielle and Sebastian. They were alone as the others prepared food around the campfire. The water was so cool and refreshing after the long day of backbreaking work. Indeed, it was the most work that they had done since before they had begun the original camel trek. They both stripped down to their underwear and dived in from a rock ledge. At its deepest point the water came up to Danielle's shoulders.

It felt so good to get the dust out of her hair and the pores of her skin. And it felt so good to feel cool. There was an evening breeze that blew between the rock pillars, evaporating the water off the skin and cooling it even further. They joked and playing in the water and then laid back on the soft warm sand until the first stars appeared. Each of them had brough a change of clean clothes, and facing different directions they changed out of their wet underwear and into dry clothes. This was the type of life she could happily live, out here in the middle of nowhere; it was like being at one with nature, like the ancient swimmers of the Neolithic. The only problem was it required water, which was so rare and fleeting, and it required a Sebastian. The world was dying, or it was tearing itself apart, she was not sure. But here and now it was serene and romantic like an evening dream.

Having changed, they washed out their dusty clothes and draped them across the rocks to dry overnight, then they headed back to the camp barefoot in the sand by twilight. During the day the Tuareg had shot and prepared a small gazelle that had strayed into range. They explained that it was cooked in the manner described by the thirteenth-century Muslim-Andalusi scholar Ibn Razīn al-Tujībī. Danielle and Sebastian kept an open mind and were thankful it didn't come with a side serving of grubs and insects. It was presented as a stew with large chunks of spiced meat and chickpeas, all on a bed of rice. It was absolutely delicious, and there was so much meat left over that they salted the remainder to make it last the journey back to town.

Sebastian said, "Do you know what would really go down well with this?"

"No, tell me," Danielle said as she greedily ripped hunks of tender juicy flesh from a bone, like a ravenous cave woman.

"A nice cold beer," he said with a chuckle.

She replied, "You know I read somewhere that the brewing of beer was one of the first inventions after the discovery of farming; maybe even before it."

"That figures," he said with a smile.

CHAPTER 11

It was a peaceful night's sleep, and this time Danielle didn't even wake up in the early hours. Perhaps in the past it had been hunger that triggered her light sleeping, because now with a full belly her sleep was undisturbed. Each night Danielle and Sebastian sleep together they edged closer, both physically and emotionally.

She awoke just before dawn, still dark enough for stars, but light enough to see where she was going. Leaving Sebastian to sleep, she silently slipped out of the tent. The others were already awake and doing Fajr, morning prayer. There was food left over from the previous night, and it was heating in a large pot on the campfire. The Tuareg also had a kettle of coffee simmering away at the edge of the coals. But before she ate or drank, she wanted to have another swim in the pool. She asked the other woman, through the Tuareg, if she would like to join her, and she was very pleased to be invited. The old woman's escort accompanied them to the pool, but then stopped short and out of view, such that he remained within earshot but could not watch them.

The water was clear and still. The waterfall still trickled, perhaps no more than a faucet's worth, and when one stood beneath, it felt like being in a shower. The woman had a natural product that worked like soap. Danielle had seen it before and believed that it was made from pulverizing the leaf of a plant. She took some from the woman and lathered it up to wash her hair and skin. It was extremely refreshing and tingled like a combination of comfrey and peppermint. The bubbles floated across the water and then quickly dissolved until they left no trace. What a perfect solution for camping; but of course, that was to be expected of the desert nomads.

After bathing they sat on the rock ledge dangling their feet in the water. Although they could not speak each other's languages, they still communicated how lovely the morning was, and how happy they were. From a small bag the woman produced a colored glass bottle with a cork stopper. It was ornate and possibly very old. It was the type of bottle that one would expect a genie to billow from if rubbed. The woman then gestured Danielle to put out her hands as a cup, and when she did the woman poured a fragrant oil into them. She then gestured for her to rub it though her hair. It was a conditioner, based on an ancient recipe, which made her hair soft and glowing.

Then she was instructed to rub it over her skin. It was a full body treatment to protect yourself from the sun and wind, and everything in the desert that ages you. It was probably why so many of the women she had seen, despite their age and this environment, had beautiful soft and clear complexions.

When Danielle returned to the camp Sebastian was sitting by the campfire eating breakfast. They had been on meagre rations for the past few weeks, so they all had healthy appetites to satiate. He looked at her as she approached, wearing a loose silky white robe with Arabic designs embroidered with gold thread. Her long blonde hair was down. It was probably the first time he had ever seen her like this. And now with the old woman's conditioning formula, it shone and swirled like threads of corn silk in the morning sun. Her skin glowed and her smile beamed. He just kept looking as if the old woman had anointed her with an aphrodisiac; maybe it was a special concoction and that is exactly what she had done.

Danielle ate lots, then they packed up camp and loaded their precious cargo onto the camels. It would be a hot day's trek, and they would arrive back at Irh Arrikine late in the afternoon. She returned to thinking about Rudy as she swayed listlessly on the back of the camel. Would he still be alive, and was it possible that his condition had improved? And what of the other people in the town, had anyone else comedown with R24? If they did start to show symptoms, Samia had been instructed to give them the potion just like with Rudy. She was sure that Samia could handle any emergency.

During their return trip they had to negotiate gorges that funneled water between deep rock walls. They were dry when they came through the first time, but now they contained water. Sometimes it was up to 1m deep. After stopping to drink, the camels plodded through, keeping the riders and cargo high and dry. In some parts of the Tassili N'Ajjer there were rumors of West African crocodiles, once common in oasis, but now thought to be extinct. Relics or those much wetter times thousands of years ago, and a symbol of resistance against change. She could imagine seeing crocodiles in these gorges now that they were filled with water, but obviously it would only be the permanent ones where they could survive until the next rain. Maybe with most of the people removed from the face of the Earth, endangered species could make a comeback, like in Chernobyl after the nuclear accident.

They entered Irh Arrikine late in the afternoon. There had been no traffic on the road they followed for the last few kilometers, and there was no movement in the town. This was not unusual for the hottest part of the day, but it did make it look like a ghost town. Fortunately, there was activity at the compound, with people sheltering under tents and awnings. The one closest to the fence had Sophie and Rudy sitting in 21st century collapsible camping chairs and wearing dark sunglasses. It was an odd contrast between the traditional and the contemporary.

Danielle immediately went over to check on Rudy. They both appeared to be asleep but then Sophie woke as the camels began their normal belching and protesting at being forced to do something they didn't want to.

She looked up and asked, "Hi, how was the trip?"

"It went well thank you," Danielle said. "We found the plants and have brought a load back with us. How have things been here, and how is Rudy?" she asked.

"It has been quiet. There have been no new cases of R24, or anything else."

"And Rudy, how is he?" she asked again.

"I think he is improving. Although he is not very active, and he's sleeping a lot, when he is awake you can hold a conversation with him. He says that the numbness is starting to subside and that his eyes don't hurt as much. I've been with him constantly, and I've noticed he is eating and drinking better each day."

Danielle left Rudy sleeping whilst she helped unload the camels and then clean up after the long hot journey. The shower in the compound was welcome but a poor substitute for the serenity of the oasis that morning.

The pace of life had slowed down. In the past it would have taken them about two hours by car to get to Djanet, now it would take them two days, via the shortcut through the mountains, and three days if they followed the road. This change in pace required a change in the way one thought, and the culture that need to be adopted. It wasn't only technology that would be regressing, it would be every aspect of life and of thinking. She wondered how they would be coping back in the UK. Compared to the Middle East and North Africa, the Neolithic, or even the medieval, were pretty harsh and brutal in the higher latitudes.

When she returned to Rudy, he was awake and being tended to by Samia. She had brought over his evening potion, and Danielle could see that he was able to hold the cup and drink without spilling. The tremors in his hands and body had stopped, and his eyes were no longer bloodshot. It was fortunate that R24 did not produce other symptoms like legions and pustules, like with plague, or bleeding, coughing or diarrhea like with so many other African illnesses. However, she could not be sure of what was going on internally. In the medical literature no one had lived long enough to develop secondary symptoms. She hoped that his neurological and nervous systems had only been affected by some form of toxin, and it was now getting flushed out of his body. Regardless of his progress, she still could not tell if he remained infectious, or if he would have a relapse.

She donned her mask and then sat on the sand beside him, "Hello Rudy, how are you feeling?" she asked.

He looked over at her and the life had returned to his eyes. He said, "I must be getting better because this potion tastes awful again," and then he managed a weak smile.

"That is good," she said, "and what about the numbness and dizzy spells?"

"That is going away, although I can't move very fast, or I get unstable. But if I just do things slowly, and if I concentrate, then I can manage most things," he said.

"And what about the sensitivity to light, how is that going?" she asked.

"It's still there, but it's not as bad as it was. There is a dull headache, as if my sinuses and ears are blocked, and it's like my eyes are connected to that, if it makes sense. I'll tell you what I *would* like, a long relaxing soak in a bath. I feel like that just might clear my head."

It was a good idea, and despite the heat, maybe some steam, and a warm bath could do wonders. Maybe the old woman would have some fragrant salts and oils to add to the water to give it mystical rejuvenating power. Even if there was no medical basis for the effect on the body and the soul, if it made him feel better, then it was as good as any drugs she could offer.

In the courtyard behind the clinic was a large stone bath. What its original purpose was, she had no idea. It looked more like something for christening a baby, sacrificing a goat, or even washing clothes. They erected a sheet about it to hold in steam and fragrance, then filled it with hot water. It was after sunset as they slowly walked Rudy from the compound to the clinic. They could have put him in the back of a pickup truck and driven him in less than a minute, but he insisted on walking. Wearing gloves and masks Danielle and Samia held each of his hands as he walked. It did not seem like the disease had affected his heart or lungs, because he did not become tired or breathless, although by the time they reached the clinic he was having a little trouble with his balance.

Samia explained to the old woman what they were planning to do, and she gave her a carved wooden box that contained a powder. It was a combination of desert salts, minerals, and fragrant oils. Samia was instructed to sprinkle this over the water and then give it a good stir before Rudy took his bath. In effect it was an ancient version of bath salts. Then when he came out of the bath, they were told to apply the same oil that had been used on Danielle. The woman handed over the ornate genie bottle that had worked such wonders on Danielle's hair, skin, and mind.

In the candlelit courtyard, preserving as much modesty as they could, they stripped Rudy bare and put him down to soak in the fragrant effervescing bath. He fully immersed himself, head and all, and then resurfaced to take in the tent full of vapors. It opened up every pore, and enter every orifice, evacuating the days of dust, sweat, and malignancy.

Finally, he was removed from the bath, rinsed off, and then placed upon a rattan bed next to a burning torch. Samia then massaged in the unguent potion. It was the type of day spa wealthy middle-aged women would have structured their entire holiday around.

It seemed there was a connection between Samia and Rudy. Sure, she was a good nurse, but this seemed like something more. The two of them had a connection that had never existed between herself and Rudy and had not developed between Rudy and Sophie. And this was despite Sophie having a longer history with Rudy and constantly caring for him since the onset of his symptoms. It was only when Samia approach him, and conversed with him, that he warmed and smiled. And it was the same with Samia. She was always friendly and empathetic with all of the patients, but with Rudy it was different, as if it were very personal and heart-felt. Like she was tending a loved one rather than duty bound to a patient.

It was ironic. Sophie should have been prime real estate. She was attractive and personable, and looking quite fit after losing a few pounds, and yet she remained the bridesmaid. There was no doubt that she would become someone's bride, in this strange new world, but it may not be with her first choice. Then again, is that ever the case? And people just delude themselves that it is and instead settle because it is the time to do so.

CHAPTER 12

The Internet was now completely down. They didn't know if it was a global outage, or if it was just at their end of the line. Thus, they had no contact with the outside world. Now everything would need to be hand delivered, a dedicated person and journey for every correspondence. They had not seen an aeroplane since before the pandemic; maybe they no longer flew anywhere. Did this mean that humans would revert to ocean voyages for travel, correspondence, and trade? If so, then how long and perilous would Danielle's journey be back to the UK, if at all possible. What would be the cost of such a journey, and how could she possibly pay.

Over the weeks, with repeated treatment, Rudy slowly regained his senses and strength. It seemed that R24 could be beaten, although why the potion worked remained a mystery. They didn't even know if it would work on other people, there were no other sick people in the town to test it on. Still, they had really dodged the bullet. It would have been so easy for others to get infected, or for more cases to arrive from out of town. If they had not enacted quarantine, then they would have had recurring outbreaks every few weeks. And then there was the potion. It was a miracle that it had worked. The planets had really aligned for Rudy to have been saved; the odds were incalculable. Those with stronger religious beliefs said that it was the will of God that he survived, and that it must be part of a greater plan.

Now that their quarantine had been lifted, they were free to move about the town and even take up residence in unused houses. These were the homes where occupants had left, perhaps to travel to Djanet, and then never returned. It was presumed they had been caught up in the pandemic and its aftermath, and likely to never return or bequeath to anyone. After a short and somewhat awkward conversation, Danielle convinced Sebastian to share a house with her. It was on the basis of separate rooms. Romantically it was 'suboptimal' but still it brought them closer together without having to say anything aloud.

Sophie and Rudy also shared a house, although in their case she lived upstairs, and he live downstair. Rudy still required assistance. Sophie would watch over him during the night and Samia would tend to him the remainder of the time. It would have been more logical for Rudy and Samia to live together, but religious beliefs and cultural customs forbid this if they were not married.

The Westerners were now responsible for preparing their own food; thus, they drew on what stocks remained in the dwellings, and what was growing in their gardens. In many regards the town was self-sufficient, with homes having vegetable gardens and fruit trees. There were also larger farms and plantations just outside of town. But still there were other things that they would soon be running low on, some of them food, and other items like household groceries, medical supplies, or batteries. They would need to venture out into what was once civilization, to do reconnaissance, to get supplies, and to get the message out that they had discovered a cure.

Danielle called for a town meeting, and everyone was asked to attend. It was organized around a community dinner in the main street. Everyone attended, and many for the first time could see the progress being made with Rudy's recovery. He wore a mask and kept his distance just in case he was contagious, but still it went a long way to allay fears.

After they had eaten, she mentioned the topic of needing to send a delegation to Djanet. Everyone agreed that supplies were running low, and that it was important to try and get some information about what was happening in the world. She wanted to get agreement from all of the people in the town because there was the possibility that whoever went may not return.

Or they may return infected, or they may cause other people to come back to the town, either as refugees or with malicious intent. Despite these risks the motion was approved.

It was decided that they would take two pickup trucks. In each truck they would have a driver and armed guard, and as passengers there would be Danielle and Sebastian in one, and the old woman and her escort in the other. They would carry extra guns and supplies just in case. That night they said their farewells knowing they would be leaving before sunrise, and that there was a chance that they may not return.

Danielle and Sebastian walked the dirt road back to their house. They had settled in as if they owned it. She said, "You realize that we have to get this potion out to the rest of the world, but I'm not sure what to do if Djanet is also cut off."

"Where would be the best place to have it delivered to?" he asked.

"I'm not sure. Maybe a military base if one is still operating, and they have aeroplanes flying, or perhaps a large hospital or university. Ultimately it would need to be coordinated by WHO, or some other United Nations agency," she said.

"I'm a bit worried that if we give it to the military, or just one country's government; they may keep it for themselves. The temptation could be too great. Just think about it, the whole world is dying, and you alone possess the cure. If you do nothing and let the rest of the world die, then you inherit the whole Earth," he said.

"Do you really think someone, or some group, would do that?" she asked.

"Unfortunately, yes, I think they would. But it's not an indictment on the whole human species, just on those that have managed to seize power. Perhaps things are different now. Maybe power structures have collapsed, and people have once again formed communities in order to survive. But that is probably being a bit too fanciful and naïve. What is more likely to have happened is that the rich and powerful managed to escape the carnage in their bunkers, and behind the police, and now they can take over completely," he said.

"A fat lot of good it does them if there are no workers for them to tread on. I prefer my version of reality," she said with a laugh.

It was amazing how even in the darkest of times people could keep their humor and their dreams. If she lived ten thousand years ago, it would have been her painting on the walls of the caves; and most certainly Sebastian as well.

After morning prayers, the two pickup trucks departed. They would head Southeast, then after skirting the mountains, would turn to the Northwest and on to Djanet. It would take them around two hours, travelling at a leisurely 80kmh to conserve fuel. Normally at dawn there would be traffic on the main road that looped the mountains, but apart from the arrivals a few weeks back, there had not been a single traveler. Not by road or by camel. It was hard to imagine that the Tuareg nomads also adhered to the travel restrictions, yet none passed through.

Djanet extended over a large area and had a collection of settlements around its outer perimeter. As they approached, there was the turnoff for the airport on their left, and on their right the road went through the settlement of Eferi, then on to Djanet proper. They passed some government offices, including Inspection Divisionaire des Douanes Djanet (Customs Office), all of which looked shuttered and uninhabited, and then finally they pulled into a gas station. Normally it would be busy, especially this time of the morning with trucks, tour busses, and taxis going to the airport. But it was quiet and appeared abandoned. There were some cars and trucks in the carpark, but none were at bousers for refueling.

Fortunately, due to the extensive reliance on solar power, the pumps and all other electrical equipment were operating. Although for how much longer, they did not know. They began refilling the vehicles and fuel cans they had brought with them. The two guards, brandishing their guns, went over to the building that served as both shop and restaurant. Danielle and Sebastian also carried rifles as they walked around the outside of the complex.

Sebastian spied what appeared to be a new, and likely expensive, SUV. It had probably been owned by a wealthy businessman or high-ranking government official. He signaled Danielle to come with him to look at it. It was unlocked and there was no one inside. They noticed that the ignition was turned on but there were no lights illuminated on the dash. It was common for vehicles to be left running so that the air conditioning would keep them cool. It was likely that this vehicle had been left running, and for some reason the occupants had fled and not returned. Thus, it probably idled for days until it ran out of fuel. He said,

"I think if we put some fuel in this and get a new battery, then it may run. What do you think?"

"It sounds like a good idea," she said. "But I suppose we better see how the guards are doing in the service station, just in case the owner is in there and still alive."

They continued their sweep of the perimeter, inspecting other vehicles, and then finally approached the front doors. Through the glass they could see the guards helping themselves to snacks from the shelves. The automatic doors opened, and they were surprised to find that the air conditioning was working. Speaking in French, Sebastian asked the guards,

"What have you found?"

One replied, "There are two dead people in a room at the back. It smells unbelievably bad, so I don't suggest that you go there. Other than that, there is no one else in the building."

Danielle put on her mask and decided to look, just to assure herself that the people had died from R24, as opposed to something else like violence. She did a quick inspection, and although it was difficult to be sure, she could not see any evidence of bullet wounds or other trauma. And based on other indicators, such as the dribble stains down the front of their clothes, they had been infected with R24.

They grabbed a new car battery from the shop, along with some tools and more fuel cans, and then set to getting the SUV re-fueled and running. It was not a difficult job, and when it roared to life, the air conditioning started to blast. With its leather seats and tinted windows, it was much more comfortable than the beat-up pickup truck in which they had arrived. Having observed the upgrade, the other drivers intended to get themselves new vehicles when they started to pillage Djanet.

Now they had fueled and collected supplies,

the group headed into Djanet proper. Depending on what they found would determine what their next move would be. If Danielle could contact the rest of the world and hopefully get a message out that they had a cure for R24, then they would wait it out either at Irh Arrikine, or if safe, then at Djanet with its greater resources. However, if they could not contact anyone, then the next step would be to travel to a larger town or city in the hope that it had people, some form of functioning society, and the ability to get the cure to whomever would be the appropriate authority.

They were aware they would have to guard their secret from unscrupulous operators. But how would they be able to tell who was going to use it for the good of humanity, and who was going to use it to control humanity? It would be extremely racist and short sighted to think that only the advanced economies of the Western European countries should be the responsible recipients. As far as most of Africa and the Middle East were concerned, it was the West that was the enemy of peace and freedom, despite their rhetoric to the contrary. Perhaps it should be up to herself and Sebastian to disseminate the cure as widely as possible so that no one group could monopolize it. If so, then they would have to be cagey and discerning about who they spoke to and what they divulged. It was a huge responsibility to place upon two people completely unqualified in the art of international politics.

There was a normal radio and a CB radio in the vehicle. As Sebastian drove, Danielle turned on the normal radio and began to scan the frequencies. There were two stations broadcasting, the National Government service, Radio Algérienne, and the commercial music broadcaster Radio Dzair. Presently both were playing music. They had not listened for long enough to know if it was just a default loop from an unattended studio, or if they were going to get live updates and emergency information. There was also phone reception, and she tried the international numbers stored in her phone but was unable to get a connection. Then she tried the hotel where she had previously stayed, it rang but nobody answered.

Typically, the CB radio would be busy with chatter from trucks and tour operators. Sebastian picked up the microphone and sent out a message asking anyone who could hear him to respond. They waited but there was no response. They would repeat this action as they continued further down the road, just in case someone came into range, or just happen to tune in at the right time.

The rainstorm they had the previous week apparently came through Djanet. Where the road dipped down in the usually dry riverbed, in the

Zferi settlement, there was evidence that the river had overflowed and washed debris across the road. They stopped to inspect, and to push aside some of the rocks and debris. As they stood there and looked it became apparent that no one had driven through since the river had flooded. The debris remained where the water had deposited it, and there were no tire tracks or disturbance to suggest that vehicles, camels, or people had passed though, despite this being the only road in and out of Djanet.

CHAPTER 13

They passed several shops including a supermarket, a pharmacy, and a building supply store, but everything was deserted. Then, as they continued toward the center of Djanet, where the mountains came close to the road and formed a defensive position, they saw ahead what appeared to be a barricade across the road. On the Eastern side were mountains that they could not climb in their vehicles. To the West was the sandy expanse of the dry river, and on the far bank was the historic site of Adjahil, and then more mountains.

Trucks were parked across the road, and there were other trucks on the road that crossed the riverbed. It was all to provide a defensive position from which guns could be fired at oncoming traffic. The two pickup trucks stopped some distance back, and presumably out of the range of all but the most professional and well-equipped sniper. As they discussed their options, they then noticed people on the nearby hilltops, as if taking up positions to monitor them, and possibly ambush them. It was a tense situation; however, they had no choice but to send forth a representative.

Fortunately, one of the drivers was a long-time resident of Djanet and was related to, and knew, many people in the town. He was confident that he could secure safe passage. They directed him to communicate their situation, and that Danielle was a doctor, which may afford her some cachet. But under no circumstances was he to mention the potion, or the ingredients, that they had hidden in their luggage. At least not at this early stage. Once they had established who was in charge and what their intentions were, then they might divulge the lifesaving information. He had also been warned not to come into close contact with whomever was at the barricade, even if they were close friends or family. They could not be sure who was infected, and the last thing they wanted was to go through quarantine all over again; or worse, catch R24.

The man drove up to the barricade, and as they watched though binoculars, they could see activity. Firstly, people talked from a distance, but then, as more people arrived, the contact was closer and seemed to be friendly. After about 30 minutes he returned and said that they could approach the barrier, and after they had confirmed his story and vetted the party, they would be allowed into the central district of Djanet. But even though they were allowed in, they still must respect quarantine rules.

They progressed toward the barricade, being

watched from all sides, and no doubt being held in gunsights. Each of their party was taken aside for interrogation. It seemed that the men of the barricade had military or policing experience. They had an English interpreter for Danielle, and she was able to show them her MSF credentials.

The barricade guards were extremely pleased to learn that she was a doctor and thereafter treated her as a VIP. They had lost all but one of their doctors to the pandemic, and now relied mainly on junior nurses. She also learned that they still had infected people living within the city. They were locked up, wherever they could be secured, and given rations of food and water to keep them alive. Apparently the 'patients' were in extremely poor condition and were not expected to survive much longer. They were also getting new cases, almost daily. It was obvious that at least three weeks ago people were still getting infected even though the first wave had passed; a result of poor crowd control and breaches in quarantine.

There was a large hospital in the center of town and Danielle asked if she could go to meet with the doctor and nursing staff. She insisted that Sebastian accompany her, and this they understood and approved; assuming he was her male escort. Of all the remote Southern desert towns, Djanet was one of the more tolerant and cosmopolitan by virtue of all the tourists that frequented the area via Tiska Djanet Airport. In the town there were many hotels, travel agencies, and tour operators catering for international arrivals. They also had a 'faux' authentic souk and various other tourist attractions.

Thus, the locals were used to Western women being unaccompanied, and less than modest. But despite this, or perhaps because they believed she was sensitive to culture, they applauded that Sebastian would accompany her, and when necessary, speak on her behalf. Something else that endeared her was the fact that since the start of the trek she had worn a scarf or veil over her head and face. It was not to please the Tuareg, for it was the men that covered their faces instead of the women, but because on most occasions, especially during the day, it was practical. The loose fit allowed air to flow over perspiration, whilst keeping the sun and desert wind off the head and face. It was like being under one's own private tent. Thus, she entered Djanet dressed as a local, despite her blonde hair, blue eyes, and pale complexion.

Sebastian had also adopted local garb, wearing loose white robes, and with his darker skin and mannerisms, he somewhat resembled an Arab. He even wore a traditional goat hair agal, the black cord atop his white keffiyeh, the head scarf, such that he could have been at home anywhere on the Arabian Peninsula or Levant.

Clearing the barricade, they followed a car that led them to a house a short walk from the hospital. As was the case in Irh Arrikine, there were many houses left vacant when their occupants fell to R24. Houses ready to live in and full of food, clothes, and even jewelry. The world must have been flush with once valuable trinkets that for all their luster could not save a single life. Danielle and Sebastian were allocated a house, and by local standards their new home was up-market. It also came with a peaceful courtyard that had perfectly manicured plants and a water feature.

It was explained to them that the people had died in the house. There was a local crew that were tasked with removing the bodies and cleaning up. This house had been cleared out a couple of weeks ago, and it was presumed that after being disinfected none of the disease remained. There was a great deal of wishful thinking attached to this assumption. A pestilence like anthrax can survive up to 70 years in enclosed spaces, 140 years in soil, and nearly 50,000 years in permafrost. The life cycle and persistence of R24 was still a mystery, thus every day, and activity, had inherent risk. However, the impermanency of life now changed people's outlook and behavior.

After settling in they walked down the street to the hospital. It was a dissimilar experience than in the previous town. Now there were other people walking on the streets, and from time-to-time vehicles drove past. Still, everyone kept their distance and watched each other with suspicion. Symbols had been painted on houses, to denote the dead, and others that signified the still alive but almost dead, being the zombies. Often, they would past a house and there would be the horrid stench that made one want to stop breathing.

Out here in the desert everything dried up quickly. One could only imagine what it was like in the tropics, or the temperate climates, with all those dead bodies. And, the problems with flies and other insects, especially if those insects could spread R24. Then of course there was the issue of secondary disease caused from all the death and decay. In so many places around the world drinking water must have been poisoned and even become infected and dangerous to touch.

Yet Danielle did not know what was required to kill R24. Would boiling water do it, or bleach, or alcohol? She just did not know. The only way she could find out was to gather data. Maybe that data had already been gathered and was being analyzed and tested all around the world. But maybe it had not. Maybe here in Djanet, and only by her efforts, would they get answers. She had to carry on as if that was the case. She had to assume that it would be her efforts that gave humanity the best chance for survival.

The hospital was a modern multi-story building. Inside it was clean, tiled, and hospital-like. A lady wearing a mask sat at reception and greeted them. At first, she spoke in French and then continued in English at Sebastian's request. One would have thought that during a pandemic the hospital would be overwhelmed with patients and rushed off their feet. But here on the ground floor it was silent, and their voices echoed. Danielle showed her medical identification and said, "I can't believe how quiet it is in here."

The receptionist replied, "We stopped bringing R24 patients in a few weeks ago. It was a disaster. It spread the disease to the other patients and staff, so it was decided to leave them locked up in their houses. And then with all the deaths, well there were very few people left to treat. We have a couple of women patients with newborn babies, a few elderly people, and then some children with conditions unrelated to R24. We have everyone together on the first floor, but other than that the hospital is empty."

"Do you have a pathology lab in the hospital?" Danielle asked.

"Yes, we do," the receptionist said, "and it is very new and well equipped. It hasn't been touched since the outbreak. There is no one to staff it, and there has been no demand for its services."

"Excellent," Danielle said. "Can I please have a look at it?"

"Sure, just follow the corridor to the end," she said as she pointed, "and then turn to the left and you will see the door with the sign above it."

"OK, thank you. I will have a quick look and then I want to go and meet with the doctor," Danielle said.

"You will find him on the first floor, just ask any of the staff and they will help you," the receptionist said in a friendly almost normal way, as if there was no apocalypse.

They thanked her and walked the long white corridors to pathology. Upon entering they found it was an impressive facility. There was a plaque on the wall commemorating a wealthy doner for funding the facility. There was also a list of partners across the world, including WHO in Geneva, and OIPH, Office International d'Hygiène Publique, in Paris. These were significant credentials, and if she could contact these or similar agencies, then she could get the message out that there was a cure.

A quick survey of the facility revealed that they had bio-hazard suits and other protective gear, electron microscopes, as well as high-tech equipment like mass spectrometer and spectrophotometer. In adjoining rooms, they had MRI, X-ray, and ultrasound equipment. All of this would be extremely helpful for studying R24 and its effects on the human body. Now she just needed to get infected patients in here without placing herself and others in danger. She needed them to be subdued, or even lucid like Rudy. In fact, it would be helpful to bring Rudy here so she could properly analyze and treat him. To see what damage had been done, and how his body was repairing itself.

She also considered where and how they may synthesize the potion. Perhaps they may be able to do this in the hospital's kitchen. It would need to be done under hygienic and controlled conditions. She could experiment with concentration and dosage rates and perhaps identify the active chemical compounds to discover how it worked. In a normal world this would have earned her a Nobel Prize in medicine, but today it only justified her existence, and the food she consumed.

Danielle beckoned to Sebastian that it was time to take the elevator to the first floor and met the resident doctor and staff. They went to the elevator just outside in the corridor and pushed the button. Nothing happened. It seemed that although the power was on, the elevators, or maybe just this elevator, was not working. She noticed that there was a smell coming from the elevator, that horrible smell of death, thus they elected to walk back to reception.

"Excuse me," Danielle said, "The elevator next

to pathology is not working, and there is a horrible smell coming from it."

"Oh yes, I'm sorry I forgot to mention it. The elevator has been locked. A zombie was in the hospital, and in the emergency, it was locked inside the elevator. The cleanup crew hasn't removed it yet. We have put in a request, and they are expected to come soon."

Danielle thought about it and then said, "Perhaps we should look at the victim ourselves, given it is so close to pathology. Do we know who it was and any other medical history?"

"Yes, actually we do," said the receptionist, "It was one of the laboratory staff who fell ill during the second outbreak," she said with little emotion.

"OK, then cancel the clean-up crew. We will deal with it ourselves. I'm hoping that we can do an autopsy on the body to see how the disease works and what damage it did."

The receptionist said, "We also have a morgue in the basement. It already has some bodies in it, but it hasn't been used for a few weeks because it was suspected to be a source of infection. So, you are free to use it, but I would not enter without a biohazard suit."

"Thank you, yes that is good advice. Now how should we get to the first floor?" Danielle asked.

The receptionist pointed to the nearby elevator and said, "This one is working."

They thanked her and proceeded up to the first floor.

CHAPTER 14

The elevator doors opened to what could only be described as a normal scene. There were people at the nurse's station, pushing trollies, and folding linen. The doctor, wearing a white lab coat complete with stethoscope, was discussing issues with one of the staff in the doorway to a private suite. It was what one expected to see when entering a ward. It was perhaps the first sign of normality they had seen since leaving Djanet to begin their trek into the Tadrart Rouge.

Danielle introduced herself and presented her credentials. Immediately she was taken over to the doctor and introduced. He looked very pale, drawn, and overworked, but still he managed a smile. Fortunately, most of the people on the ward spoke English, including the doctor. He took them to his office where they sat around a desk. There was a computer that was turned on and seemed to have some open emails. Danielle's first question was, "Do you have Internet access?"

"Yes," he replied, "but it is terribly slow. I can send and receive emails from colleagues using a server located in Algeria. It seems to be working across North Africa, from Morocco to Egypt."

"So, no word beyond that?" Sebastian asked.

"Well only indirectly," he said. "People have travelled from Europe and from the East, either by boat or by car, sometimes even on private aeroplanes. They tell stories and then I hear of them from my colleagues."

"And what do they say. Is there any news from Canada?" he asked.

"I'm sorry, I have neither asked nor heard anything about Canada. However, I was told that things were unbelievably bad in the Americas. But they were unsubstantiated stories. How much truth is in them I cannot say."

"What do you mean by bad?" Sebastian enquired.

"I heard that there was an exceedingly high death toll, and there was lots of rioting and civil unrest. But then that was common in many cities around the world, even Algiers. However, it seemed that the more isolated a population was, the less the impact from the pandemic."

Sebastian could only speculate that the Canadian cities had gone through the same troubles, but that many of the remote locations, such as in the wilderness, may have been refuges like in the Sahara.

The doctor continued, "I am told that there was less trouble in some of the European countries. They were very quick to close their borders, and to set up strict quarantine. This is why there are no passenger aircraft flying.

Basically, all international flights have stopped. There was talk of re-opening, but then the second wave hit, and in some ways that was worse than the first. That was because so many people were infected but did not realize it. And it was these people that were in the refuges, hospitals, military, and the governments. Thus, the disease penetrated what was thought to be safe areas and threw all the response plans into disarray. It even happened here at our hospital." He shook his head and then said, "We lost so many doctors and staff."

"Yes, we discovered one in an elevator over by pathology," Danielle said.

"Oh yes, he was a good friend," the doctor said. "It was sad what happened, but we had no choice. If we could have shot him, we would have. But as soon as we were able to isolate him in the elevator, we took that opportunity; and then it was just too risky to open the doors again."

Danielle asked, "And what of a cure, do you know if there has been any progress anywhere in the world?"

"No... I have not heard of anything. The only thing that is currently available is quick death, and we certainly know how to do that," he said in a melancholy tone.

She looked at Sebastian, he nodded his head, and then she looked back at the doctor and said, "We have a man back in Irh Arrikine, his name is

Rudy. He came down with R24 transmitted by a friend through close personal contact. The friend developed the classic symptoms, and within the hour she was a zombie, and we had to shoot her. A few days later Rudy became symptomatic, however, prior to becoming a full-blown zombie, large doses of a potion, derived from local desert plants, was administered. This appeared to stop the progress of the symptoms, it kept him lucid, and then over time he has slowly recovered. When we left him this morning he was able to walk and talk, as well as feed himself. I will stress, he is still weak, but based on the current trajectory of recovery, the prognosis is good."

The doctors' eyes were wide, and his mouth hung aghast. Finally, he said, "This is amazing. I have heard of nothing like this anywhere. Have you isolated the active compounds, or know how it works?"

"No," she said, "that is why we are here. We have brought the ingredients with us so we can use the equipment here to better understand what is so special about this 'potion', and why it works. We would like to bring Rudy here for further study and treatment. Also, we would like to start treating infected people, the ones that are locked away, to see if we can duplicate Rudy's recovery."

"This will be extremely dangerous, but it is necessary and urgent. My colleagues in other hospitals will be extremely excited when they hear of this," he said.

"About that," Danielle said, "let us do some tests first before we tell anyone. We should make sure that Rudy wasn't just an anomaly, and that we can duplicate the results. And, we must make sure that the information goes to the right people. This really needs to go to the United Nations, or a benevolent organization that will use this knowledge to benefit all humanity, and not just a select few. I am concerned that if the wrong people find out, they may arrive here with soldiers and take all the knowledge and supplies and then use it to take over the world."

"Yes, I see what you mean," he said. "I do have people that I trust, but there are others that I do not. There are bad actors and militant ideological groups across the region. Many of them would not like to see the West rise to power again, but instead see this as an opportunity for change, and a sign from God."

The two pickups were ready to return to Irh Arrikine with supplies, and also some relatives of people that resided back in that town. They would need to go through quarantine, but at least they could see and talk to their families. Later a larger truck would be sent back to the town with additional food and groceries. Danielle then arranged for one of the vehicles to return with Rudy and Samia. To ensure that Samia was replaced, she sent one of the more qualified nurses from the Djanet hospital to fill Samia's position in the clinic.

She wanted Samia's help because she had spent time with Rudy, and she would be very capable as an assistant. She also figured that it would reduce the stress on Rudy, having that familiar face, and maintaining the bond that the two of them had formed. The invitation was also be extended to Sophie, given that she would otherwise be left alone in the town, culturally speaking, and thus may appreciate following the rest of the Westerners to Djanet. Despite all her dictates, it wasn't that Danielle was in charge, per se, it's just that in the absence of any real or formal authority, she filled the vacuum and became the default arbitrator and counsel.

Part of the hospital's commercial sized kitchen was cordoned off for producing the potion. Also, crews of Djanet locals were charged with scouring the nearby mountains to harvest more of the plants. They were instructed to do this in the manner the old woman had taught, such that it would be harvested sustainably. It would be a day or more before the crews would return with new supplies. In the meantime, Sebastian and her set to brewing the potion with the stocks that they had on hand, under the supervision of the old woman.

It wasn't that it was such a difficult or intricate process, but it was an extremely specific process that one was not likely to chance upon. Primarily it was time critical, both in the preparation, and the length of time that it retained its potency. Using the current method, they could not make up large batches and store it indefinitely, for it would only stay fresh for a few days, even when refrigerated. Thus, like working with fresh milk, it had a short shelf life, and they would need to constantly be making batches based on forecasted demand. What didn't get used up within those few days would get thrown away. They had to be very diligent because there just wasn't enough ingredients and human resources to be wasting it.

Danielle and Sebastian worked well together, and although he didn't have her knowledge or skills in medicine, he had complementary attributes that empowered her. For one thing, being an artist, he was particularly good with his hands and had fine motor skills that most people lacked. He was a person of very practical and direct thinking. Thus, he would encourage her to jump in and do things that she would have otherwise procrastinated over.

Sometimes it is very handy to have someone around who knows their own thoughts and has conviction. They are presented with a dilemma and immediately they have an answer. They may not be able to articulate their reason with any degree of sophistication, but still they believed that their choice is right; just because it feels right. Perhaps they aren't deep thinkers, or perhaps it is because they are always deep thinkers, thus the scenario has already been mulled over, in various guises, time and time again.

The new batch of potion would be ready the following morning and then be administered to a couple of newly turned zombies. Thus, there was nothing gained by staying at the hospital any longer and wearing themselves down, so they decided to walk back to their new home.

It was a shock to the system to walk out into the evening heat after spending the day in air conditioning and artificial light. Apart from the occasional smell of death it was otherwise a pleasant evening. If everything were normal, it was the type of evening that one would go out to dine at a restaurant. There used to be many here that were on upper-level terraces and looked out across the city to the giant rock pillars that broke through the sea of sand. It was views like this, on travel brochures, which had drawn Danielle to the region.

The two of them had a pleasant night at home. They went through the well-stocked kitchen and worked out what foods were closest to their expiration dates. Then with what they had assembled they devised a meal. Tonight, they would use the gas stove but going into the future they would need to change over to electric or charcoal. Djanet had electricity to spare, and up until the pandemic, gas was trucked in from distant locations. But now there had not been a gas delivery in weeks, and there was nothing to suggest there would be any in the future. Thus, what gas remained in the town, like petroleum and diesel, was rationed and used carefully.

They ate their meal on the open-air roof terrace. Although there were lights across the city, there were no vehicles on the streets this evening. The only sounds were from the breeze stirring the palm fronds, and the occasional ring of wind chimes that hung on the terrace. They lit some incense and ate by candlelight, discussing their plans for tomorrow and beyond.

Sebastian said, "You know what, it is so pleasant on the terrace, I think I'm going to sleep out here tonight."

"Ooh," Danielle said, "I like that idea. Do you mind if I join you, or are you wanting solitude?"

"No, not at all. I'd love for you to join me. So long as you don't mind sharing the day bed, because I have no intention of sleeping on the floor."

"Sure," she said, "I'm happy to share, that way the mosquitoes will go for you instead of me."

"Yes, well, what did you expect? They go for

the people with the sweetest blood. Not those that are bitter and anemic," he said with a laugh.

"Haha," she said, "aren't you just the comedian."

They got up and cleared away the meal, being sure to seal and refrigerate any leftovers. They had plenty of food at the moment, but how long it would last, and how it would get replaced, was still unclear. Fortunately, Djanet was an oasis city, established because of its abundant fresh water and agricultural potential. There were many farms on the Western side, although most were currently palmeries. They would have to change their focus toward edible horticulture if the city were to become self-sufficient.

The population of Djanet were mostly literate, but poor Kel Ajjer Tuareg people. Many made their living though employment that depended on the steady stream of tourists. No longer would there be any tourist, but then again, there were not enough people left to fill even the jobs that currently needed to be done. Heaven knows what was happening in the rest of the world.

Djanet had lost around half of its population to the pandemic. It was significant but they should be able to manage through the hardship, and then slowly re-build both population and 'industry'. However, with losses greater than this, as was rumored to have occurred in the densely populated regions of the temperate climatic zones, then populations may be below sustainable levels. Large areas could become abandoned until new, or ancient, technologies allowed people to re-colonies and sustain themselves in those environments. For many thousands of years people had survived in the Sahara, in semi-permanent settlements, even after much of the water had disappeared. The people of Djanet were confident that they could continue that tradition.

Unlike in areas on the Southern edge of the Sahara, Danielle and Sebastian did not need to use mosquito nets. The desert acted as a barrier to many of the sub-Saharan diseases, including malaria and yellow fever. Thus, surrounded by fragrant candles, they reclined on the large soft bed that was graced with intricately embroidered pillows. Danielle made a point of putting a pillow on Sebastian and then flopping down onto it, and him. Thus, they almost slept together, and they both seemed wonderfully comfortable with that.

CHAPTER 15

Danielle and Sebastian waited at the barricade for Rudy and Samia to arrive. They were expected to arrive around 9AM, but they were already 10 minutes late. Danielle was running scenarios in her head of what may have gone wrong. Perhaps in her absence Rudy had a relapse, or maybe the vehicle had broken down. She asked Sebastian if they should drive toward Irh Arrikine to look for them.

She wasn't usually the type of person to over analyze or fret, but the events of the last few weeks had change her, had changed everyone. Each person became more precious than before, each opportunity more valuable, and each decision more critical. She could not afford to lose Rudy; in fact, the world could not afford to lose Rudy. As far as she was concerned, he was the only proof of a cure.

Sebastian calmed her and suggested there could be many innocent things that caused the delay. He also reminded her that running on time varied from culture to culture. And that the pace of life was slower out here, and slowing down further as modern technology faded away. The Djanet guard network had people positioned all the way out to the intersection with the main road heading West and South. Men were placed at vantage points and had radio communication back to the barricade. They heard a crackle on the radio and then the operator turned and said something to Sebastian in French. Danielle tugged on his arm before the communication had even finished. Impatiently she asked,

"What did they say. Is everything all right?"

"Yes, they just past the first check point. They will be here in five minutes. There you go, nothing to worry about."

She breathed a sigh of relief and lowered her shoulders. They had explained to the barricade guards everything about the people that would be coming, including how Rudy had been infected and that they should keep their distance. It was agreed that they would just get waved straight through and thereafter Rudy would be Danielle's responsibility.

As the car approached the barrier, they backed up one of the trucks to allow the pickup through, and then after a brief exchange, it followed Danielle and Sebastian back to the hospital. Rudy was in good spirits but still weak. He was able to walk by himself to a specially prepared hermetically sealed room. It was on the ground floor and not far from the radiology and pathology laboratories.

Samia and Sophie had accompanied Rudy,

with the former taking residency in the hospital, and the later taken back to the house where Danielle and Sebastian were staying. She would be taking one of the spare bedrooms. Danielle wasn't sure if she wanted her there, but she also didn't have the heart to put her in a house by herself. Of course, the right thing to do would have been for Sebastian to move out, or at least move downstairs, and for the two women to live together. But Danielle didn't want that, and as far as she could tell, neither did Sebastian. It was one of those topics that they should have talked about last night, but they didn't.

Rudy fell asleep. It seemed the two-hour journey had drained him, and then maybe the air conditioning and the comfortable bed made the environment conducive for taking a nap. Whilst he slept Danielle and Samia began to familiarize themselves with the medical equipment at their disposal. They found the operating manuals, and the laboratory guides, and did their best to make sense of all the technical information.

The hospital also a had a small library of medical books, and a digital database of papers and procedures that Danielle was able to access. Through their combined efforts, assistance from Sebastian, and several discussions with the resident doctor, she was able to produce a research plan. It included what samples to take, and what tests to do, in order to get a better understanding of what had, and was, going on in Rudy's body. Then they would also start to do internal examination using ex-ray, MRI, and other tests, to see what they could see. Danielle didn't have much experience in radiography, but fortunately the other doctor did, which included experience using the equipment that they had on hand.

Samia and an assistant nurse were left to begin taking samples from Rudy and then preparing them for analysis. Meanwhile, Danielle and Sebastian, along with a couple of other men, armed themselves with the necessary biohazard protection and left the hospital to visit some of the still living R24 victims. What they really needed, but no one was hoping for, was someone who was a fresh victim, who is just turning into a zombie, like at the stage when they caught Rudy.

The first house they stopped at was the most recent victim. It was a teenage girl, who after turning, was lured into a house and then locked in two days ago. When they approached the house, they could see her through the window. She was a small, slight girl, sitting upright on the floor, and swaying side to side. She looked passive enough, but Danielle had been assured that when they first locked her in, she was extremely aggressive.

Their plan was to put on the suits, then the men would unlock the door and rush her, hopefully pinning her face down on the ground. They would bind her hands and feet before rolling her back over and sitting her up. Only then would Danielle be able to administer the potion orally. But if that was unsuccessful, she had prepared a concentration to inject directly into the girl's blood stream. It was unknow if it would work, or actually if anything would work. But it was the girl's last hope. Without a reversal she would be dead within a day or so, either from the internal damage rent by the disease, or just from dehydration.

The girl was fortunate that the air conditioning was running in the house. Anyone who had become a zombie and stayed out in the desert sun would be dead within hours. The desert heat, and the isolation of Djanet, is what had saved them from the wandering zombies that plagued both the cites and countryside in the temperate climates.

They suited up and then unlocked the door. As it slowly opened it got her attention. She began to make noises, loud horrible growling and screaming noises, like she was possessed. The two men rushed her, followed by Sebastian who would be using zip ties to secure her hands and feet. She lashed out at the men with surprising speed and intent, but they were prepared and pushed her off balance and then managed to get her face down on the floor. From her actions she seemed that she wanted to bite and scratch them. If she had been successful, it is likely they would have been infected. Indeed, even if the seals on their suits failed, and they were exposed to the air in the house, then they ran the chance of getting infected.

Once she was restrained, they rolled her over and sat her back up. The two men had to continue holding her, it seemed that the disease gave her significant strength, even in her rundown state. Approaching from behind Sebastian put a twisted towel around the front of her head that also covered her eyes. With this he could pull her head back against his knees in order to immobilize it. All she could now do was kick her bound legs up and down, but it did her no good. She was effectively immobilized for their purposes, and because her eyes were covered, she could not see Danielle approaching or resist what she was about to do.

Danielle had prepared a plastic squeeze bottle of the potion that had a tube attached to the nozzle. The intention was to get the other end of the tube into her mouth and then squeeze the liquid in. They couldn't do it too fast, or she would aspirate the potion, which would not only cause her to cough, but in sufficient quantities could drown her. However, they also didn't want to go too slow. It would give her more time to fight back, and the longer that they were under these conditions, the greater the risk to their own health.

The girl opened her mouth and Danielle quicky shoved the tube in and squeezed. It wasn't enough to overwhelm her, but enough for her to have liquid in her mouth, and to stimulate a swallowing reflex. As soon as she swallowed, Danielle did it again. Then she would let the girl breath and then repeated the process. The girl seemed to calm down a little, perhaps her brain, or limbic system, were being distracted by what was happening in her mouth and throat. Or perhaps there was still some sentience there that recognized she was getting fluid into her severely dehydrated body. It took about five minutes for Danielle to administer 500ml at the same concentration she had given to Rudy.

Perhaps she should have made it stronger, given that the girl's symptoms were more advanced, but at the moment she could only go by what had worked in the past. Perhaps with the next zombie she would increase the dose. It would be tantamount to experimenting on these people as if they were guinea pigs; but so what? At the moment they were not human, they were just dangerous animals.

Now that phase-one had been completed, the next step was to get a hood over her head. They did not want her to be breathing directly onto them, or the surrounding environment, nor spitting and biting. They also didn't want her to react to the bright sunlight once they got her out of the building. Sebastian removed the towel and replaced it with a hood. With speed and conviction, she tried to bite him, but fortunately he got his hand out of the way in time. Then the two men picked her up from both sides, and part walking and part being dragged she was taken out onto the road where they had a stretcher and ambulance waiting. She was forced onto the stretcher and then strapped down with belts before being loaded into the ambulance and taken back to the hospital.

Back at the hospital they had to clean her up. She was an absolute mess, having urinated and defecated on herself, as well as dribbled and seemingly vomited all down her front. Somewhere underneath was a pretty teenage girl, but presently she looked evil and smelt the same. Four female nurses wearing biohazard suits took her to the shower. Whilst keeping her hands and feet bound, they cut off all her clothes and then gave her a thorough wash with disinfectant and detergent. After they had done the body, they dimmed the lights and removed the hood. Then with great care not to get bitten they washed her hair and face. There was a positive sign when she opened her mouth and tried to drink the shower water. They let her do it and it seemed to calm her down.

After drying her off and carefully fitting a gown, she was placed in the room next to Rudy, strapped into bed, and using what materials they had on hand they sealed the room. Whilst she was accepting it, they would continue to administer the potion orally. Danielle also fitted her with an intravenous drip to provide salts, minerals, and dextrose, in the hope that it would reverse the effects of dehydration and improve her cognitive functions. Thereafter, every two hours she would receive the potion, and when necessary, have her bedpan emptied. Danielle took all manner of samples from the girl and then ran the same tests that she had with Rudy.

It was early enough in the afternoon to retrieve another zombie. This one was further advanced and if they didn't get him now, there was a chance that he may die before tomorrow. They went through the same procedure as before, however, when they entered the house where he was imprisoned, they found him lying on the floor. Every minute or so he would open his eyes and spasm, and then seemingly go back into an unconscious state. They were told that when he was first locked in he had been extremely dangerous and had actually killed someone. At the time they intended to shoot him, but seeming they were able to lock him in a house, they decided to just let him die instead of wasting a bullet.

Like with the teenage girl, they took every precaution to restrain him and shield themselves. Danielle was not confident that he would be capable of taking the potion orally, so she injected a concentrated dose directly into his veins. It took several attempts to locate a suitable spot. Yet each time she jabbed the large needle into him, there was no reaction. Rudy had described one of his symptoms as being numb. It appeared that this man was numb all over and felt no pain.

They brought him back to the hospital and he went through the same induction process as the girl. It was a challenge to clean him because he was effectively comatose whilst also having his hands and feet bound. He was so dirty that he couldn't just be sponge bathed in a bed. Instead, he had to be hosed down, thoroughly disinfected, and then dried and clothed. Finally, he was strapped down in a bed and administered the potion, and other liquids, intravenously. His condition was poor, and Danielle did not expect him to survive. He not only had to deal with the damage done by R24, but also the damage done through severe dehydration. He also had various injuries that were likely sustained whilst raging, evident from the lumps and bruises on his body. She suspected that he may even have some fractured of broken bones. If he lived through the night, then she would see what could be discovered by scanning him tomorrow.

Before sunset they went back out to assess the zombies that remained locked in houses, and other secure spaces. Unfortunately, all of them were dead. They hoped that no more would appear, but they suspected that they would, and they were prepared for that eventuality. She told the militia to notify her of anyone who showed the slightest of symptoms, even if it was in the middle of the night. She also asked them not to shoot anyone unless there was imminent danger to someone. She explained that she needed them alive, and that there was good chance of curing them.

Sebastian had overheard some of the guards talking, and as he and Danielle drove back to the house he said, "Some of the guards are grumbling about what we are doing. They seem to think we are just keeping the zombies alive for sentimental reasons. They think that this is a risky strategy, and that the zombies may get strong again and then attack and infect people."

"I suppose I can relate to that," she said. "I'm sure that's how it looks. Hopefully tomorrow we will see some progress with the teenaged girl. The potion worked remarkably quickly on Rudy, but then again, we caught his symptoms early. All we can do is cross our fingers and see what tomorrow brings."

CHAPTER 16

Sophie had been alone in the house all day and had prepared dinner for the three of them. It was laid out on the upstairs terrace, and using a tajine, mutton and apricot, had prepared a Moroccan style meal, served on a bed of couscous. It smelt and looked marvelous. It was such a shame that the former residents of the house were no longer with them to enjoy the evening. Many of the survivors felt guilty; they felt like the meek inheriting the Earth.

Sophie had continued to slim in the desert culture. No longer did she have the subdermal thermal layer, a product of London's fish, chips, and pork pies. Her paleness had also gone as she bronzed like an Australian surfer. During the day she had gone through the clothes that were neatly left in the house. Several of the former residents must have been women with expensive taste and abundant means. Thus, she was dressed in linen and silk of the most stunning colors and embroidery. This was complemented with gold jewelry inlaid with sapphires and emeralds. With her dark hair, and the way she had done her makeup, she looked like she could have been the lady of the house. Perhaps married to some wealthy merchant and hidden away behind doors and veils from the prying eyes of other men.

Maybe she was sick of being dusty and disheveled, and wearing the same old cargo pants and t-shirts. Everyone likes to feel clean and attractive, and to play dress up from time to time. But Danielle suspected there was more to Sophie channeling Jezebel. She convinced herself that the intention was to infatuate and seduce Sebastian. And oh my God, from what she saw, how could any mortal man resist if they were led by their eyes, and by their desires. Furthermore, she had never seen Sophie conduct herself with such airs and graces, gliding about the room with flowing silk and hair, attending to their every need. What a perfect host she was being in *their* house. If Danielle had not developed such an attachment to Sebastian she could have enjoyed being spoilt by Sophie, but she had, and she didn't.

The rest of the evening was spent watching Sebastian from the corner of her eye and listening to every word and dissecting every laugh. Amongst all of the death and upheaval across the whole human population, this is what she was reduced to. The matters of the heart and the basest of desires. If nothing else, it showed that deep inside she was still human.

After clearing away the meal they relaxed on the terrace. Danielle was getting tired and wanted to sleep as they had the night before, with just her and Sebastian on the large day bed surrounded by a cloud of soft white pillows. But now it was awkward, and she had to force herself to stay awake. Sophie was sitting right in the middle of her dreams.

To his credit Sebastian was diplomatic and at least appeared impervious to Sophie's seduction. Danielle just hoped that Sophie wasn't going to demonstrate how she had taken belly dancing classes back in London or maybe try to read his palm or the bumps on his head. Fortunately, she did not. If they had alcohol with their dinner, then maybe these and other tropes would have been played; thank God for sweet tea. There was a hookah in the house, along with tobacco and syrups, and possibly cannabis, but they had no desire to use it.

'Damn' she thought to herself, why did I miss all of those opportunities. Life is too short to fiddle about at the edges, and there was no way she was going to be just another woman in some man's hareem. Sophie got up to return something to the kitchen and Danielle took a sneaky chance. She stood up, and as she walked past Sebastian, she grabbed his arm and said, "Quick, come with me."

She led him over to the day bed, sat down and then pulled him down next to her. She then proceeded to arrange the pillows and lay down, but not before pushing him into the position she wanted him to recline into. 'There', she thought, 'that should be the end of that'. Sophie would go to her own room and sleep whilst Sebastian and her could share the day bed out under the magical stars, as they had the night before.

When Sophie returned, she said, "Oh, how sweet is that."

And then proceeded to approach the day bed and wait for them to make a space for her. Neither of them could rightfully refuse, given how she had prepared such a lovely meal and was being so sickly sweet. Did Sebastian really mind? Probably not given that by default he was in charge of the two women's emotions and dreams. That bastard was getting his harem without even trying.

Fortunately for all concerned Sebastian fell asleep soon after all the birds were in the nest. Danielle followed shortly afterwards. The day had been too long and draining to lay there and stew over third wheels and sabotage. And at least, and thankfully, Sophie kept her hands and body off of Sebastian. Indeed, he had even placed a pillow between Sophie and himself, that she then pressed against him, but advanced no further. Regardless, Sophie made it abundantly clear that she was available and willing should that be the path he wished to wander.

Given their early starts, and the long hot days, they were asleep by 9PM. However, at 3AM they were awoken by a ringing sound. It was the mechanical door chime. A bell upstairs was connected by cable to a pull next to the front door. It was Sebastian who got up to investigate. When she returned he said that there was a person somewhere showing symptoms of R24. Unfortunately, it was one of the barricade guards, and he had been in close proximity with other people.

Danielle and Sebastian immediately switched to their 'emergency services' mode and were out of the house within a few minutes. They would worry about showers and clean clothes later, for now they had to get this patient dosed with the potion, and isolated in the hospital. In case of such an eventuality, they carried all the protective equipment, and other items, in their vehicle. Thus, they followed the man's car directly to where the patient was being detained.

Like when Rudy first developed symptoms, the patient was still lucid, but this time he alternated between passive and raging. For everyone's safety they were forced to restrain him. Right there and then she began to administer the potion. He could not detect its bitter taste; thus, they knew how far R24 had already progressed. They transported him in the back of a pickup truck. Danielle rode in the back with him, along with another man who held him secure. Sebastian followed her in their own vehicle back to the hospital.

As with the other patients, he was cleaned up and strapped to a bed. He was then given a second dose of potion, along with an intravenous solution. A nurse stayed with him whist he was awake, constantly conversing with him to keep his mind focused on reality.

Danielle took all of the samples she could and put them through the same testing as the others. They were slowly building up valuable data, and an understanding of how R24 progressed, what it was attacking, and how the body responded.

With just the preliminary results she had identified that the disease produced a very potent and complex suite of neurotoxins, as if the patent were bitten by several snakes and scorpions at the same time. But that was only part of the problem, the other aspect was its high transmissibility and survivability. She was yet to identify the pathogen, be it a virus, bacteria, or spore, outside of the host and ready to infect. But it appeared that once it entered the host it transformed, as if it were going through a life cycle, thus what was inside the body was different from what was originally outside.

It was extraordinarily complex, and almost the perfect weapon against humans. Indeed, it was so perfect that she wondered if it had been deliberately engineered. What a highly effective tool it would be for ridding the planet of humans. Who or what would want to do that she could not fathom. Maybe it was natural. Mother Nature seemed to attack humans with frightening regularity. And if it was her, then what a collision of coincidences to exploit all of the specie's weaknesses in the one disease.

By midday two more patients had presented with symptoms and were quickly isolated. They were beginning to catch them earlier in the disease's progression, which made them easier and safer to handle. But it would be the nighttime that would prove most challenging. People that developed the symptoms whilst they slept, and not watched over by others, could wake as zombies. It only took a few hours for people to lose the ability to reason and be overtaken with rage.

She said to Sebastian, "I get the feeling it's going to be a busy night tonight, and maybe each night for the rest of the week. The nurses are competent in processing and treating each of the patients during the day, but still I want to be here at night, especially when they first come in."

"Sure, so what are you suggesting? he asked.

"I'm thinking I should go home and sleep whist its quiet and then come back for the night shift."

"Yes, that's probably a good idea. Sleep whilst you can get it. There may be dozens of patients about to come in, and they will all need to get processed before they start to rage."

She stood there silent and just fiddled with a piece of equipment on a nearby trolley until he said,

"Do you want me to come with you? Perhaps I should do the night shift with you, given how we work well together."

"Would that be OK. Do you mind?" she asked coyly.

"No, of course not. I think it's a great idea. We're a team, wherever you go, I go," he said.

She liked the sound of that for a range of reasons, and amongst them was that she would not be leaving him alone with Sophie. It was one of those fortunate coincidences that solved several problems at once. But what she really needed to do was to find someone for Sophie.

Although she had thought in the past that Sophie and Rudy would hook up, it seemed that since he and Samia had become closer, it was unlikely to ever happen. It was heartening to watch Rudy light up each time Samia entered the room, and it was amusing to observe how many times she found excuses to tend to him. Danielle, and everyone else, hoped that he would recover from R24, and it would not leave any disability. So far Rudy was progressing well. His numbness was reducing, and his cognitive abilities were improving. Fortunately, he had not suffered dehydration to the same extend as the two zombies they had rescued and were treating.

The teenage girl had stopped raging and although she did not talk, it seemed that she was becoming lucid enough to respond to simple commands, like drink or move fingers. She was now hydrated and was almost ready to start taking solid food. The other man that they had retrieved, who was found semi-conscious on the floor of the house, had stabilized and remained in a semi-conscious state. He was wired up to an electroencephalography device (EEG), and they could measure his brain activity. It seemed erratic, and yet it looked like it was trying to function, as if it were a computer trying to reboot after being corrupted. Danielle had neither the skill nor the desire to expose him to any invasive procedures that would normally be done by a neurosurgeon. Thus, she did what she could with what she had and just watched for any signs of progress.

Danielle and Sebastian returned home at 3PM and found that Sophie was not there. It was a short walk to the souk and given that there wasn't much else for her to do in the city, they assumed she was probably there shopping. Money was basically worthless, so what she shopped with they did not know. Maybe she traded jewelry or food. No doubt as she got to know more people she would be invited to shop, embroider, and gossip with the other women. Her former life as an accountant was probably obsolete now, or at least for the foreseeable future. No, instead she would either re-skill, or she would keep house and produce babies, such was the dry pragmatic view of the future.

They showered, changed, and after eating, like a married couple, they retired to his room. It was the darker and cooler of the two, again a happy coincident. Sebastian hung a sign on the door that said they were sleeping because they were on night shift. Danielle closed the door to her own bedroom. She was modest and didn't what Sophie to realize that she was actually in Sebastian's room. The walls and doors were solid, and excellent at deadening sound. Thus, even if Sophie was noisy, they were unlikely to hear her. It was dark, cool and peaceful, a whole world away from the reality and concerns all around them. This was enough for her, for now. Maybe he wanted more, but he hadn't said or acted in any way to start anything. And that was OK, just so long as this was how they finished each day. Just the two of them a touch away from each other. This, or he, was the reason that she kept fighting when it would have been so much easier to give up.

CHAPTER 17

Another week had passed. They were averaging two or three new cases per day and were getting better at early detection. They were also ramping up production of the potion and had a sufficient amount to begin vaccinating people deemed to be at high risk. Predominantly people that had been exposed to those who had become symptomatic.

Rudy was getting better by the day, so his dosage was reduced. He was the guinea pig to establish when and how they should begin weaning patients off the potion. Obviously if there was a relapse, he would go straight back to a full dose. But at present there was no sign of a relapse. If there had been, then that would prove disastrous. A whole generation of people needing access to a potion to stop them turning into zombies; it would have been a logistical nightmare.

The teenage girl was also showing signs of recovery. Although she was still dizzy, and parts of her body were numb, they could now hold a conversation with her. Both her, Rudy, and the man that was near to death, and was still in a critical condition, did not appear to be contagious. Danielle had identified what she believed to be the pathogen that caused R24. It was a robust and long-lived spore that was extremely small, thus it was likely to be a product of nature. It was possibly from Earth's distant past that had been liberated by melting permafrost. Like anthrax, it could endure on surfaces and in soil, was impervious to the cold, but it did not survive well when exposed to direct sunlight. Ultraviolet radiation seemed to be its weakness, and thus all sterilization was steered toward ultraviolet germicidal irradiation (UVGI). As each new patient came in, part of the check-in procedure was a session in what would otherwise be described as a UV tanning pod.

Still there was no contact with the outside world apart from the Internet that only spanned North Africa. Danielle was coming to the realization that her work was done in Djanet. She should now try to push North toward a major city, and then perhaps across to Europe. Ideally the ingredients and the formula for the potion should end up in a facility that could synthase it and be able to produce industrial quantities to distributed all around the world. The highest concentrations of pharmaceutical manufacturing were in Germany, followed by the UK, although the largest companies were in Denmark and Switzerland respectively. Of course, even larger companies existed in other countries, predominantly the United States and India, but at the moment she considered that a stretch too far.

Danielle and Sebastian were on their way home from the night shift. It was dawn and just before the first call to prayer. They walked the dusty road and were pleased that there was no longer the stench from decaying human corpses. She said to Sebastian, "I think the doctor and the staff here will be able to manage from now on. We have a successful response in place, and if they can keep me updated with recoveries, then that will help to perfect that response."

"I'm not sure I understand why you are saying this," he said, being both polite but also confused.

"We need to get the news of our success out to the rest of the world. I'm scared that if we don't, then soon there won't be anyone else left in the world besides just us in Djanet and Irh Arrikine."

"Oh, I see," he said.

"This is what I was thinking," she said, "We need to take the information out into the world, and we also have to get medical professionals to come to Djanet and get a crash course in how to set up their hospitals to deal with R24. We need to talk to industries about growing or synthesizing the ingredients for the potion, so they can mass produce it. I believe that I am the best person to do this, I've got the most knowledge and would be the most convincing. There isn't really anyone else in Djanet that I could send on such an important mission."

"Well, if you're going, then I'm going with you, he said. "When do we leave?"

"I've enquired if an aeroplane could be sent to Djanet airport to pick us up. I had no luck. I mean..., I know there are still planes flying somewhere, be they private or military, but no one I was able to contact had any way to connect with the right people or otherwise organize such a thing. Hence, we will have to drive, at least until we find the right people who can make things happen."

"That is assuming there is anyone left," he said rather gravely. "So, when do we leave?"

"The sooner the better," she said. "I was thinking maybe tonight."

"Sure, why not. We can make up a three-vehicle convoy and get the militia to prep everything during the day whilst we are sleeping, then we can head out just after sunset," he suggested.

They arrived at home and Sophie was already up and preparing her breakfast, and their dinner. It was very thoughtful of her. When they were sitting on the terrace Danielle said, "Sophie, I've got some news for you, although it might come as a bit of a shock."

"OK, go ahead. Nowadays I don't think anything could shock me," she said, but with a hint of trepidation.

"Sebastian and I are going to be leaving Djanet and head North. We plan to go to Algiers, and then after that it's a bit murky. Depending on what conditions are like in Europe we can try to head overland to Paris, or further across into German. Or, if conditions are better in the UK, then we may try to head straight for there. But, at the moment, the only thing we are sure of is driving from here to Algiers, which is 2,230km. So, we figure a few long days on the road, provided we don't run into any trouble."

Without hesitation Sophie said, "I want to come with you. I desperately want to get back home to the UK, and this may be my only chance. Please take me with you. Please," she implored.

How could they say no? Of course she was not crucial to the mission, and indeed could even prove to be a hinderance, being one more mouth to feed and one more person to look after. But then again, she could share the driving, perhaps help out in other ways, and maybe she could learn to fire a gun.

Danielle looked at Sebastian, he had a blank expression and just shrugged. He was probably thinking the same as her. She turned back to Sophie and said, "Sure. It wouldn't be the same without you."

A big smile came across her face, like a child being told they were going on an adventure, even though she knew full well the risks. She asked, "When do we leave?"

"Tonight, at sunset, so be sure to have everything packed." Then Danielle added, "Also, it is likely that we will not be returning. I cannot say or even imagine what the world is like beyond the desert, but I suspect that travel will not be something that is done often or easily anymore. So be sure to say sayonara to everyone."

"That is very sad," she said. "Will Rudy be coming with us?"

"No, unfortunately he is not well enough for such a difficult journey, and we cannot risk a relapse, or to have him scare any of the people we meet along the way."

Sophie had a downtrodden look and then said, "I will go and see him today and say goodbye."

After they had eaten and showered, they locked themselves in the darkened room, and once again Danielle slipped into Sebastian's bed and fell asleep beside him.

They woke mid-afternoon and packed their bags. They had more luggage than before since collecting what they had left at their respective hotels before going on the camel trek. There were some items of clothing and jewelry in the house that Danielle was particularly fond of. With their owners and heirs now gone, she decided that she would take a few trinkets with her as a reminder of her time in Djanet. Sophie had also selected items, so they both would be leaving with some of the forfeited treasure.

They went back to the hospital with Sophie to say goodbye to Rudy, Samia, and all of the staff that had become good friends over their time there. In this new world of impermanence and the overriding hand of fate, friends were made quick and easy, because those people may also be lost the following week. It was an emotional farewell, and they did pledge to come back and see them again, but everyone knew that the chances of that were very slim. Their journey would be full of peril and unknowns, so they may themselves be dead within the week.

The SUVs had been prepared and carried additional fuel and food. They also carried supplies of the potion and samples of the ingredients required to manufacture it. Their escort vehicles were nearly new, having been commandeered, and each vehicle carried several guns and boxes of ammunition, just in case. They said their final farewells at the barricade and then put Djanet behind them. They turned onto the main road that headed Northwest, keeping the Tassili N'Ajjer mountains to their East, and the broad flat plains of the Sahara out to everywhere else. It was 140km to the next town, a small settlement called Bordj El Haouas, and then they would cut through the mountains to Illizi. From there they would cover a long, lonely stretch through the dunes to arrive at In Amenas, where they would probably stop to sleep, and if anyone were still alive, to render assistance.

When they arrived in Bordj El Haouas, the streetlights were on, but the houses were dark and there were no signs of life. If it had been impacted like Djanet, which was likely because it was on the main North-South road, then it was possible that some people fled into the desert, and those that remained turned into zombies and were now dead. They went to the only doctor's clinic, but the doors were locked and there were no lights. They banged on the door just in case someone was inside sleeping, but there was no response. When they walked around the back there was the horrible stench of death. That told them everything they need to know. They stopped at the gas station and topped up their fuel tanks before heading back out into the dark desert.

Danille had promised Samia that she would keep her updated with their progress when she could. She noticed on her cell phone that she had reception, although it was likely no good for voice calls, they hadn't figured out why. Thus, she sent a short email explaining where they were and what they had found. Samia would inform the other survivors in Djanet, and would no doubt be the bearer of bad news for those who had relatives in that now dead settlement.

The mountains rose to over 2,000m and were noticeably cooler than the Saharan lowlands. At one of the highest points, they stopped at a lookout to stretch their legs. Of course it was dark, but still the moonlight, and the impossibly bright stars, gave the barren mountains a faint ghostly glow. A cool breeze blew through the mountain pass and Danielle had to wrap her arms tight about herself to keep warm. There were also quite a few animals out in the night. And in their light tan through to white colored fur, and eyes that reflected like gems, they resembled ghosts that watched them drive past.

It was 270km of winding mountain roads before they reached Illizi. As they descended toward the town, they could see streetlights, but this time there were also lights on in the buildings. Coming in from the South, the first major building in town was the large hospital. They could see through the windows that the lights were on inside. This was a welcome surprise, but it also presented danger. They did not know how they would be received, and they did not know if the people they encountered were clean or infectious.

As they approached the hospital, there was a large roundabout in the center of the road. To the right it went into the center of town, and straight ahead the road skirted the town boundary and then continued to the North. There was a barricade blocking entry into the town proper, and then there was another barricade, about 100m further along placed across the entrance to the hospital. They stopped a little back from the barricade and found that it was guarded by men with guns. The local drivers from Djanet got out first to talk to the guards, everyone kept their distance, and the conversation was best described as yelling past cars and bollards.

The Djanet men explained the situation and then brought Danielle out with her MSF identification to support their story. They asked to see whoever was in charge at the hospital. Fortunately, the town had three doctors and all of them had avoided contracting R24. One was awake and the other two were asleep. They waited at their vehicles for around 20 minutes before all three doctors came to the barricade. Danielle then discussed the potion and the results they had achieved. The doctors said they had no zombies left, but they were fearful of an outbreak, suspicious that some people in the town were carriers. She gave them a dose of the potion and then told them to go down to Djanet to get informed on how to make it, and what procedures to follow when dealing with patients.

All of this occurred under the blaze of vehicle headlights, and with no member of either group coming within 10m of the other. Despite keeping their distance, they were very thankful, and two of the doctors said they would make the trip to Djanet at first light. Danielle and her group were then instructed where to get fuel and water before they continued another 240km North to the next town In Amenas. After getting fuel Danielle and Sebastian alternated the driving. Sophie had fallen asleep in the back seat and would drive during the day if it were needed.

CHAPTER 18

The moon sank lower in the sky, and each time they crested a dune, all they could see was an endless gritty sea. They had come down from the mountains and onto the hyper arid Maghreb region of the Sahara. There were no large animals out here, just the odd insect. And there wasn't the slightest breeze.

It was almost three hours before they saw the first lights from In Amenas in the distance. The town existed to service the oil and gas industry. It had pipelines and heavy industries, with foreign workers housed in company encampment. It was only 30km from the Libyan border and had been the site of recent conflict and hostage taking by Islamist militants. As such there was also a significant military presence in the town. None of them expected the welcome here to be very friendly. Sure, it had a large modern hospital, but more than likely the whole town was now under the control of the military, or worse, private security.

The main road skirted the Western side of the town, but to reach the hospital they would need to travel right through the center. Thus, they could bypass In Amenas completely, of take a chance and try to get to the hospital, and on the way stop at the only gas station. They elected to turn off the main road and head toward the center of town. As they approached, they found a barricade had been set up at the entrance to the center of town, directly out front of the gas station. Instead of cars and trucks blocking the road, it was armored vehicles with mounted machine guns. One burst from the many guns pointed at them would have ripped them and their vehicles apart.

As they had done in the previous towns, they stopped a comfortable distance from the blockade, and this time a Djanet man and Sebastian got out and walked to within yelling distance. It was figured that because this was a company town, and that there may be expats from Algiers or France, then Sebastian may communicate better, and possibly be held in higher regard than the Arab-Berger from the South. As soon as they were detected the soldiers shone a powerful spotlight onto them, but thankfully after a minute it was turned down to a less blinding intensity.

They explained their situation, as they had done before, and asked if they would be allowed passage through to the hospital. The person in charge of the barricade called someone up on the radio. Apparently, there was a chain of command, and permissions had to be granted.

They were granted permission to go directly to the hospital and nowhere else, but only under the condition that they surrendered all of their weapons. They were given assurances that the weapons would be returned when their business was finished, and they were leaving. The Djanet men in their group did not believe this to be true. A hushed discussion ensued among the party before they replied to the border guards. They reinforced that they had medical experience and a medicine that would help in dealing with R24, and they would only speak to the doctors at the hospital. And furthermore, they were not prepared to give up their weapons.

It seemed that they did not have as much bargaining power as they had hoped. Two of the armored vehicles started up and drove toward them. One parked behind and the other remained in front. Then a troop-carrying truck arrived, and they were ordered at gun point to get into the back. Fortunately, they had left their guns in the vehicles, so did not get them confiscated.

Given no choice, they climbed in and took a bumpy ride to what appeared to be a military barracks. They were ordered out and then marched in the dark to a building that had been converted to a prison. If left alone they could have escaped with little effort, but they were not alone. Two armed guards sat on the other side of a mesh glass panel watching them, however, they didn't look too interested but instead read magazines.

Due to the noise, four prisoners were woken and came from a separate room to greet them. Two appeared to be of Pakistani origin, and the other two, a man and a woman, were European. It turned out that all four were contract workers for companies that operated in the area. They had arrived from remote sites in the desert after the first wave of the pandemic. They had been kept in the prison officially for reasons of quarantine, but unofficially for suspicion of being spies, or in some way foreign actors that had spread, or benefited from, R24. They acknowledged how stupid it sounded; especially given they had papers and credentials to support their stories.

The prisoners showed the new arrivals the adjoining rooms for sleeping and the bathroom. It seemed that it was going to be very crowded, and with little privacy afforded to the women. One of the Europeans, a Swedish national called Andrea, who also spoke English, was their spokesperson. After welcoming them he asked where they had come from, and they gave him the full explanation, which he then relayed to the others. Danielle then asked, "How long have you been locked up?"

He replied, "We have been here for almost a month." Danielle and her party breathed a sigh of relief. Due to their long isolation, they probably weren't infected, otherwise the symptoms would have shown by now."

But still she asked, "And you haven't had close contact with anyone outside of this prison since you have been here?"

"No, they will not come near us," Andrea replied. "They deliver the food wearing masks and then they leave. Once a day they let us out into the yard to walk about and get some sun. They just stand at a distance with their guns watching us."

Sophie enquired, "Why don't you just run away?"

"To where?" Andrea replied with a shrug. "The yard opens out to the desert in every direction except for the front where the guards are standing. No, it would do us no good. To run into the dunes would mean certain death, and they know it. Maybe they are hoping we will try it; it would save four bullets."

"Who is in charge?" Sebastian asked.

"It is one of the soldiers. A low-ranking officer who found that he now held highest position after his commanders died from R24. But he has gone power crazy and turned this town into his own kingdom. I expect that you will be taken before him today. He has set up his headquarters like a palace in one of the hotels."

Then Andrea looked at Danielle and said, "I worry for you. He is rather fond of blonde women. He keeps two of them at the hotel, and I do not think they are there by choice."

They all looked at Danielle, whilst she looked at Sebastian for help. Sebastian put his arm around her and then asked, "What about at the hospital, are there any doctors or staff left there?"

"As far as we know there are no doctors. There were a few nurses, but most died in the second wave, so I do not know how many are left or what condition they are in."

Sebastian said to Danielle, "I don't think there is any good we can do here. We are just going to be kept as prisoners, or worse. I say we try to escape."

Everyone looked at each other and then started to nod in agreement. Sebastian turned to Andrea and said, "Surely you have thought about this, what do you think is the best plan for escape?"

Andrea said in a soft voice, "If I had enough people, which I believe we do now, then this is what I thought of doing."

He then continued to outline a plan, and the others offered additional ideas and strategies until they had an agreement. It was important that they executed it now, whilst it was dark, and presumably whilst their vehicles were still parked beyond the barricade.

Although the guards at the prison were armed, they were not in radio contact with other soldiers or headquarters. That meant that if they could incapacitate the guards, then their escape would not be detected until someone came to check on the prison.

There was a heavy wooden bench at one of the tables. They slowly moved it toward the door that led out into the exercise yard, and ultimately the desert. The window to the guards was sufficiently high that they could not see the bench being moved. Their plan was to use the bench as a battering ram and break down the door. Sure, it would be loud and draw attention, but that was actually what they wanted. The guards would expect that as soon as they busted the door down, the prisoners would scatter into the dark dunes. However, that was not their plan. Instead, they would wait outside the door that the guards were expected to come rushing out from. Then when the guards came out, they would collectively jump on them and overpower them. They realized that perhaps one or two of them may get shot, but the guards would not be able to get all of them before they were overpowered. It was risky, but even if they couldn't all get away, then at least some of them would.

When they had moved the bench into place, they waited till the guards were distracted, and then the eight men picked up the heavy bench and at as much speed as they could muster, battered it into the door. If it had been a solid older building, or one designed specifically as a prison, then it would have been almost impossible to break through. However, it was a relatively cheap modern building, so the lock just burst out of the frame and the door swung open. They continued through the door with the bench, and the women followed. Then they rushed over to the door where the guards would be coming out from and stood the bench upright. On cue the guard's door burst open, and they threw the bench down on top of them, knocking them to the ground.

Quickly the guards were disarmed, taken back inside, and then bound and gagged. A couple of the drivers wanted to shoot them but were talked out of it. Firstly, because the shots may alert other soldiers, and secondly, if they were recaptured, then there may be serious retribution. They were on the Southern edge of the town, and open to the desert, so they could disappear into the dark dunes and then trek back toward the vehicles. It was going to be a couple of kilometers creeping silently through the sand.

As they walked, Sebastian whispered, "Is there an airport here?"

"Yes, it is a few kilometers in the opposite direction," Andrea said.

"And are there any aeroplanes or helicopters there?"

"Yes, there are, one of them is even a military helicopter. But here is the problem, all of the pilots have died. So, unless any of you know how to fly an aeroplane or helicopter, then they are of no use anymore."

"Can anyone fly?" Sebastian asked.

Everyone remained silent, so that gave him the answer.

After about 30 minutes they arrived in the dunes opposite their vehicles. They appeared to be as they had left them, and they hoped that the ignition keys were still inside. It was fortunate that they had parked a fair way back from the barricade. It was dark where the SUVs were, so they could approach them undetected. They could not see any guards near the vehicles. It seemed they were all at the barricade sitting about a campfire, talking, and occasionally laughing. Hopefully this would be an easy escape.

They crept as a closely bunched group until they were standing at the rear of the vehicles. The man with the darkest clothes and skin was chosen to go up to each vehicle and see if the keys were still inside. He had a small torch with him, and hopefully when he flashed it through the windows, the guards would not notice.

After a few tense minutes he returned and confirmed that all of the vehicles had keys inside them. Thus, on the count of three they quickly went over to their allocated vehicles and as quietly as possible opened the doors and got inside. They quickly turned off the interior lights, but no one closed their door properly, instead they were only pulled to the first safety catch. Once they were moving, they would close them properly.

They had agreed that when the last person got in and closed their door, they would all count to five and then turn on the ignitions simultaneously. Then, keeping the lights off, in a line they would do a U-turn, then switch on the headlights and travel as fast as they could back to the main road, then continue North. There was no action at the barricade as Sebastian, in the lead vehicle, counted down to starting the motor. It seemed that the solders had not noticed them and were not prepared for their escape.

Three, two, one, he turned the ignition, the vehicle started. He immediately put it into drive and turned the steering wheel. From his side window he could see that the other vehicles were also moving. They had all turned around and put on their headlights by the time the spotlights came on. He could also see in the rearview mirror that a couple of the army vehicles had their lights on and were pulling onto the road.

Andrea, who was travelling with them said, "Don't worry about the armored vehicles. There is no way they will catch you; they are too slow."

But then Sebastian noticed that the army vehicles had left the road and were heading across the open ground between buildings and crashing through fences. It seemed that the soldier's intention was to cut them off. The road they were on headed West and then turned North when it hit the main road. If the military vehicles could get in front of them then they would have to leave the bitumen and head across country. In those conditions the military vehicles would easily outperform their road-going SUVs, and they would either get captured, or just shot up with the machine guns.

Sebastian was driving a turbocharged diesel V8 and was already doing nearly 160kph. Surprisingly the other escapees were close behind in their respective vehicles. They were probably glad they had commandeered late model SUVs for this mission. Up ahead was the 90 degrees turn onto the main road. He would have to slow right down to avoid losing control or tipping the vehicle over.

They took the turn on the wrong side of the road with the tires screeching, then headed past rows of industrial sheds. He was wary of other vehicles coming in from the left, but there was nothing, only the lights from the military vehicles coming in from the right. It looked like it was going to be close. Hopefully, if the soldiers were forced to stay off road, then they probably wouldn't be able to aim their guns on the bumpy terrain.

They were up near 200kph now, and with his lights on high beam he could see that the road was straight and clear. It would have been a disaster if they had another barricade, or even an obstacle on the road. Sure, he could slow down or swerve off the road to get around it, but anything that slowed them down would probably allow their perusers to get in front or shoot their vehicle. Just one bullet in a tire or the engine and it would be over. They had agreed that if anyone did get caught, that the others would not stop for them. Whoever could get away should go for it without feeling guilty.

They managed to get just in front of the military vehicles where their paths would have otherwise crossed. They could see though the side windows that soldiers manned the roof mounted machine guns. And then they saw flashes coming from those guns, so they knew they were being shot at. But it was all over within a few seconds. They were traveling so fast, and with the pursuers coming in at almost a 90-degree angle, they were able to just fly past and continue at high speed until they were safely out of range. Thank goodness the micro-junta couldn't use the helicopter; they would have been sitting targets out on the straight road in the barren desert.

CHAPTER 19

When they could no longer see any lights behind them, they slowed down to 80kph to preserve fuel. Africa is a huge continent, and Algeria is a huge country. They still had a long way to go just to get out of the Sahara, and they did not know what perils lay ahead in the populated North. It was daybreak, and after putting 100km between themselves and In Amenas, they pulled off the main road and parked behind a lone craggy butte.

There was some dead wood about, so they lit a small campfire and for breakfast made tea and flatbread that they dipped in olive oil and then finished with dried dates. They did have packaged food, collected from gas stations and supermarkets, but it was kept in reserve. Everyone was tired from driving through the night and then burnt out from the adrenaline rush during the escape.

They decided to pitch the tents and sleep during the day. It was still and hot, peaking around 43°C in the mid-afternoon. Given they had picked up four more people, and none of the party were Tuareg nomads, then all but one of the tents would need to house three people. The tents were really only sized for two people, and three would be 'cozy', in the heat.

Danielle had done the calculations as soon as they were erected and tried to organize bedding to put herself between Sebastian and the inevitable squeezing in of Sophie. But she was wrong, it was her and Sebastian that ended up in the tent for two. Sophie had decided to bunk with Andrea and the other woman, Mishka, who looked and sounded Eastern European, but was Dutch. There was nothing romantic between Andrea and Mishka, probably because she was considerably younger than him. She would have been in her mid-twenties, and he would have been early forties.

So, Sophie, being the ever-flexible opportunist, began to cultivate a friendship with Andrea, and maybe she would now snuggle up to him. In a dangerous shrinking world, it was probably not such a stupid strategy. He may have been married with children, but if he was, then he probably didn't know if they were alive or dead. Danielle didn't know if the two of them had had that conversation yet, but she did get the impression that Andrea was honest and honorable.

They broke camp just before sunset. A few kilometers ahead the road forked, one way continued North and the other East. They decided to turn to the East. It would mean they avoided more towns on their way to Algiers. About 20km up the road was the oil and gas town of Ohanet. Most of the buildings were a kilometer from the main road, but there was a gas station all by itself on the main road. They pulled in and found that it was deserted. Quickly they topped up the vehicles whilst keeping watch through binoculars to see if anyone was coming. It was a corporate administered area, so it probably had private security or even a military presence in the town. If there was anyone alive in the area, they may be friendly and even offer them assistance or information, but after their last experience, they were not willing to take that chance.

Now that they were carrying as much fuel as they could manage, it was possible that they could make it all the way to Algiers without stopping. The Muslims amongst them conducted prays and then they hit the road. It was now a 600km drive though one of the Sahara's most inhospitable regions, to the city of Hassi Messaoud, with a population of 50,000. The last 360km before the city would be nothing but sand dunes carved up into oil and gas leases. Fortunately, the road was good, and the strip of bitumen just undulated over the dunes as if it rode an ocean swell.

They reach the point where they could finally see lights on the horizon. If there were lookouts around the city, then they would see them approaching as their headlights shone across the flat treeless plain. They stopped and poured over maps. It was decided that they would approach to within a couple of kilometers of the main city and then take a series of dirt roads, and even cross-country routes, to avoid the city. They would also turn their lights off from now onward and instead tape a small flashlight to the front of each vehicle. Thus, they travelled in near darkness to avoid giving themselves away. This also meant they would be travelling much slower, at around 40kph, and it would take them an additional 30-40 minutes to navigate their bypass of Hassi Messaoud.

They crept down the road barely able to see five meters ahead. Fortunately, the road was straight and level, and they should start their detour before reaching any barricade. Lots of lights were on in the landscape around them as they got closer to the town. These were the mining camps and drilling rigs owned and managed by multi-national corporations. They would have private security protecting them, and probably the whole city was heavily guarded. Not that it was done for the benefit of the local inhabitants, but instead to protect leases and profits. This business model was now obsolete, but it had a long half-life, and thus people would continue to fight for lost causes long into the future.

They bumped down the dirt tracks that

radiated from the city, and where necessary went cross-country to link up with other tracks allowing them to weave their way North. If they had already been spotted, then no one responded, and after about 30 minutes they rejoined the main road to Algiers, turned on their headlights and increased speed. After they had put the lights of Hassi Messaoud behind them, they looked for a place to camp before sunrise. Somewhere off the main road and away from any settlements and infrastructure.

From tomorrow onward there would by many more towns and cities on their route. The next city would be Touggourt, where they would turn East before arcing to the North again. This time they would approach that town before sunset and then bypass it by driving though the desert before linking up with the road heading East. They figured that they wouldn't meet anyone in the desert, and that they could complete the detour before it got dark.

They found a gully that would conceal their camp, lit a fire and set up the tents. Whilst driving they had been eating packaged snacks, but now they could have a proper meal without the excessive sugar and carbs. Dried and salted meat with beans was cooked into a stew and accompanied by rice. It was delicious and hearty and ensured they would all sleep well. Again, Sophie bunked with Andrea, and this time Mishka asked if she could share the tent with Danielle and Sebastian. Perhaps she was starting to feel like the third wheel. Of course, they said it was OK, but Danielle made sure that it was she that slept in the middle.

They were back on the road by 4PM and as they drew closer to Touggourt they saw palm plantations and civilization on their right. The Northern boundary of the Sahara wasn't too far away. When they were about 20km away from the city they turned left into the desert, trying to take the most direct route back to the bitumen, which by their rough calculations was 18km to the Northeast. However, the sand was so soft that it wasn't long before they had to deflate the tires to stop the vehicles from getting bogged. It was slow going, slower than they had expected. It was also extremely hot. Each time they stopped and got out of the vehicles to survey their route or dig themselves out from the sand, it was like opening the door to a furnace. It was hard for the Westerners to fathom why some people in North Africa did this kind of four-wheel driving for leisure.

Just on sunset they finally returned to the main road, and it was about 100km to the next town called Guettara. They really needed to reinflate their tires, but they had no pump. Of all the items they could have forgotten to pack, an air pump was probably the most crucial in the desert. There was no choice but to drive slowly on the underinflated tires, and then stop at Guettara to pump them up, and if possible, get some fuel. The challenge was to do all of this without being noticed. The gas station was located on the other side of town, and they didn't really want to do another cross-country detour. It was dangerous in the dark, especially given there were farms with fences and irrigation channels that surround the town.

They took the chance and drove straight into the center of the town, which by coincidence was where the hospital was located. The lights were on, and they could even see people through the windows. There was no barricade or security, so they decided to stop and run into the hospital and talk to the staff. With the vehicles left running just outside the entrance, Danielle and Sebastian hurried inside. There were a few people at the reception including one of the doctors. Danielle pulled out her ID and in the most official voice she could muster announced that she was from MSF and needed to talk to whoever was in charge. The doctor at reception responded and said that it would be him.

She produced a bottle of the potion, a sample of each of the ingredients, and then the formula written out on a few sheets of paper for how to prepare and administer it. She also told him about Djanet and the success they were having there, and that if he wanted to verify it then a delegation should go and investigate. However, she also told them to avoid In Amenas due to the military takeover.

The doctor took all of the information seriously and acknowledge that it was important that her convoy got to Algiers. He was amazed, however, that they had managed to get to the hospital without the police stopping them. He said that they still had zombies roaming the streets, and that the police were patrolling and killing anyone out after curfew. This now presented a problem; how would they get through town and out to the gas station if the police were patrolling?

The doctor devised a plan. He had a radio for contacting the police. He would call them and report a zombie had been seen in the street behind the hospital. As soon as they got that call all of the police would converge. Then, when the police were investigating the back of the building, Danielle and her party could slip away, driving quietly down the road with their headlights turned off.

This plan was put into action and one of the nursing staff was used as a spotter. When she saw all of the police cars at the far side of the hospital, they quietly slipped away, getting through the town and then finally stopping at the gas station about 1km further on. Like a race car pit crew, they quickly re-inflated their tires and topped up their tanks with fuel. Someone ran inside and stole an air pump for the tires, and then like bandits they slipped away back into the desert.

There was now only 170km of Saharan sand left before they were officially out of the desert and entering the savanna of the North. The next obstacle was the large city of Messaad, with a population of over 120,000. The doctor at Guettara had said that they should avoid the city. Apparently there had been lots of rioting, and that there was a breakdown in law and order. He could not say if conditions were the same in Algiers, but that they should expect a similar situation there. He said that the further North they went, the more difficult conditions were likely to be.

They stopped on the side of the road in the last stretch of desert and plotted out a course that would bypass the roads of Messaad. It was going to be difficult, but there was a dry river that ran right through the center of the city and then met back up with the main road further North. It was hoped that the police and military would be focused on the barricades erected on the road network. They had to have faith that the riverbed was not boggy or otherwise impassable. With the help of the city lights, and the moonlight, they just may be able to sneak right through the center of the city, with their lights turned off, undetected.

It was the early hours of the morning when they reached the edge of a plateau and saw the lights of the city below them. It was built along the meandering river valley, with the dry riverbed at the center. They turned off the main road, reduced their tire pressure, and without using their headlights, travelled about 2km overland until they reached the river. The drop-down into the channel ranged between 1-2m relative to the surrounding land. Hopefully it would be enough to conceal them as they quietly crept past security, militia, and zombies.

Right in the center of town there was a large concrete road bridge that linked two sides of the city. The river narrowed and the banks either side became much higher. The center of the city had been built on higher ground to escape flooding. Indeed, it was the location of the Roman Fort city Castellum Dimmidi, circa 200AD.

There were vehicles and spotlights on the bridge. It was a checkpoint set up to control the movement of people in the city, but hopefully not set up to monitor the river. Of equal concern, at the narrowest part, which was directly under the bridge, there was water in the river channel. There was mostly a dry path through, but in a couple of places the water extended all the way from bank to bank.

They stopped the vehicles and stealthily

walked up to the bridge to check how firm the bed was, and also the likelihood of them being spotted. As they approached, they could hear a noisy portable generator that must have been powering the spotlights. They were hoping it would be sufficiently loud to mask the sound of their vehicles. As for the water, one of the men waded through and found it to be about half a meter deep. This was at the very limit of what their vehicles could tolerate in their un-modified condition. They did have tow cables with them, but the last thing they wanted to do was pull someone out of water or mud whilst right under the nose of police and soldiers.

The SUV that Sebastian drove was the fastest and fanciest, but it was also the one that was least capable in rugged terrain. Therefore, it was decided that the other vehicles would go through first. They did not want to risk him getting bogged and blocking the path for the other two vehicles. If worst came to worst, they could abandon his SUV and all pile into the remaining vehicles. There were so many abandoned SUVs on the streets that it would not be difficult to find a replacement. However, all of this was just contingency, hopefully luck would be on their side.

They edged forward until they went into the dark under the bridge. The water rose around the vehicles and started to come in through the bottoms of the doors. But still they kept moving forward, bumping over rocks, and from time to time spinning in mud. They couldn't gun the engines; all they could do was let the vehicles crawl along in low gear. First one, then two, and then three vehicles climbed up out of the water on the far side of the bridge.

But they could not stop and celebrate or drain the water that sloshed around their feet. They were in full view should someone just happen to glance over the side of the bridge and down into the river channel. So, they kept moving forward, slowly picking up speed, and being sure not to touch their brakes. It would only take one driver to tap the brakes, and their taillights would give them away.

They continued along the river for another 7km before it met up with the main road again. Palm plantations lined both sides of the river and then the road. It was about another 10km before they were truly away from civilization, climbing back up out of the valley and finally being hidden in another small mountain range. They pulled over, pumped up their tires, then continued North.

There were lots of hidden spots to camp not far from the main road. So, although they were only 350km from Algiers and the coast, they decided to make camp, de-stress, and prepare for what would be a difficult day tomorrow. The doctor at the last hospital had given Danielle the name and address of someone he knew was still alive and may be willing to help them. He was located in Port Madrague, which was a Western coastal suburb of Algiers. If they could get to him, he would be able to give them accommodation and hopefully connect them with others who could help. They sat around the campfire and planned out the best route, intending to avoid the freeways and the most populated parts of the city.

It was a warm night, but they could already start to feel the moderating effects of the Mediterranean and their drift to a higher latitude. Since leaving Djanet they had travelled 1,900km, mostly in a Northerly direction, so unless the wind blew in from the desert, it would continue to get cooler. They were all asleep before sunrise and aimed to be back on the road by noon. This would likely put them at their destination around sunset. They figured there would be lots of zombies in the city, but they would be less active during the day. Also, the daylight may help them to navigate the urban backroads and give them advance warning of roadblocks and other surprises.

CHAPTER 20

They began the final push for the coast. Their vehicles and bodies were covered in dust, and their clothes crusty with sweat and mud. No one smelt or looked good anymore; well, that wasn't quite true. Danielle found Sebastian looked rather rugged with his beard and spiked up hair. She could only wonder at what he thought of her though, but if Sophie or Mishka were anything to go by, then she must have looked like something the cat dragged in.

As they approached the city limits, they were surprised how many people and cars were out on the streets. There were also police and military vehicles, but they hadn't erected barricades, and neither were they stopping anyone. Perhaps they had been overwhelmed and all but abandoned the outer suburbs and settlements. Instead, maybe they had consolidated into the inner city. Maybe they protected the central business district and the government buildings.

There was lots of evidence of conflict, probably from rioting, and nothing had been cleared away. Broken shop fronts burnt out cars, and even human bodies, still littered the streets and sidewalks. Unlike in the smaller towns, there were no crosses on the doors to signify if someone had died inside, it was just all left to sort itself out, which included left to decay.

Up ahead was a road tunnel. It wasn't exceptionally long, maybe a few hundred meters, but inside there were many people. Some wandered slowly across the vehicle lanes, and others either sat or lay on the ground.

As they got closer Sebastian said, "Zombies. The tunnel is filled with zombies."

"They must be sheltering from the sunlight. I imagine they will come out again at night," Danielle said.

He stopped the car about 100m back from the entrance and then conferred with the other drivers. They could have driven through, swerving to miss as many as they could, however, some that lay on the road may prove more difficult to get around. And they did not know how the zombies would react. Would they actually be attracted to the cars, stand in front of them or even surround them? It would be a hell of a place to get stuck. There would be no way anyone could get back out of the tunnel on foot without getting scratched or bitten. Also, what if the air in the tunnel was filled with the spores that caused R24. Could they make the vehicles airtight to stop them from getting inside? Probably not.

They looked again at their maps and devised

an alternative route. It was a bit longer, but it would mean they could stay in the daylight. They had to backtrack and find an off ramp and then weave through the narrow streets until they were back on their original route. Thus, they continued through suburbs that seemed to be partially functioning. Everyone wore masks and rushed from place to place, cars drove around the streets, but with no longer any regard for traffic rules. It was a slow anarchy.

They came over a rise and just a few streets in front of them could see the sun setting over the Mediterranean. The coast was lined with modern bleached white holiday apartment blocks and hotels. They looked perfectly normal. The marina was full of boats, indeed there was an overflow, and boats sat at anchor out into the bay, hundreds and hundreds of them. Were these refugees who had fled from Europe? A reversal in the tide of boat people?

Finally, they found the building they were looking for. It was a ten-story apartment block with underground parking. They followed the driveway down beneath the building only to find that there were zombies, both alive and dead down there. Immediately they turned around and parked out on the road in the orange glow of sunset. It was an unbelievably beautiful view in an otherwise very ugly world. They noticed that there was a restaurant next door that appeared to be open. Masked people were going in and out. It didn't seem that anyone was staying to eat, but they were certainly ordering food and then taking it with them, probably back to the many other holiday apartments.

They walked up the white stone steps to the large, tinted glass doors. They were locked, so using a nearby stick, they pushed the button for reception. A man answered in French, whereupon Sebastian explained that they had been sent by the doctor in Guettara. The man was pleased to hear that his doctor friend was alive, and immediately the automatic doors opened. They walked inside, all wearing masks, and then the doors closed behind them and locked.

It was a small but opulent foyer with lots of marble, brass, and exotic potted plants. The man behind the desk was impeccably groomed and wore a suit. It was as if they had stepped into an alternative reality. On one side of the doors was a world falling apart with zombies, riots, and curfews, and on this side, it was clean and orderly, as if they were checking in for a week's holiday at the beach.

The man introduced himself as Farid, the co-owner and manager of the complex. He looked at them with empathy and said, "We must get you settled and cleaned up before we talk. Give me your car keys and I will have your luggage brought in, and then we will park your vehicles in a secure location."

They were a little apprehensive, with trust being in short supply. Therefore, two of the Djanet drivers elected to assist, just to make sure that everything was above board, and the vehicles or luggage didn't go missing, especially the potion.

Farid grabbed a handful of keys and asked the party to follow him as he walked to the elevator. It was a squeeze to fit them all in, and in the confined space they could really appreciate the stench of several days on the road. The elevator stopped at the tenth floor, and everyone shuffled out into the immaculately clean carpeted corridor. Farid laid the keys out onto a small decorative half-table next to the elevator doors.

He said, "Please, choose your rooms. They are all doubles and there is more than enough space for everyone. There are no other guests on this level so you can use it how you wish for as long as you like."

They thanked him and then started to look at each other and negotiate who would go where. It was like when school children are picking teams for sport. Who would get picked last? Danielle pushed niceties to the side and just grabbed a key and then said to Sebastian, "Come on, you're with me."

He did not raise an eyebrow as he turned and followed her down the hallway. They did not even stay to see how the others divided up the rooms, but it was probably in line with the sleeping arrangements over the past few days.

They found their room at the end of the hall; Danielle inserted the key and opened the door. It was a pleasant and welcome sight, being a rather lavish room on the corner of the building. Two of the walls were glass sliding windows that looked out across a wraparound balcony. One direction faced the marina and Mediterranean, and the other had a view of the city. It was extremely beautiful, the perfect holiday destination. There was only one bathroom, so Sebastian insisted that Danielle have the first shower whilst he investigated the kitchen and mini bar for something to snack on and drink.

She picked up the towel and robe that had been laid out neatly on the bed and then locked herself in the bathroom. There was a wide selection of soaps, oils, and hair products, thus she had a long hot shower and indulged. The water about her feet was the color of the desert as the dust washed away from her skin and the grains of sand dislodged from her scalp. It felt so good to be clean and smelling of rose petals. When she finished, she put on the fluffy white guest robe, stepped into the disposable slippers, and wrapped a towel around her head.

She came out to find Sebastian had opened the glass sliding doors and was stretched out on a reclining lounge taking in the view. In his hand was a glass with a clear cold bubble drink. She stepped out into the warm evening breeze and asked, "What have you got there?"

"A gin and tonic," he said with a smile. He reached over and picked up another glass and handed it to her.

"Oh, yes please," she said, took it from him and had a sip.

These rooms catered for the international tourist market; therefore, they had minibars with alcohol and other Western contraband. The two of them certainly weren't going to judge or complain. They sat on the balcony and watched the evening turn to night. Surprisingly there was a lot of boat activity, with most of the craft looking like commercial fishing boats. However, there were no people having parties on their luxury yachts. It seemed like serious fishing was the only thing happening. It kind of made sense. People needed to be fed, and if agriculture was breaking down, then the fishing industry could probably pick up some of the slack.

Sebastian gulped down the remainder of his drink and then disappears into the bathroom to shower and shave. Danielle sat there giving out deep sighs at the view, the luxury..., and then she heard a knock at the door.

Upon opening she found a member of staff, in full steward uniform, standing next to a trolly that contained their bags. How he knew which room they were in was a mystery. Perhaps the others had told him as he made his deliveries. He brought in their bags and then in broken English he said, "Please put clothes in…" as he handed her two laundry bags. Then he continued by saying, "I come back in one hour, leave outside door, yes," as he held up his index finger and then pointed it to the floor.

"Yes," she said, and then nodded to acknowledge. 'How nice', she thought, they would get all of their clothes washed.

She began to stuff everything she had into a laundry bag and then a chime came from the telephone. She answered by saying her room number.

"Hello Danielle," Farid said. "Have you settled in and enjoyed a shower?"

"Yes, thank you. It is very lovely, we are very happy," she replied.

"Very good. I just wanted to inform you that the kitchen has prepared a small buffet dinner for yourself and the other guests. The dining room will be open in 30 minutes if you would like to come down."

"Oh.." she said, "that is very kind of you, but I don't have anything to wear."

He laughed and said, "There is no dress code tonight. Everyone is in the same situation; it will be OK to wear the shower robe. If this is not enough, I can send up a swimsuit to put underneath."

"No, that will be OK. So long as I don't offend anyone," she said with a laugh.

He replied, "These are exceptional times; no one will be offended. So, we will see you and Mr. Sebastian in 30 minutes?"

"Yes, we will be there, thank you."

Sebastian came out of the bathroom clean, shaved, and with his wet dark wavey hair reaching down to his shoulders. She could have thrown him on the bed there and then, but instead she threw him the laundry bag and told him they would be collecting the dirty clothes. She then informed him of their dinner reservation, so he needed to hurry up.

They walked into the hallway to find everyone else had left their rooms at the same time and were congregating about the elevator. They were all dressed in their white hotel robes, and as a group they looked like a church choir about to sing from the ambo. Sophie was sharing a room with Andrea, and she clung to him like a child who had just won a fluffy toy at the fair. He seemed pleased with this but remained dignified like the senior engineer that he was. What a lovely couple, an accountant and an engineer. Two people who found each other under the most improbable and ridiculous of circumstances.

They filed into the dining room and were surprised by how many staff, dressed in crisp white uniforms, were there to attend to them. Seafood buffet steamed under bright lights. It made sense that it would be seafood given the boats were being unloaded right at the front door. Getting other meats, like beef or lamb would have involved finding a working farm or butchery, and then transporting such goods through the broken city. It would have been fraught with danger and just not worth the risk given the ready access to seafood.

They sat at dining tables, set for two and four. Danielle and Sebastian shared with Sophie and Andrea. They had plates overflowing with prawns and fish, accompanied by steamed vegetables and buttered dinner rolls. How they secured vegetables for the kitchen was beyond what they could fathom. Maybe they were grown nearby in someone's garden or came in on a boat from some partially functioning town further along the coast. Regardless, they were a welcome addition to their diet.

And then there was wine, white and red, still and bubbly, by the glass and by the bottle. They chugged greedily as if they had forgotten their manners, with each glass washing away the traumatic memories and filling the head with a pleasant fog. Was this the aristocracy's last meal before the revolution? They dined as if it were, with no thought to the cost, or who would pay the bill. Perhaps they were dining on the past, every accumulation and privilege poured into one glass and eaten from that one last plate of decadence and vice. But still they did not stop until the last cream stuffed desert was served and eaten. And they were neither ashamed nor felt guilt. Instead, they toasted the fallen and wished the survivors the best of fortunes and happiness.

Farid was the host of hosts. Was he really the co-owner, or now the full owner? Or did he masquerade, living high on someone else's misfortune? Did he really have the authority to open the vault and spoil them like this? These were valid questions, but they did not care for an answer tonight. Instead, they would be partners to any crime and claim ignorance and repent in the light of the next day.

Cheerfully bloated they drifted back to their rooms. Sebastian being witty and wisecracking in a way that Danielle had not seen before. He was a long way from that introverted stoic she had first met in the desert. Now they had their own private jokes and routines, and ways of touching that were allowed, or even expected. They were a couple in every way but being physically intimate. 'What is wrong with him', she thought. She knew he was not gay; this she would have certainly noticed. And neither did he seem emotionally damaged, well no more than anyone else including herself. Then she questioned if it was her, was she so unapproachable, or unfathomable? Could he not read her, or did he maybe fear her? Surely, she wasn't that dominant and intimidating? Should she sleep in the other bed tonight, by herself, and see what happens? No, that would just be childish game play, and it may hurt her more than him. It wasn't worth the risk.

Within a few minutes of the door being locked she found that she had worried over nothing. Be it the alcohol, the safe environment, or the city lights that sparked on the sea breeze, all inhibitions dissolved and now she felt like she was truly on a romantic getaway.

CHAPTER 21

When they woke up all of their clothes had been cleaned and pressed by the valet service, neatly presented outside their door. It was a bright clear morning, but without the desert glare and heat. A full continental breakfast was waiting for them in the dining room. Everyone was well rested and refreshed. Sophie was in an extra cheerful mood, if that was possible. Obviously, things were going well with Andrea. Danielle just hoped that he wasn't just using her whilst the opportunity presented itself.

After breakfast Farid call them into the adjoining conference room. It was all rather formal, like they were there for a company retreat, but in a way it was still nice to hark back to convention. Whist they sat he stood at a whiteboard and commenced a very business-like presentation. Perhaps this was the stage where he was most comfortable, and where he could rationalize the world beyond the glass doors.

After greeting them, as if they had paid to attend his seminar, he said, "Let me tell you everything I know. Some of this is firsthand, but most of it is stories I have heard from other people, mainly the people that have arrived by boat from Europe and the Middle East.

"Many places in North Africa have fared much better than other areas. It was because of its relative isolation, and the effect that the Sahara, Sinai, and Arabian deserts, as well as the Mediterranean have had had on restricting people's movements. It is like we are an island," and using a marker he drew a rough map of the world and then emphasized North Africa buy putting a rig around it.

"And speaking of islands," he said, "many island nations have done much better than those on the continents. Some of the countries that weathered the pandemic better than the others included Iceland and Greenland, Japan, Pacific Islands and Australia," and he made dot points and wrote out their names.

He continued, "I am told that even the UK and Ireland have fared reasonably well, or at least outside of London. The only exception is Denmark, they closed their borders very early, basically closed themselves off from the rest of the world.

"So, all those countries, or regions, that I have not named on this list have been, for want of a better word, decimated. Some still have governments, hiding in bunkers or something similar, but as for their populations and economies, totally decimated.

"I have been in touch with my doctor friend

down in Guettara, and he tells me about the important mission you are on. I applaud your effort and can only guess at how difficult it has been to come as far as you have."

He then started to clap his hands and encouraged the staff to also clap and to praise God. Ironically a God that had forsaken all but those that had not yet contracted the disease. To the Westerners, at least, it felt almost staged, but it was not. It was genuine. They were the first sign of hope that these people had experienced since the start of the pandemic. Perhaps this explained why they were being treated like royalty.

Then he said, "This is what I can now say and advise. Copenhagen in Denmark, and Birmingham in the UK, which is now the new capital for the English, are coordinating whatever effort the World can muster. However, it isn't much besides putting information on the Internet, when it is working. For the most part they put every effort into protecting their borders and keeping refugees and the disease out. They do, however, have functioning medical research facilities, and I am told they are trying to find a cure. It is my suggestion that you take your cure to them so that they can work on it and spread it around the world.

"To help you with this I can organize a boat for you. It can cross the Mediterranean to Palma de Mallorca in the Balearic Islands, refuel and then continue to the Costa Brava, dropping you near Tossa de Mar, about 100km Northeast of Barcelona, Spain. This will put you around 100km South of the boarder with France. Unfortunately, after that I cannot help. You will need to cross France, which will be 1,000km to the English Channel, then somehow cross the sea, or travel another 1,000km overland though Belgium and Germany if you wish to get to Copenhagen. From what I understand you will have trouble getting into both of these countries, but probably England would be the easiest if you have a passport," and he looked specifically at Danielle.

The news was grim, and the challenge was great. Each person had something to say, some of it supportive, and some not so much. It seemed that only five of them would be continuing the journey. This would be Danielle and Sebastian, Sophie and Andrea, and lastly Mishka. For good reason none of the native Africans wanted to cross the sea, especially given they did not have passports, not that they meant much anymore. The two Pakistanis were happy to throw their lot in with their Muslim brothers in Algeria.

Farid put a positive spin on travelling as a smaller group. He said that the boat was small anyway, so it would have been difficult to take all of them. And, when it came to sneaking around the countryside, then maybe the fewer of them there were, the less conspicuous they would be.

They decided to rest up for a few days at the apartment hotel. They ate well and indulged, including using the pool and sauna. There was a gym on site, but they hardly needed to get into shape given the workouts they had gone though over the past few weeks. As a group they even ventured outside and went to the marina, and then to a sandy beach for a swim. In the midday sun there were no zombie, and apart from fishermen tending to nets and boats, there were very few people about, either on foot or in cars. It seemed that there was a degree of adjusted normality. One could live life if one followed basic rules. These included, stay away from dark places and be inside before sunset, and to avoid close contact with anyone unless they had gone through quarantine. Also, unless in a sterile environment, wear gloves and a mask at all times; and wash everything.

Fifteen minutes' drive from their hotel was the Hôpital de Bainem. Danielle, Sebastian and Farid drove there in the hope that they could get in to see whoever was in charge. It seemed that Farid was well known, and his name carried some weight. After discussions with security guards and reception staff they were able to get an appointment with one of the senior administrators of the hospital. Danielle had used one of the computers at the hotel to type up everything that she knew about the disease, the potion, and the methods of treatment. She then printed and bound it into a small booklet. She presented the administrator with this along with a bottle of potion and samples of the ingredients needed to make it.

The administrator was very please and immediately called in several other doctors. They turned the plant samples over in their hands, and all of them acknowledge that at least two of them grew locally, indeed they were considered useless weeds; how ironic. But the third one, the small black seeds, they had never seen before. They said that they would collaborate with their colleagues at the nearby Issad Hassani University Hospital and try to better understand the potion and also try to produce a synthetic version. This was a great weight off of Danielle's shoulders. At least someone would be working on it, therefore even if she were not successful in her push North, all would not be lost.

It was unfortunate that there had been no Internet connection through to the UK or Denmark for the past few days. The hospital said they would continue to try and contact those countries with news about the cure. If they were able to get a message through, they would inform the authorities to expect Danielle to arrive in the next week or so.

They left the hospital mid-afternoon to ensure they would be back to the hotel before dark. It was a pleasant drive along the foreshore, and in places it looked normal. Then there would be a reminder, like an abandoned car in the middle of the road, burnt-out buildings, or dead bodies on the sidewalk. The cleanup hadn't reached the outer suburbs yet, and probably wouldn't until this current wave of infections and zombies had passed.

Their last night in the hotel was a celebratory occasion, as well as sad, now that the group was breaking up. They had formed strong bonds with their Arab-Berber and Pakistani compatriots. They were sad that they would probably never see them again, but everyone knew the risks and the realities of the times. It was another seafood buffet, fortunately each meal was prepared in a different style, so as yet, no one was sick of the good things they had. How sad it would have been to be sick of oysters and crab, and to lose the appreciation of washing it down with fine wine.

Those that were leaving would be going to bed earlier than the others. They would be leaving on the morning tide just before sunrise. It would be a five-hour trip, and hopefully the seas would be kind to them. This time of year, it was typically calm, and the breeze was blowing offshore, so it should be fine and smooth sailing.

During their dinner they discussed as a group

how they should proceed. And even though the Africans had never travelled through Europe, their input was still valuable. The consensus was that they would travel as a group through to Northern France, and then they would split into two. Danielle and Sebastian would head for the Channel and then England, whilst the other three would head for Denmark. Each group would carry samples of the potion, plants, and the instruction booklet. If the freeways and autobahns were clear, and they could requisition vehicles, then the journeys may be relatively quick and straight forward. Of course that was the best-case scenario, but it helped to look on the positive side.

Everyone agreed that probably the hardest part would be getting across the Channel and also crossing heavily guarded borders. Of course, if the hospital was able to get a message though, then they may get straight in, and even escorted or airlifted to their destination. However, if they arrived just like any other refugees, then they may end up getting lost in some disease-ridden internment camp. Maybe even stripped of the potion, plants, and identity, and left to wither.

Danielle and Sebastian sat on their balcony drinking gin and tonic as the steady stream of boats plied the marina. And out into the distance, on the glass-smooth sea they could see the lights of many more boats, most of them anchored and dropping nets, but some moved slowly like satellites amongst the stars.

Danielle asked, "You are OK going to England, aren't you?"

"Yes, no problem at all. It seems that I couldn't get back to Canada even if I wanted to. And based on what I have heard, I don't really want to. I hope that doesn't make me sound unpatriotic. But the way I figure, the Canada I left doesn't exist anymore. So, wherever we can make a home, well that becomes my country."

She though it was nice that he used the term 'we', but did it mean the two of them, or was it just a generic we, the royal 'we'?

They had already discussed his family, and he had no siblings and few relatives. His parents were both gone before the pandemic, so he didn't really have much of a familial connection to his former home. He probably now had a stronger affinity to Algeria, and to Danielle, than he did to his past life. So, it made sense to follow her wherever she went.

Then he said, "I hope I don't have any trouble getting through the border into the UK. It's all right for you; you're a citizen and still have your passport on you. I'm not sure how they're going to treat me even though Canada is a member of the Commonwealth. I'm just worried they may try to split us up."

She reacted saying, "Noo... I won't let them." Then she thought for a while and said, "I could always tell them that you are my husband, but that your paperwork has been lost in all of the chaos. I can say we were away on holiday in Algeria, which is true, and we have just managed to make it back."

"Yes, but won't they be able to check that?" he said, "Surely there is a database, and they'll find out straight away that it's not true, and then you'll be in trouble for lying."

"Ok then, we can say that we got married whilst we were away. We got married in Algeria. I'm sure that Farid knows someone who can make up a marriage certificate. And the border guards, they are not going to know what an Algerian marriage certificate looks like, are they."

"So, you're talking about a forgery?" he said.

"Yeah... I suppose," she said rather coyly.

"Or a real one?" he said as if fishing.

"Well yeah, if it comes to that," she said in an even more shrinking voice.

"Do you want to get married, like for real?" he asked in a rather clumsy and insensitive way.

"No, I mean not if you're going to ask like that," she said in a rather indignant tone.

He realized, finally, how stupid he had been and then started again. He knelt down beside her, pulled a piece of string from his pocket and asked, "Danielle, will you please marry me, so we can live together happily ever after?"

"Now you're just making fun of me," she said

as she pushed him away, and in fact pushed him over as he lost balance.

He got back into the kneeling position and took her hand and then tied the piece of string around her ring finger and said, "I am serious, will you marry me, please? We can get Farid to organize it tonight. I don't want to lose you, and I don't know if we are going to still be alive tomorrow. So, every day is the rest of our lives, and I want to spend all of those days with you, starting right now, tonight."

How could a girl say no?

CHAPTER 22

Danielle and Sebastian went downstairs to find Farid. Everyone was still in the dining room, including those that had said they were going to bed early. Sebastian said, "I have an announcement."

Everyone went quite as he put his arm around Danielle and said, "I asked Danielle if she would marry me, and she said yes."

There were cheers and applause as everyone began to congratulate them. He then gestured with his hands for them to quieten down, and said, "But the thing is, we want to make it official tonight, as in before we get on the boat and leave."

He turned to Farid and asked, "Is this possible. Can you make it happen?"

Farid cupped his hand around his chin and mulled over the question, and then he said, "All of the churches and mosques are across the other side of the peninsular. It wouldn't be wise to drive there at night, although we could go by boat, which would take about 30-40 minutes each way. But then we have to get from the boat to the church, which would be dangerous without cars."

Danielle said, "I don't care if it's not in a church or mosque," then she looked at Sebastian and asked, "Would that bother you?"

He shook his head and said, "I don't care, as long as we get married, that's all that matters."

"Well then," Farid said, "then, this is not a problem; we can do it here. Do you prefer an Imam or a Priest?"

Sebastian said, "I don't care, so long as it is official and legal."

Then Danielle responded, "A Priest if we can. It's just that we are going through Christian countries, so it just may make it easier."

"Yes, yes, I see," Farid said. "We have the Catholic here in Algiers. Will the Catholic do, or does it have to be some type of Orthodox?"

"Catholic will be fine," she replied, "and would they do it; do it tonight?"

"He is my good friend; he will do it for me. I will send a car to get him. You must get ready. I will have him here in 30 minutes."

Sophie was pulling hard on Andrea's arm and fizzing almost to the point of bursting. She looked at him mouthing something and then he finally said, "Sophie and I will also get married. It is the right thing to do now that we are in love."

She let out a squeal of excitement and gave him a huge hug and kiss. They weren't even sure if he had actually asked her, but it seemed that it didn't matter to her. It was time to grab hold of life and live it to the fullest. Sure, they had only known each other for a few days, but that was no indication that they wouldn't be happy for the rest of their lives. Indeed, knowing someone for years was no guarantee either, based on the divorce rate.

The women rushed back to their suites to get ready, Farid sent for the priest, and the men had an impromptu bachelor's drink at the bar. When Danielle returned, she was wearing the most beautiful of white Arabian inspired gowns. It was something that had been left in a guest's room that one of the hotel staff presented to her. She wore a white silk veil and then gold chains and pendants across her brow, and more down her arms that connected to her fingers. One of the female staff had done her makeup, giving her the mysterious and seductive eyes of a Muslim woman. She could have been a princess in the 'Tales of Arabian Nights' gracing a palace one thousand years ago. Sebastian was floored and could not believe how lucky he was that this was his bride.

Sophie was equally stunning and exotic. She wore a bright red gown, heavily embroidered with gold. Real gold that was heavy and pulled everything perfectly into place. It was amazing what people had travelled with, and what was now left behind. Perhaps the former owner was on her way to her own wedding but never lived to enjoy it. Both women had bare feet and a mesmerizing collection of bejewel anklets. It was probably more wedding regalia than Sophie had ever dreamed to be wearing, and more spontaneous and romantic than could have possibly been fanaticized in a Victorian novel. Andrea was a lucky man. No woman in the history of wives could have ever been as adoring and faithful as Sophie; she was love and butterflies personified.

Sebastian set up his camera and began taking photos of both couples and the wedding party. They were important for their memories, and equally important for convincing border security. They looked authentic, and when the Priest arrived, they include him as well. The preamble and wedding vows were really just a formality, the true weddings occurred when the woman first entered the room. The whole service was brief and succinct; Do you? Yes, do you? Yes, then I pronounce you husband and wife. Papers were signed, toast were made, and vol-au-vent and other delicacies were passed around. It was the most beautiful and romantic of weddings that one could have in such an ugly world.

The morning came on soon and they were packed and down at the marina early. There were zombies about, and those that got too close were either shot, or herded into the sea; they discovered that Zombies could not swim. After a bit of a splutter, they just floated face down and finally found peace.

Sophie had acquired more luggage; curtesy of items being abandoned at the hotel. No doubt she had packed her wedding dress, the jewelry, and anything else that wasn't bolted down. For now, it wouldn't be a problem, but if they had to travel by foot further along their journey, then it would all get jettisoned, and some other survivor would lay claim to it.

The boat was a modern cabin cruiser, probably costing $1 million, with a powerful inboard motor, and lots of timbered deck for lounging in the sun. They were out of the marina before sunrise and powered past the numerous fishing boats and abandoned craft. Across the calm sea they made good time. Upon talking to the skipper, it was revealed that he regularly did the voyage between Algiers and Palma and had been doing it long before the pandemic. He had relatives and friends on the island which would allow them to dock safely.

However, he said that it was unlikely that they would be allowed to leave the boat due to the very strict quarantine on the island. Palma had almost totally avoided the R24 plague, and what zombies they did have had died out without infecting anyone. Thus, they considered themselves disease free and they wanted to keep it that way. Life on the resort island went on as it had before, although now there was no high or low season. There were just the people who were fortunate enough to be there when the walls went up, and that is where they would stay. No one would trade their good fortune, for if they left the island, they would not be permitted to return.

The skipper maintained a courier service. Previously it was just people and the odd case of wine, but now it was all manner of food stuffs, household, and mechanical items. He would ensure that the products were uncontaminated, drop them at the wharf, and then bring back items that they wished to trade. His boat carried enough fuel to travel to Palma and back to Algiers, about 200km return. However, to get to the Spanish coast, he would have to do another 200km. Thus, he would have to refuel at the wharf, and for this he would have to trade. Money was no longer any good, so instead he had small gold ingots. These were less bulky than sacks of potatoes or bunches of bananas, which were worth almost as much.

The island was very picturesque from the sea, and as they approached Puerto de Palma, they saw row after row of luxury yachts. It seemed that the rich and famous knew where to go at the first sign of trouble. People were walking up and down the piers, the restaurants were busy, and the beaches were full of swimmers and sunbathers. It was busier and more decadent than it had ever been, protected by the sea, and the police at every point of entry. They had a paradise on Earth, and they guarded it jealously.

A mooring was kept free at the nautical gas station for boats just like theirs. No one else was really going anywhere, so all the boats, and yachts, and mega-yachts, just sat there like apartments for those that had not secured a terrestrial dwelling. The skipper knew the man at the gas station, and they watched as he handed over a wooden crate of something and then a few gold bars. At no point since the pandemic had their group be asked to, or had to, paid for anything. It was now such a different world where paper and digital money meant nothing. Fortunately for them, they were able to salvage and scrounge what they needed, which in the old world would have been called theft. From now on maybe they would have to think about things they could trade, such as food or gold, and in Danielle's case, medical services.

The whole re-fill and transaction took less than 10 minutes, and then they were powering back out into open water and the island disappeared behind them.

The skipper said, "My friend at the wharf has given me the name of someone who can help you. Where I drop you off there will be an old man there. You will ask him for this other person called Mateo, and he will take you there and introduce you to Mateo. Mateo will get you transport and papers, and he will tell you which way is the safest to travel."

This was going to be extremely helpful, even if Mateo turned out to be a people smuggler. In this new world, who you knew was perhaps more important that what you knew, and who you knew came down to connections. Making enemies would be a very bad survival strategy. It could only take one person to give you the wrong directions and your life may be over.

It was late in the afternoon when the Spanish coast came into view. It was very built up, with large stone villas and resorts looking out from the rugged cliffs. As they cruised toward the Northeast, remaining safely offshore from heaven knows what, they could not see any people or vehicles. Nothing moved or showed any sign of life. Was this what Farid had meant by describing the continents as decimated?

Finally, the skipper pointed the boat toward the shore and backed off the engine. There was a small cove with a rickety wooden wharf jutting out behind a headland. He motored up to it and then stopped short, about 10m or so from being able to step off.

"Why have we stopped?" Sebastian asked.

"I'm waiting to see if the man comes down. I need to make sure it is the right man, and not bandits or infected people," the skipper said.

They waited for around 5 minutes before

an old man appeared from the trees and then proceeded down the path to the wharf. He walked to the end of the wharf and asked what they were doing coming into the cove. The skipper explained that he had been sent by the gas station man back on Palma, and that he had some parcels for him, and that he needed to unload passengers, and that they were to be taken to Mateo. The old man understood every part of the conversation as if the skipper had whispered a secret password, and just like that they were taken under his care. They helped unload the luggage and parcels, and also carried the latter for the old man, as he took them back up the path to his house. Andrea had to make a second trip for the rest of Sophie's luggage, but he didn't seem to mind.

It was quite a steep climb, and they had difficulty keeping up with the spritely old fellow. No doubt he walked the path several times a day and had probably done that all his life. The home was very Spanish and very pleasant. It was of the typical stucco masonry with a broad multi-arched veranda across the front and side. It had an impressive view of the Mediterranean, but from this distance there was no sight of Africa or the islands from which they had just come. It may as well have been the Pacific Ocean, except without the waves.

They saw their boat disappearing back across the sea to the Beleric Islands. The skipper seemed to have no desire to hang around near the mainland. Perhaps for fear of catching the disease or maybe being attacked by pirates. Thus, with his departure, their only way was now forward.

They introduced themselves to the old man and upon learning that Danielle was a doctor, he presented with all manner of ailments that required her urgent attention. She was happy to oblige, and between his household pharmacy and her medical case, she patched, repaired, and administered on everything from boils to gout.

The others walked the ancient gardens, with its groves of citrus and olives that hid the villa. Later they congregated about the large outdoor table where a wife, and children, and grandchildren, appeared, as if from thin air. They were there to share in a giant paella, olives, and cured meats. There was also a jug of home-made sangria. It was watery thin transparent red, and everyone drank it including the children. It would have taken a concerted effort to get drunk on it, given how watered down it was, but it was perfect for quenching the thirst and cutting through the soaking of olive oil.

They kept their distance as much as possible, even though they were given assurances that no one had R24. It was hard not to trust these people, and their absolute acceptance and hospitality. Blessings were bestowed upon them as if they were pilgrims walking the Camino de Santiago.

Bonafide travelers that must be given sanctuary; for God above tallied their every good deed.

If this was the wedded couples' honeymoons, then they were rustic, homely, and surrounded by love. They drew straws with Sophie and Andrea winning the only spare room. This was OK. It was a spacious villa and the day bed under the veranda was perfectly comfortable, and romantic, for Danielle and Sebastian on this warm Spanish candle lit night. Mishka slept around the corner, under the other veranda, on a mattress laid upon the tiles.

Their first day on the Continent was much better than they had expected, and it raised hope that they would find more enclaves of peace and safety as they travelled. Still, they held a small amount of fear for zombies that roamed in the night and hoped that the area had been cleared of them. They still had their guns, and they slept next to them just in case.

CHAPTER 23

In the morning there was just the old man and his wife. The rest of the family had disappeared back into the countryside. They must have had their own villas, children out in the orchards with their parents, picking olives and pulling grapes from the vines. There would be no school, not for a while, maybe never for this generation of children. But in this new world they may do just fine, as long as they can read and write. Perhaps the most valuable thing they could offer society was the ability to grow food and feed those around them. That would be so much more important and worthwhile to humanity than being a lawyer or a stockbroker. Yes, civilization would rise again, but not for a while. There would be peace until the markets began their exorable march toward greed and destruction.

After breakfast the old man took them to meet Mateo. They left all of the luggage and belongings at the villa and walked well-worn paths through the groves and up to the top of a hill. After about an hour of considerable effort, which did not in any way fatigue the old man, they arrived at a rather grand home. It was more in the Italian style, three stories high, and looking like the keep of a castle.

With his walking stick the old man wrapped on large wooden doors. They had been mounted 500 years ago, and seen off knights and bandits, being solid oak and studded with iron bolts and knobs.

Everything in Spain happens when it happens, thus it was a few minutes before a small portal opened and a man peered out and greeted them. The old man relayed the message of who the group were, and on whose recommendation it was that they sought his 'masters' assistance. The face in the portal disappeared, perhaps for another 5 minutes and then there was the sounds of timber and iron thumping on the other side of the door. Finally, it swung inwards, and they were invited to enter.

A stately man of means greeted them. He wore expensive clothes, and sported a fedora hat, introducing himself as Mateo. His manners were impeccable, and he enjoyed charming the women. One could imagine that he had a garage of Ferraris and convertible Alfa Romeos that he used to take his many mistresses to restaurants or equestrian events. They sat and drank lemonade, or was it limoncello and soda, in a courtyard that looked out over his estate, and they explained their mission.

Mateo sat quietly, just nodding, and occasionally saying, "I see."

When they had finished there was a long silence as he looked out to the distant horizon. Then finally he said, "A truck. That's what you need. A large prime mover with a box trailer. That will get you where you need to go. It will break though barricades and keep you safe from zombies and bandits. It will travel all the way across France without needing to stop and refuel."

Sophie said with incredulity, "Really! Are you suggesting we travel in the back of a truck, as if we are being smuggled?"

He gave a small laugh, as if to say, 'No my silly child', but he was more tactful than that.

"You will travel in the front," he said, "in comfort. Five plus a driver," then he stopped and corrected himself. "No, maybe we get two trucks, yes two trucks might look better and could even be safer. And we will load supplies in the trailer. We can go to a warehouse and get pallets of food, but not too heavy or this will slow you down. Perhaps something like cartons of potato crisps." He seemed very pleased with his idea and talked about it as if it were the final word on the matter.

But it did sound like a good idea. If they were in big trucks carrying food, then they would seem important and official, they would have a reason to be on the roads.

"And these truck, you can organize them?" Andrea enquired.

"Oh yes, the trucks are no problem, although finding the drivers may be a bit more challenging. It's not that there aren't any drivers about, it just finding one that is willing to drive across France and then back again. It is very risky, and all for what? The money is worthless, and a house or a car can just be taken as easy as picking an apple from a tree. I need to find someone who is doing it because they need to go there for their own reasons, or because they want to support your cause. I have people in mind, and I will talk to them tomorrow," Mateo said.

"I can drive one of the trucks," Andrea said. "I have the correct license. I may be a bit rusty, but these modern trucks almost drive themselves, so I shouldn't have too much trouble getting back in the saddle."

"Excellent," Mateo said, rubbing his hands together. "Then I shall find you two trucks and one driver. Give me two days and I will have them here. So, we will leave not tomorrow but the day after, first thing in the morning. You shall stay here tomorrow night. I will send someone tomorrow afternoon to collect you and all of your luggage."

An early light lunch arrived and as they ate, he talked about his estate, and what he grew upon it. It had been just a hobby; he had worked as a CEO for a shipping company before the pandemic. That job didn't exist anymore. But he still had connections in the transport industry, at last until the world completely unwound, and this was how he could get trucks and give advice on which routes to take.

Although he was in his 40s, and Mishka was in her 20s, he really did lay the charm on thick for her. In turn she seemed to enjoy his wit, wealth, and sophistication. He made a point of saying that he was divorced, several times, and that he had this lonely castle, which is what he called his home, all to himself. Could Miska see herself out here? She could certainly do much worse with a boy half his age. She was tall and he was tall, so at least they had that in common.

Mateo invited them to tour the estate with him. The old man from the villa said that he could not stay and thus excused himself. When it was asked how they would find their way back to the villa without the old man to guide them along the maze of paths, Mateo said that he would have someone drive them back later.

And so, the courting began in earnest. As they walked the manicured gardens, he linked his arm with Mishka and extoled the virtues of the estates. Upon returning to the house she was given the grand tour, as opposed to the others that were left to roam at their leisure. At the very top it was like a castle. One could walk onto the rooftop terrace and look out from the battlements for kilometers in all directions. How many of these grand houses now lay vacant? How many chateaux would they pass during their drive across France. Properties that were left to ruin after the Revolution, then restored by new money in the last few decades, now only to be overrun again by creeping vines and the hungry earth.

It was late afternoon and time to leave. A Mercedes limousine with a chauffeur pulled up out front to take them back to the old man's villa.

Sebastian commented, "I don't think we are all going to fit. Will we be doing it in two trips?"

Mishka replied, "No it's OK, Mateo has invited me to stay tonight. So, you can go ahead without me, and I will see you tomorrow."

The ever-protective Danielle said, "Are you sure? I know we can make room for you. It's not like we have to travel very far."

"Oh no, it's OK. It was actually me who asked if I could stay, and Mateo kindly obliged. He said he would love the company."

What more could be said or done? They were both consenting adults, and Mishka was certainly no innocent choir girl.

On the drive back Sophie said, "I think it is so sweet that they are hitting it off."

Danielle said, "I suppose she is lost and scared. Based on all reports she doesn't have any place to go home to. And well, I must say, it is a lovely house and property, and he does seem kind and thoughtful."

"I hope it is just not all an act," Sebastian said, but then he realized that he was sitting next to one of Mateo's employees and thought it wise not to say anymore, lest it get back to him. Andrea kept his thoughts to himself. He was about the same age as Mateo, therefore about ten years older than Sophie. Could he see himself with someone twenty years younger, sure, most guys could. Indeed, it was very common until the twentieth century. Perhaps this was another reversion to come from the pandemic. Pragmatic and opportunistic marriages; living in the moment and letting the future take care of itself.

When they arrived back at the villa the old man's family had rematerialized. Again, there would be a celebration. Perhaps every night was a celebration. What a blessed life they lived. After dinner they relaxed on the veranda. As a change of pace, probably inspired by the house and the people within, they selected books from a library that graced the walls of the study. It seemed that the books had been collected over decades, perhaps centuries. Thus, on their second night of wedded bliss they read in bed like an old couple, one the story of Antoni Gaudí's Sagrada Família, and the other Miguel de Cervantes' Don Quixote.

In the quiet of the evening, they could hear Sophie doing her best to make babies. It wasn't inappropriate or embarrassing, just giggles and squeaks as she played for attention. That was fine, her and Andrea were putting their privacy to good use, and it was probably for the best that they had won the rights to the room. The world needed repopulating, and she would be one of the vanguard.

Sleep came easily and Danielle did not stir again until the sun was almost up. She felt about her only to find that Sebastian was gone. She got up and looked about, eventually finding him in the kitchen squeezing fresh oranges. 'Yes, that's right' she though, they have an orange orchard; so many oranges that one must eat them every day to prevent becoming overwhelmed. He handed her a glass and winked, saying, "One more day in paradise."

He was right. She really didn't want to leave. But it wasn't their home, they were just travelling through. She was sure that if they stayed longer, they would probably wear out their welcome anyway. But truly, how could the cold grey of Yorkshire compare to this. Everyday a perfect temperature and ambience for the human body. Perhaps she had forgotten what home was like. The green fields, the old dark forests, the moors, and those oh so wonderful summer days. Yes, she was sure she would love it when she got back home. This was just a holiday infatuation.

They spent the day helping out around the farm where they could. And then in the afternoon they packed up their belongings ready to be collected, presumably by Mateo's driver. Two cars arrived, the chauffeured Mercedes and then Mateo and Mishka in a Range Rover. She already looked like his mistress, but not like they had been rolling in the hay, but in the way she had seemed to pick up some of his sophistication. She acted better, not like a snob, but like she was better trained and woven from a finer cloth. Danielle thought to herself, 'How malleable and impressionable the young are'. It was a better version of Mishka, not changed, just upgraded.

They said their goodbyes and were very genuine in expressing their gratitude, and how much they wanted to return, if it were ever possible. They were told they would always be welcome, and then 'hasta luego', and they drove away. By the time they arrived at Mateo's castle it was coming in dark. There were lights about the outer walls, and around some of the garden sculptures and trees. It made the estate look like a national monument, or maybe a period themed restaurant. It certainly added to the grandeur, and it was obvious how impressed Mishka was, and wanted the others to be.

There were plenty of rooms, all well-kept, and surprisingly Mishka had her own room. Perhaps Mateo was more the gentlemen than they had given him credit for. Of all the rooms Mishka's was the grandest. It had exquisite tapestries on the walls, thick satin curtains, and its own private Juliette balcony. If she wanted to feel like a princess, then this was the place and the stage for her to play upon.

As they were freshening up for dinner, Danielle said to Sebastian, "I bet Mishka doesn't leave here. And that they end up getting married, having lots of babies, and she lives a full and happy life in her Andalusian castle."

Sebastian laughed as if she had said something silly and then stopped and thought. Finally, he said, "Now that I've thought about it, I think you may be right. They are perfect for each other."

Where they ate was not so much a dining room as a dining hall. The long wooden table, which was probably hundreds of years old, could have sat twenty people, and as such they only occupied one half of its length. A suckling pig complete with an apple in its mouth sat center table, surrounded by tureens and platters holding all manner of good things. It had been a few months since they had eaten pork, given they had been in a Muslim country. After Mateo said grace, which caught them off guard, but then again this was pious Spain, one of the kitchen staff calved and then loaded their plates.

Mateo said, "Eat heartily, for you don't know where your next meal will be coming from."

And so, they did eat and eat. It seemed like everywhere they went they were fed like royalty, perhaps it was the last hoorah of the age of decadence. Guilt aside, it was extremely enjoyable and complemented by his excellent wine cellar. Of course he had wine, local vintages of grenache and resiling, a whole cellar full of them. So, this was how the privileged and wealthy lived. Would this be how all survivors live; had things actually got better rather than worse?

When they finished the meal, they retired to what he called the sitting room. It had high ceilings with heavy dark wooden beams, and at one end Mateo stood next to an open window smoking a cigar. The others sat on sumptuous leather couches, probably purchased new just after the Spanish Civil War, and there sipped on shots of Madeira. Then it came, and it was absolutely to no one's surprise.

Mishka said, "I have something I need to say. I have really enjoyed travelling with all of you, and I believe in this mission. It is very honorable, but I also have to make some decisions about my own future.

I'll get right to the point. I've decided I'm going to stay here and… and help Mateo run the estate."

That was one way of saying become the lady of the house; perhaps she hadn't yet admitted it to herself, or she was worried the others may judge her.

Sebastian spoke first, "I think that is a marvelous idea. Don't get me wrong, we will miss you terribly, and if we were to be purely selfish, we would beg you to continue with us. But that would not be fair to you. I can see that you belong here. I can feel it in my bones, and I think that you and Mateo will be extremely happy here; you complement each other."

He said it without saying it; they would become husband and wife, soon.

Everyone in turn echoed his sentiment to the point where Mishka was perhaps now more assured that she was making the right decision. She was young and strong-willed. If anyone would end the relationship it would be her, and it would be Mateo's heart that got broken. But it was not their place to warn him about her. But in equal measure, she would not likely do any better for protection and devotion. For her, for now, it was the smartest move; and if she outlived him, which was no guarantee, then more power to her.

CHAPTER 24

The fortified home was solid and silent like a crypt through the night. And the drapes were so thick that they blocked the morning sun. Thus, when they arose, they were surprised that it was already well into the morning. Breakfast was made to order, a fry-up of eggs, bacon, tomato, mushroom, and asparagus, all on toasted ciabatta. And then fresh orange juice, as much orange juice as one could ever want to drink.

The trucks had not arrived as expected. There could have been many reasons for their delay. Mateo was not concerned and invited them to sit with him on the terrace and enjoy coffee. They discussed how much longer coffee would last, and if they could maybe grow it themselves. Apparently, Mateo had already researched the topic and suggested that it could be a lucrative business to import the beans directly from Ethiopia. He was the type of person to make the most of any opportunity, even if that came from misfortune. It would be easy to picture him as a coffee baron.

Finally, the trucks arrived, reversing from the main road all the way down the long driveway. They were expensive, new semi-trailer trucks, with company logos down the side of them. Strangely it was not any company that Mateo was connected with. Perhaps they were from a competitor that had not survived the past few weeks.

Andrea and Sebastian went to the front to inspect the prime-movers and their cabs, followed shortly by Danielle and Sophie. Mateo was more interested in what was in the trailers. He had the drivers open them up and inspected the shipment as if he were checking if off against the manifest. Was there maybe something secret inside? Were they transporting drugs or some other contraband? It didn't really matter what was in there.

The cabs were ultra-modern and spacious, with each of the trucks having a sleeper compartment. Neither truck had been fitted with long-range fuel tanks, but they could easily travel over 1,200km before re-filling, more than enough to get across France. They climbed down and went to the back where Mateo was having a heated discussion with one of the drivers. After a few minutes of back and forth between them, Sebastian asked, "Is something wrong?"

Mateo threw his hands up in the air with exasperation and said, "He will not drive the truck. Neither of them will drive the truck. They say it is too dangerous and not worth it for them, even though I said I would double what I would otherwise have paid them. They are saying that it is not worth their lives, not for any amount of money."

"Oh, that is a problem," Sebastian said as he looked around at the others.

"I am so sorry, señor," Mateo said. "I have failed you. I have the truck and not the driver."

"Then we'll drive it," Danielle said with conviction. "Sebastian and I will learn to drive it today, right now, this morning. How hard could it be? We can both drive cars and pickup trucks, and we are only going in one direction, it is a one-way journey." And then she looked at Andrea and said, "You said yourself; these modern trucks practically drive themselves. Well, if you can do it then so can we."

Andrea smiled and said, "Hell yes, why not. I can teach you the basics and you can figure out the rest on the road. They both have radios, so we can talk to each other. I can warn you of what is coming up, and what gear you should be in to safely handle the conditions."

Danielle looked at Sebastian and asked, "What do you think, are you game?"

"Sure, why not. Just another life skill. Oh, and you forgot to add, I can already drive a tractor and a snow mobile," he said with a laugh.

Mateo then said, "This I think changes the route that you take. I was going to send you North, straight over the mountains to Toulouse in France, but this will now be too dangerous for the inexperienced. Instead, you will have to take the main highway, which is shorter and easier, but there are many more towns. You will basically follow the coast up to Narbonne in France, and then Northwest to Toulouse," he said as he pointed to a map that he had spread out against a truck.

Then he continued, "From there you head Northwest to Bordeaux and then stay on the far West of the country until you reach the English Channel. After that you will travel along the coast until you find someone with a boat who will take you across.

"But you cannot go to Calais, there are many refugees there and you will not be allowed to go through the tunnel. Instead try for Cherbourg-en-Cotentin, the next shortest crossing point."

He made a gap between his finger and thumb and put it up to the scale on the map and said, "Maybe it will be 100km, so you will need a good boat."

Andrea took the four them, including Sophie, out in a truck for driving instruction. They figured that she may as well learn at the same time, just in case something happened to Andrea. Both trucks had automatic transmissions, cruise control, and lane keeping assist, so short of any obstacles or emergency situations, they *were* pretty much self-driving. Hopefully they wouldn't have to do much reversing, or unhitching of tailers, but still he ran through the basics with them.

It was decided that they would spend one more night with Mateo and leave early the following morning. This would allow them to get in a bit more practice on the trucks. Also, Mateo was getting some official looking paperwork so that he could forge shipping orders for them. If they were stopped, they would at least have the correct paperwork for transporting food and perishable items through to Calais. The hope being that it gave them a reason to be on the road during any curfew.

It was one more evening of perfect sunset and feasting. However, it was different from being at the villa, with no children playing, raucous family, or simple homely food. Now it was more mature and refined. It was enjoyable but in a different way, and it gave couples more alone time.

In a remarkably short time Mishka and Mateo had moved closer. No longer did they look like an odd couple, like a fit suave father and his twenty-something daughter. No, they looked more like a lord and his lady. Later that evening, when Danielle got up to get a drink, she spied Mishka sneaking into Mateo's room. Only one more day and they wouldn't have to pretend. Not that they need to, no one was judging them. However, modestly is modesty, and people will play their games.

After their false start they were ready to leave in the morning. They said their goodbyes to Mishka, Mateo, and his staff, and there were even some tears. For the first part of the journey, it would be the women driving. In part this was to build up Sophie's confidence whilst they were still on the backroads of Spain. The first 15km was smooth single lane B-road that wound through a low range of hills. There was almost no traffic, and both women enjoyed the experience. Then they turned onto a multi-lane freeway that would take them all the way to Toulouse in France. They would bypass every town, and with luck they could follows the freeway network all the way across the country.

They were travelling at a comfortable 100kph on an almost deserted freeway. From time to time, they would see a tuck similar to theirs. Then on the side of the freeway, when they could see into the countryside and the villages, they would spot someone driving a car. But in reality, it was like a quiet Sunday morning. Everyone but Sebastian had forgotten what day it was, or the date. These things just weren't important anymore, and he only kept track because of his wristwatch.

When they crossed the border from Spain into France there was no barricade, no obstacles on the Viaducte de Roma, just a seamless European Union. They did not know if there were people watching them via the many cameras that monitored the freeway. But what of it, what would they do? As far as the authorities were concerned, there were two trucks shipping food across the country. That should be innocuous enough.

In just over 3 hours they reached Toulouse, and still it was only mid-morning. They did not stop there, or even enter the city, instead they remained on the freeway, skirted the outer perimeter, and then continued North. From vantage points they could see the city clearly. It looked perfectly normal, with its stone and rendered concrete buildings and the terracotta tiled roofs. It was a large city, but with three quarters of its people removed. All of those missing people had cars parked in driveways and on the streets, never to be recovered. They would gather dust, and the tires would go flat. Maybe one day they would be collected for scrap.

It was another 40km North before they took the freeway to the Northwest, the sign said Bordeaux, 200km. At their current speed they would be in the famous wine region by lunch, and about a quarter of the way across the country. It seemed that their understanding of the word 'decimated' was ill-conceived. What decimated had meant was only devoid of life. It was the people that had gone, not the physical infrastructure, well at least not as far as they could see. And the freeways were clear. Sure, they could see cars abandoned on the off-ramps and the side roads, but the black top of the freeway just lay clear in front of them.

Swapping over the driving at Saintes, another 100km to the North, they continued staying on the Western side of the country and after another 5hrs reach Laval. This put them about 50km from the coast facing Jersey and the Channel Islands. From here on if they continued to the North Northeast, they would lose the freeway and be back on the B-roads. Passing through towns and dealing with whatever challenges may be there. It was getting near sunset, which would mean the zombies would be coming out. They hadn't seen any so far in France, but they had seen the occasional dead body on the side of the road, so they presumed they were still lurking in the shadows.

They took the road to Ernée and things now started to look grim. There were more abandoned cars, signs of rioting, and more dead bodies. No one had been through to clean anything up, and often they would have to slow the trucks in order to negotiate obstacles. And sometimes they even ran over obstacles, which included dead bodies.

Everyone was tired, and they discussed over the radio if they should perhaps find somewhere safe to park the trucks for the night. They planned to sleep in them, for their own safety, and to also ensure they didn't get stolen or vandalized. However, they didn't just want to park on the side of the road, like in a tuck pull-off bay, because this would leave them very exposed.

Up ahead Sebastian spotted an old farmhouse that was surrounded by a high stone wall. There was an iron gate across the entrance to the property, and at the front of the house was a circular drive that would allow them to turn the trucks around without needing to reverse. He pulled the truck over and Danielle jumped out to see if the gate was locked.

As she climbed out, she immediately felt how much cooler the air was. It had been a few hours since their last toilet stop, and that was hundreds of kilometers South, and in the afternoon sun. Now it was evening, and they were nearer to the coast. The wind was blowing in from the Northeast and it had a distinctive chill. One thing that they had not thought to pack was warm clothing. They had begun their journey in the central Sahara and had been in constant heat all of the way though to central France, in mid-summer. But now it felt more like autumn, and they would need to scavenge appropriate clothes for somewhere. Perhaps this farmhouse may have something practical for them to wear?

She crossed the road, and then the gravel, up to the large black iron gates. They were latched but not locked. She slid the bolt and pushed them, and although heavy, they swung freely. She looked down at the farmhouse and there was a car parked under an awning, but there were no other signs of life. The grounds were neat, but the glass looked like it could have done with a trim, thus it was hard to tell if the property was still occupied or not.

She stood inside as both of the trucks entered and drove up to the house. They turned and parked in such a way that should they need a quick escape they were already pointed in the right direction. She mulled over whether she should close the gate or not. If it were closed then they knew no zombies would come in, at least not from the road. However, if they got surprised by something during their first inspection, then a closed gate would delay their departure. In the end she decided to close the gate and slide the bolt. They had chains and straps in the truck's toolboxes. They could make it more secure later should they intend to stay.

When she returned the engines had been switched off and the others were standing next to the trucks. It was the first time they had silence since leaving Mateo's estate early that morning.

It was cool with just a slight breeze rustling the leaves in a nearby tree. Sebastian handed Danielle her rifle and then as a group they began to walk the perimeter of the main building.

CHAPTER 25

Andrea pushed at the window until it began to slide.

"I've managed to get one to open," he said to the others.

They were around the back of the house trying to find their way inside, but without doing any obvious damage. After knocking at the doors, they soon established that there was no one home; at least no healthy people. So, they just assumed that the people were dead, either inside the house, or somewhere further afield. It's not like the homeowners would have been out shopping, or visiting neighbors, at this late hour of the afternoon.

The yard was muddy, the fields were green, and everything was very provincial and agricultural. There was evidence that there had been dogs and chickens in the back yard. But now they could see none. Perhaps the dogs had wander away to find food, and the chickens had been taken by foxes. Still there were sheep and cattle in the fields, and they seemed unaffected by the absence of people, or by the intruders. They also did not appear to be infected with the disease, which was a relief.

Like a cat burglar, Andrea climbed through the window, was gone for only a few seconds, and then opened the back door. He tried the light switch but there was no power. The sun had just set but there was still enough light coming inside to see by. The others gingery walked inside to find they were standing in a cute rustic kitchen. However, everything was rather messy, as if things were left undone. Food scraps were on the bench, dirty dishes next to the sink, and the bin almost overflowed with rubbish. Then, staying close together, and each with two hands on their rifles, they crept into the living room. The curtains were drawn, and it was quite dim. Again, it was messy, as if someone had been in a hurry. There were clothes and other items scattered about. It was a single-story dwelling, and down a dim hallway they presumed they would find the bedrooms.

They sniffed the air as they proceeded, to detect the stench of death, but they could not. Instead, it smelt like mothballs and camphor, like an old person's house. Carefully they went through each room but there was no one in them, and neither were there any dead bodies. Thus, they finally declared the house clear. There were some outbuildings that they had not checked, but it was presumed that they just contained farm machinery and feed, which they could see through partly opened barn doors. It appeared that the farm had a milking cow. She stood near the fence and bellowed from time to time, complaining that she was not being led to a small lean-to where there sat a three-legged stool and a food trough.

In the kitchen they found a kerosine lamp and some candles. They hunted for matches and then lit them, distributing the light between the kitchen and the lounge. There was also a large antique woodstove in the kitchen, along with a stack of tinder and wood in the corner. Sebastian set to lighting the stove whilst Danielle looked over the shelves and through canisters until she found the coffee, tea, and sugar. She also opened the refrigerator, but it had been off for weeks. It smelt rank and was filled with spoiled food.

She joked to Sebastian, "Amongst your many skills, did you ever learn to milk a cow?"

"No can't say I did mam, but I've ridden a few bulls if that helps," he said with a laugh.

"Not today, but I'll keep it in mind. Well, it looks like we'll be having tea and coffee without milk."

Sophie piped up, "I've got a tube of condensed milk in the truck. I took it from Farid's apartment block in Algiers. Do you want me to get it."

"Yes please, then we can put it in the drinks."

Danielle then found some unopened packets of biscuits. How pleasant, they could sit around the woodstove and dunk them into their hot drinks.

With a cute spring in her step Sophie went back out through the back door into the fading light of evening. It had come over cloudy and felt like it would start to rain soon. It was such a contrast from a week ago in the Sahara. Sebastian got the fire going, and through a small glass window at the front of the unit, it gave a soft comforting glow to the kitchen.

The tap water was still working, so Danielle filled an old, enameled, enameled, kettle and put it on the stove top. The three of them just stood there in the kitchen and watched the fire, lost in thought as the old kitchen came back to life.

The crackle of burning wood in the otherwise silent house was shattered by a chilling scream from outside. It could only be Sophie. They immediately ran outside only to almost crash into her as she ran toward the door. Behind her was a man and he was running at almost the same speed as her. As they caught her, she yelled zombie. Quickly they all rushed back inside and managed to get the door closed before it reached them. Andrea held her while Sebastian pushed against the door.

The old key was still in the lock, but he didn't think to turn it. Fortunately, there was no window in the door, but he could hear the zombie banging against it as it made an angry sound. It was going through its rage stage. Then they heard a noise, and they all looked down to see the door handle was turning. Quickly Sebastian put his hand on it to stop it turning, then Danielle darted forward and turned the key. This was something new, zombies that could open doors.

After Sophie had caught her breath, Andrea asked, "Are you OK, did he manage to touch you?"

"No, he didn't get close enough. I went up into the truck, got the condensed milk, and then when I got down and closed the door he just came out of nowhere. I got so scared I just screamed and ran."

"Lucky you did," Sebastian said. "I can't believe how fast he was moving. That is frightening."

Danielle had gone over to the kitchen window, drawn the curtains, and now was looking out of a small gap. She said, "I can see another one, no two. I can see two more. They are over by the sheds. Maybe they were hiding in there during the day."

"We should have checked; I knew we should have checked. We just can't get sloppy like this," Sebastian said admonishing himself.

Andrea grabbed the lamp and said, "I'm going to check all of the other doors and windows to make sure they can't get in anywhere."

"I'll come with you," Sophie said as she held tight to his arm.

Danielle said to Sebastian, "I'm really worried about the zombie trying to open the door. It shows a level of intelligence, or at least a connection to reality that we didn't see in Africa. The only thing I can think of is that because it's cooler here, then they are not so dehydrated and worn down with heat. Perhaps they can also drink, especially given that there is so much water around. That could mean that instead of being dangerous for a few days, as they were in Africa, they could be dangerous, as in both highly physical and intelligent, for weeks. Maybe that is why the countries, and especially the cities, in the temperate climates have been so badly affected."

"Well, that would explain a few things," Sebastian said.

Andrea and Sophie returned, and he said, "House is secured. We made sure to close all of the curtains and blinds so that they couldn't see in or see any light coming out."

They huddled in the kitchen near the woodstove, taking comfort in the glow from its small glass window, the lamp, and the candles.

"What are we going to do?" Sophie asked the others. "How are we going to get back to the trucks?"

Then she said, "What if they get into the trucks? I didn't lock ours," then she looked at Danielle and Sebastian and asked, "Did you lock yours?"

"They both remained silent but shook their heads."

Andrea said, "What if we got them all out the

back, like created a distraction, and then we ran out the front door straight for the trucks? I'm sure we could make it to the trucks before they could get there."

Sebastian replied, "But what if we don't make it, or if there are more zombies over by the trucks? And then where would we go? There might be zombies everywhere. They could be all over the roads, and we may not be able to find anywhere safe to stop for the night."

Danielle added, "And the front gate is locked. We'd have to stop, and someone would have to get out and open it. There could be more around there, and we wouldn't even see them. They could just come out of nowhere and grab you."

"So does that mean we stay in here, in the dark, with them all around us trying to get in?" Sophie said in a panicked voice.

"It seems like the least bad option," Sebastian replied as he accepted the reality of their situation.

"As unpleasant as it sounds, I think it is what we will have to do," Danielle said. "My greatest fear now is that they may have some level of intelligence. There are lots of glass windows that they could break to get inside. I think we should try to barricade where we can, and to also have a fallback position, like one of the bedrooms where we can seal ourselves in until morning. Maybe one that has a window or a door that we can escape though if they do get inside."

"You're scaring me," Sophie said, as if she was ten years old.

Andrea hugged her and said, "It will be alright, we'll get through this, just like we got through everything else."

The largest windows in the house were in the lounge room. They moved some bookcases and a couch to barricaded them the best they could. All of the locks on the doors seemed sufficiently secure, but there were no locks on the internal bedroom doors. They decided upon one particular room that seemed both the best to secure and the easiest to escape from. It had a separate locking door to the outside. And although it was further from the trucks than the other rooms, the door could be opened and afford a quicker escape than climbing through a window. They would prop a chair up against the inside door handle to hopefully secure the bedroom. The bed would be stood up to barricade the window; thus, they would sleep on the floor using the mattress and some of the couch cushions from the lounge. It was the best they could do with what was at their disposal.

They sat around the lantern in the kitchen. Outside the wind gusted and from time to time there would be rain. The house creaked sometimes, and then something would bang as if being moved by the wind. So far, the zombies were quiet. They didn't know how many were out there, or if they still surrounded the house. It was too risky to look through the curtains, not that they could see anything because it was completely dark outside.

They found some cans of food in the pantry and put together a meal. It was pathetic compared to what they had been spoilt with over the previous few days. After eating there was very little to do other than sleep, so they decided to retire to the bedroom at around 9PM and prop the chair up against the door. They huddled into two couples, with the lamp turned down low in the corner. One person would stay awake as sentry, which they would change over every two hours.

It was about 4AM when Sophie woke everyone.

She said, "I heard something. It wasn't just the wind. It was a banging against the house."

"Was it like someone knocking at the door?" Andrea asked.

"Yes and no. Yes, it was like the sound of someone knocking, but it was too slow. It was more like someone testing the doors and walls," she said.

They sat in silence listening, and then they all jumped when they heard the sound. This time it was right outside the room they sheltered in. It sounded like someone had a lump of wood and rammed it against the door. It was probably an hour before dawn, so they still could not peep outside and see what was making the noise.

It did not repeat on the door, but a few minutes later they heard it further along the wall, probably somewhere outside the loungeroom. It was a distinctive heavy thump. If it struck a window, it would easily break it, and then it happened. The silence was broken by the smashing of glass. About 10 seconds later there was another crashing sound, and then every ten or so seconds for the next minute. It was as if someone was slowly moving along the wall and thumping it until reaching the window, and now it had taken all of the windows out. Each time the glass crashed the couples held each other tighter.

The thumping and smashing stopped; they just listened, ears straining into the void. Then there was a God all mighty crash. They knew exactly what that sound was. It was the couch and bookcases being knocked over and slamming on the floor. This meant that the zombies had breached their first defense and were climbing in through the front windows. Were they really that smart, and that determined? Was it just one zombie or was it all of them working in a coordinated fashion? And if they were organized, then would that mean that several of them would start to push against the bedroom door, or maybe there would be some zombies outside blocking their exit?

They remained silent and motionless on the floor as they heard bumping and scraping now coming from inside of the house. There was no lamp or candles left burning in the other rooms, so that meant the zombies would be feeling their way in the dark. The noises got louder as they progressed through the house toward their hide, and then finally there was a noise at the bedroom door. The handle turned slowly. They could see the door flex as it was being pushed upon.

It stopped and they breathed a sigh of relief. But then a little while later it started again. This time more forcefully and a small crack opened between the door and the frame. They could hear heavy breathing coming from the other side, like someone doing strenuous work. The chair started to slip and was at risk of losing its effect as a block. Sebastian and Andrea quickly got up to secure the chair and to hold the door closed.

Whatever was on the other side was strong. It felt like it was several zombies pushing, and that the zombies could tap into superhuman strength. It just kept pushing. A normal human would have given up by now or at least stopped to have a rest. But that was not the case, it was relentless and with single purpose. Sebastian turned back toward Danielle and whispered, "I don't think we will be able to hold on for much longer. It's just too strong."

Then she said with a calm determination,

"Then we will have to make a run for it."

Sophie gave a look of horror and whispered, "But what if they are just outside the door, or over at the trucks?"

"Do you have a better plan?" Danielle said with a hint of frustration.

Sophie looked at Andrea and he said, "She's right, we'll have to make a run for it."

It was rather ironic because Sophie was probably the fastest sprinter amongst them. She was an athletic powerhouse, a coiled spring, and she was the only one amongst them that was actually wearing trainers; she had grabbed them from abandoned luggage back in Algiers. The women cleared the bedding out of the way to make a clear path across the bedroom from the internal to the external door. They then agreed which direction the trucks would be in, and approximately how far away they would be. Danielle put one hand on the door handle and the other on the key in the lock, she looked at Sebastian and said, "Tell me when."

Sebastian looked at Andrea and then said, "Three, two, one."

They grabbed the guns and then Danielle opened the door, and both of the women burst out, not even looking to the sides they ran straight out onto the gravel driveway. There was a hint of light coming from the East, just enough to discern dark figures and obstacles. The men were not far behind them also carrying their guns. The lamp had been left in the room and as they ran toward the trucks, they looked over to see a silhouette coming through the door and breaking into a sprint. What was it with these creatures, and their rage? It was like they had been programmed to hunt down and kill other humans. Like an autoimmune disease, but on a macro societal scale.

Sophie took the lead with her quick legs and could see the outline of the trucks emerging from the dark fast in front of her. She then looked to the side, saw dark figures, and said, "Zombies to the left, zombies to the left."

They all caught a glimpse of them. Presently they were just standing still but then they started to move. First it was a walk, and then a jog, until they became a blur of running. There was a crowd of them. What were they doing here, and how did they know to come here? It was just ridiculous; like a B-grade horror movie. It was hard for them to believe that they were stuck in the middle of it; a bad dream from which they just couldn't wake.

Sophie reached the first truck and scrambled like a monkey up the steps and bundled herself inside then locked the door. Everyone was slowed down by their guns, but still they carried them. Yet they were useless in the dark and at close quarters. They may have provided as sense of security back at the house, but in reality, they were just a hinderance. Sophie sat there panting and not giving a thought as to whether she was alone in the cab. Andrea was next inside of a truck and slammed the door behind him. The key fob was in his pocket, so he just hit the starter button and then turned on the lights.

Ahead they could see Danielle and Sebastian climbing up into their truck, with the zombies close on their heels. Danielle just managed to get her door closed as one started to climb up the side of the truck. It pulled at the door, and it swung open before she had a chance to lock it. They could see her leg come out as she kicked it and then she closed the door again with the zombie still swing from the side of the truck. This time she must have gotten it locked, but still it persisted and banged on the glass.

Sophie screamed as she turned and saw a face on the other side of the glass. It was a zombie, dribbling, bloodshot, and distorted by anger.

She yelled at Andrea, "Drive, drive, there here, just drive."

Andrea put the truck into gear and began to move. Fortunately, Sebastian had also started to move, even before turning on the lights. Then his lights came on and smoke was seen billowing from the exhaust stacks as he worked his way through the gears.

"The gate," Sebastian said, "I'm going to have to drive through it."

It was a solid truck, but it did not have a bull bar across the front, just the normal bumper bar. He didn't want to do damage and end up ruining their escape, so he slowed down. He looked in the mirror. The zombies were far enough away for a bit of leeway, but still close enough to cause Andrea and Sophie some concern. It was crazy that the zombies still chased. It was as if they recognized that the gate was closed and that the trucks would need to slow down or even stop.

Danielle yelled, "Just... %$#@ push it over." It was the first time he had ever heard her swear.

He edged up to it and then kept the truck rolling. The gate was heavy and the latch unyielding, but where the hinges joined to the concrete pillars was a weakness. Thus, the gate broke free from its hinge mountings and crashed forward like a pancake onto the gravel. The truck bumped and lurched as it drove over the top of it, bending the iron into a curve that scrapped the bottom of the chassis.

Finally, they were on the main road and heading North. Sebastian looked in the mirror and could see Andrea finally reach the road as well. However, the gate had hooked up on the back of his truck and was dragging near the back of the trailer. Sparks streamed out and it probably made a terrible noise. He got on the radio to inform him that the gate was hooked up, but just as Andrea answered it broke free and spun off to the side of the road.

CHAPTER 26

It was a 250km journey before they finally hit the coast near Cherbourg-en-Cotentin in North central France. England lay around 100km across the Channel. From what they could see the conditions looked quite rough on the water. The large swell broke against the rocky headland at Fort de Querqueville, just North of the main urban area. There was a small marina behind the long breakwater, and moored in it were small pleasure craft. What they really needed was something substantial, like a commercial fishing boat or a large power yacht.

They drove down into the carpark, and after determining that it was large enough to turn the trucks around, they stopped and jumped out. The area was open enough to see anyone, or anything, approaching. The breeze was strong and cool from the Northeast, holding the seagulls overhead, ever vigilant for scraps of food. Andrea got out the binoculars and scanned their surroundings, making a slow 360-degree sweep.

"It looks all clear," he said.

With each person carrying a rifle, they slowly walked down to where the boats were moored. They were all in perfect trim, and although abandoned, were ready for the taking. Andrea went to climb aboard one of them, but Danielle said, "Probably not a good idea. You don't know if there is anyone in the cabin."

He thought better of it and said, "Yes, you're probably right. Anyway, I don't think any of these boats will be suitable, just look at the weather. You will really be needing something bigger, and maybe with a greater range."

"I agree," Sebastian said, "Perhaps we are looking in the wrong place." He said as he looked out across the bay. Then he said, "Over there is the main port, I'm guessing we will find a bigger boat there," as he pointed in the general direction of the breakwater marking the entrance to the harbor, with its cranes standing idle on the docks.

It was a 10-minute drive along the foreshore to the harbor and its several marinas. They passed a locked entrance to a naval base, then past a marina housing hundreds of small to medium sized pleasure craft and sailing yachts. Finally, they arrived at what looked like the commercial dock, complete with trawlers and other steel hulled fishing boats. One particular vessel stood out as being seriously sturdy and able to brave the North Sea swell. It wasn't the prettiest boat that was there, and it even had some rust bleeding through the white paint. But it had a heavy gantry and winch on the back for hauling in nets, sturdy railing along its sides, and a fully enclosed cabin.

This boat probably went as far as the arctic circle, and braved gales week after week. Surely it would be more than adequate for their short voyage across the Channel.

They jumped down again from the trucks and once again Andrea scanned the immediate surrounds. They were near a row of warehouses that appeared to be locked. Sophie walked over and put her hands up to the glass peering inside a window. Then she jumped back and said, "There are zombies inside."

They all looked at her and then the window that she had the clarity of mind to step away from. She continued, "They were on the far side in the dark. I don't think they saw me."

"Just peep again," Danielle said. "Just to see if they are moving. But don't let them see you if you can help it."

Sophie quickly looked again and then bobbed her head back away from the window.

"No, I didn't see them moving. I think it will be OK," she said.

Quickly and silently, they moved away from the buildings and over to water's edge. There was a locked wire gate blocking entrance to the boardwalk. Sebastian was about to climb over it when Andrea said, "I've got some heavy wire cutters in the truck, give me a minute."

He rushed to the truck and then returned with the cutters which made easy work of the partially rusted chain link gate. They pushed through and made their way up to the boat, or was it a ship? After one last look around to make sure there were no zombie, or anyone else that may object, they climbed on board. The first thing they did was try the steel cabin door. Of course it was locked.

Danielle said, "Maybe there is a key hidden somewhere," and they all started to look about the deck and opened up small hatches to hidden compartments.

Andrea said, "Look for something that would likely float," and Sophie held something up and said, "Like this." It was a small yellow plastic float with a key attached to it.

He said, "Yes, exactly like that."

She inserted it into the door, and it opened with a click. Andrea and Sophie stayed outside to keep watch whilst Sebastian and Danielle entered the cabin. It was clean, plain, and very industrial looking. It had all kinds of electronic equipment and radios, as well as a large table with lots of charts. There was a second door that led below deck. Sebastian tried and found it wasn't locked. Carefully he opened the door and peered inside. It was dark so Danielle grabbed a nearby flashlight and handed it to him. He shone the light inside; it looked all clear. Slowly he walked down the steps, flashing the light from side to side.

Danielle asked, "How does it smell?" which

was the best indicator of zombies.

He replied, "It smells fine. Well actually it smells a bit like fish, but it definitely doesn't smell like zombies or death."

He opened the door to the washroom, and then each of the cupboards, but there was no sign of life, just equipment and supplies.

He called back up to her, "It's clear if you want to come down and have a look."

As she carefully walked down the stairs, he opened up the curtains on the row of small windows to let some light in. There were bunks for six people and then forward there was a double bed in what they presumed was the captain's cabin.

"Oh yes," Danielle said, "this will do nicely," as she opened some of the panty doors in the galley and fiddled with the knobs on the gas stove. There was another doorway that went aft to the engine room, and presumably the catch tanks. Again, he slowly opened the door and shone the flashlight inside. There was no smell of death, just a whiff of machine oil and diesel.

He called out, "All clear," and then proceeded to walk inside.

There was a walk-in freezer, obviously for storing catch, and maybe storing supplies. When Sebastian looked inside there was a good supply of frozen meat and vegetables. It seemed like the boat had been prepared for a voyage lasting several weeks out into the Channel, or beyond, but the pandemic must have hit before they could depart. There were solar panels and propane tanks, that somehow, in some combination, had kept all of the onboard systems, like the freezer and the batteries, up and running.

They went back upstairs, whilst Andrea and Sophie went downstairs to have a look around.

Sebastian stood at the wheel surveying the switches and knobs. Danielle said,

"I suppose you're going to tell me you know how to drive this thing?"

He looked at her, smiled and said,

"I've got absolutely no idea, but I suppose together we can figure it out. Couldn't be any more difficult than the truck."

She stood next to him and had a look, and then called down to Andrea and Sophie, "Do either of you know how to dive a boat?"

They both answered at the same time, "No."

"OK let's see," Sebastian said, "Out of gear, I mean neutral, check. Ignition on, check."

He turned the key and lights illuminated on the consol, and then there was a soft warning buzzer with a red flashing light. The writing next to it said 'voltage', and then a yellow light came on that had 'glow' written next to it. After a few seconds the glow light went out again.

Danielle said, "I bet that was for the glow plugs. I'm figuring this is a diesel, like the trucks.

Remember how we get that same symbol when we go to start the truck."

"Yeah, you're probably right."

Then he put his finger on the starter button and pushed.

A cranking noise came from the engine room and then a low drone from the diesel motor. The voltage light went out and all the other gauges seemed to come alive. The fuel tank was full, but how far it would take them they were not sure. Sebastian turned on the light switches, and when the lights came on the cold steel boat immediately started to feel more homely, it could even be said that it felt safe.

They ran the boat for about 5 minutes and then turned it off for fear that it would attract attention. There were two propane tanks in the engine room, and one was half empty. There were propane tanks in a small, caged area just inside the gate. Perhaps they may be full of gas, and it would be wise to swap out the half used one for a fresh one, just in case their trip took longer than expected.

They all sat around the map table in the wheelhouse. It had almost reached the time when they would be parting ways.

Danielle said, "There is plenty of room onboard, why don't you guys come with us."

Andrea looked at Sophie and then back at Danielle.

"Look, we'd love to, but it's not the right thing to do. If the boat doesn't make it to England, or we get stopped once we are there, then the mission fails. It would be like putting all of our eggs into one basket."

Danielle spread a map out on the table and said, "Yes, but look, its 1,500km to Copenhagen. It's going to be more of the same as we have just gone through. There is no guarantee that you will make it by road either. What if we take you there by boat?" she suggested as she pulled out another map. "It's basically the same trip, the same distance as by road, but safer because you are on the water."

"You can't really know that," Andrea said, "You don't know if you are going to get stopped by the coast guard or navy. And you don't know if the weather is going to turn bad. It is already risky crossing the Channel, and now you're talking about 1,500km on the water. No, I can't let you risk yourselves and the whole mission just to accommodate us."

Danielle looked at Sophie, expecting her to answer but without asking her anything.

Finally, Sophie said, "I'm sorry but I agree with Andrea. Don't get me wrong, I'm probably more scared of the zombies than anyone else, and I'm already sick of all the travelling. I really do appreciate the offer you are making; I know it comes from a good place and that you are genuinely concerned for our well-being. But if I was to choose between the truck and the boat, then I'd have to go with the truck."

Danielle looked at Sebastian, and he kind of winced because he didn't want to get drawn into it, and he didn't want to get on Danielle's bad side. Trying to walk the most diplomatic path he said, "I can see merit on both sides. I really don't want to break up the group, we have come so far and done so well together. But... I also appreciate that we can't force you to come with us. All we can do is respect your decision, even if we don't like or agree with it."

Then he said, "I have an idea, let's say we sleep on it. It's too late in the afternoon for you guys to head off. How about we lock up the truck and with all of us onboard we put the boat out into the bay, out of reach of the zombies. That way you can have a good night's sleep, after last night's disaster, and if you change your minds then great, and if not, you head off well rested and during the sunlight."

"Sure, that sounds like a good idea," Andrea said, "but I'm not expecting to change my mind. We will have good freeways all the way from here to the border of Denmark, and beyond. We can hopefully do it in one straight run all the way through. I think we'll be in Copenhagen whilst you two are still fighting your way through Southern England."

Danielle resigned herself to the logic and said in a defeated tone, "Yes, you're probably right." And then, "As soon as you get there try to contact us. There is probably proper communication between the two counties, so contact us straight away, and we will do the same."

They went back ashore. Danielle and Sebastian unloaded all their luggage, including their share of the potion and plant specimens. The truck that Andrea and Sophie would be using was relocated to fenced off area near the water. They used some strapping to secure the gate. Hopefully it would remain unmolested during the night.

They returned to the boat and stowed the luggage and goods safely below. Then before sunset they started the engine, cast off, and through trial and error motored out of the docks and into the sheltered bay. They put out the anchor in the lee of Fort Central, surrounded by water, and almost 1km from the coast. At this anchorage they were sheltered from both the swell and the wind, and most importantly from the zombies; that is unless they could manage to crew a boat.

There was plenty of food onboard. They ate steak and vegetables and enjoyed a bottle of wine outside on the deck. The air was cool and moist, but it was not uncomfortably cold. At one point in the evening, they   car headlights as someone drove along the coast. It did not stop in Cherbourg but instead continued back inland until out of sight. Later they saw another light further along the coast, about 10km away in the vicinity of Le Brick. As they watched it seemed to put out to sea and then disappear somewhere into the Channel. Perhaps it was other people like themselves, escaping the Continent for England.

They locked themselves inside the boat and then turned off all the outside lighting. The likelihood of them being run into by another boat was extremely slim, so they took the chance at being invisible. Everyone was extremely tired, and now, being fed, warm, and feeling safe, they slept well.

It wasn't until after sunrise that they restarted the engine and motored back into port. They brought the boat in as close as possible to where the truck was parked. After tying up, they grabbed their rifles and walked to the yard. The bindings that had been put on the gate remained untouched. That was a good sign. Danielle and Sebastian walked them to the truck and then said an emotional farewell. It must have been like when travelers met and departed back in medieval times. One would never know what tragedy may befall someone on their journey. Thus, every goodbye was treated as if it was the last.

The truck would be heading along the coast before turning inland to meet up with one of the many freeways heading East toward Belgium, then Germany, until finally Denmark. The boat would be able to stay in contact with the truck via radio for perhaps the next 30 minutes. After that they would be out of range and both couples would be on their own.

CHAPTER 27

They probably had enough fuel onboard the boat to do a return trip to the Orkney Islands, or one-way as far as Iceland. Danielle was able to calculate this after she found a logbook that recorded fishing grounds the boat had frequented, and the fuel it had used. Of course they wanted to make this trip as short as possible, but at least they knew they had options and could decide to go to Ireland or Iceland. But for now, they weren't committed to stop at the first port of call, which on their current course would be Swanage, on the South-central coast of England.

The last radio communication from Andrea and Sophie came as the truck was approaching the freeway. They reported that they had passed places that had seen rioting, but now that they were out of the towns, all seemed to be clear and safe. Everyone wanted to talk for longer, but the signal got weaker and weaker until it was just static.

The waters of the Channel got rough very quickly. The wind blew in from the North Sea and generated a large swell. They would be in it until they got closer to the opposite coast. Neither of them were sea people. They both struggled to find their legs, and both of them heaved their breakfast over the side of the boat. At least the weather was clear. It would be frightening to be out here in fog, or in the dark, with such waves. No wonder there are so many frightening tales and superstitions around sailing.

They did not envy the sailors of old or romanticize their voyages. In small wooden sailboat it would have been brutal, dangerous, and withering. They were please they had a large sturdy trawler. They set it to cruise at 11 knots, as per the mark that had been inscribed next to the throttle. That equated to about 20kph, therefore they expected it would be 5-hours to Swanage.

It was five boring hours because they had nothing to do. They had spent the last few days in high adrenaline situations, but now all they could do was sit and watch the horizon. Normally sailors would tend to lines and nets, do cleaning and maintenance, or just sleeping in preparation for a long night of fishing. They had no skill or desire to do any of this, and they didn't even drop a line over the side of the boat to see if anything would bite. Instead, they just stayed in the cabin with the doors and windows closed, looking directly ahead for the first sign of land.

They knew they were getting closer. The swell had dropped considerably, and they no longer felt as seasick as they had during the first half of the crossing. Danielle was at the wheel whilst

Sebastian looked through the binoculars; for about the twentieth time. Then he said, "I think I can see something."

They had steered due North since leaving France, but now he said to her, "Just turn the wheel a few degrees to the left."

"You mean to port," she said being cocky.

"Alright, turn to port. How did you know that?" he asked.

She pointed to a book that was in a rack beside him. She said, "It's in there. I had a quick flick through last night. It's just basic rules for navigation, like who has right of way, and which side of the beacons you have to stay on."

"Well, aren't you clever," he said. "Looks like you can be captain."

"Sure, and you can be the deckhand. Go and make me a coffee, you scurvy dog," she said with a laugh.

The mood had certainly picked up now that the end, or at least the end of this leg, was in sight.

Sebastian looked at the charts as they approached the headland and said, "I believe this is Peveril Point. There are reefs just offshore, so go wide of the headland. Then we swing a hard right, I mean port, and there will be a small pier just inside the bay."

She slowed the boat down to 5 knots as she made the hard turn to port. They were about 50 meters away from land and could see a couple of people standing on shore. They were waving, but not with one hand in a friendly way. Instead, they were waving with two and crossing them over to make an 'X'. The boat continued toward the pier where a group of people had gathered at the seaward end of it. They were also waving in a similar way, and through the binoculars Sebastian got the impression that they did not look very friendly. He said, "I think you had better cut the motor; they have guns and I'm not sure they want us to dock."

She brought the boat to a stop by reversing the propellor until they sat dead in the water. They opened the cabin door and walked out onto the deck. Both smiled, waved, and then Danielle spoke because she had her English Yorkshire accent, "Hello there. Is this Point Peveril?"

One of the men replied, "It might be. You've come across the Channel, haven't you?"

"Yes, we came from France, but we are British, and we are not infected," she said, trying to sound upbeat.

He was having none of it.

"They all say that. You've got no business here, bugger off," he said in an aggressive tone.

"No, you don't understand," she said. "I'm a doctor, we are not infected, and I have with me a cure for R24. We must get it to the proper authorities."

"Look lady, I've probably heard that one five times this week. Now off with you before we start taking potshots at you and your boat." And with that a couple of the other men raised their guns.

Sebastian put his arm around Danielle and said, "Come on, let's go. It's not worth arguing with them. There are lots more places to put in further along the coast."

She was extremely disappointed. How could these people be so stupid? She had travelled from the middle of the Sahara, had gone through so much, and had the cure for so many, and then these idiots wouldn't even listen to her, and not even let her put a foot back in her homeland.

As Sebastian powered up the boat and turned hard to starboard, he could see her disappointment. He said, "These people were likely on the front line of a mass invasion. They probably had thousands, maybe millions of people trying to escape the disease. And as you know, people will say anything to save themselves. So, you can't really blame them for not trusting us."

But she just shook her head, stewed, and said, "Idiots."

As they steered the boat around, they looked further out across the bay. There were many boats either at anchor or up on the beach. They had not noticed these when they were coming in because they were focused on the rocks, the people, and finding the pier. But now that they looked, they could see that there were so many apparently abandoned boats. These must have been from the waves of refugees hitting the shore. And now they themselves were boat people, and late arrivals at that. This probably explained why they were not welcome, even if it was stupid.

Once they got into the Channel proper, Sebastian said, "OK Captain, which way?"

Danielle gave a sigh and then said, "I suppose it doesn't really matter, we may as well head East and follow the coast until we find a place to put in."

They plotted a course that went almost due East, skimmed the Isle of Wright, and by sunset they were about 1km offshore from the Beachy Head lighthouse, East Sussex. The following day they would make a turn to the Northeast as they followed the coast around. They had seen very little traffic on the sea, and when they did it was typically many kilometers away. The shoreline looked so close and tempting. The white chalk cliffs took on the orange of sunset, and at this isolated spot they could have run the boat up into the shallow water and then jumped overboard. But that would mean abandoning their possessions, as well as risking the potion and plant specimens to the waves. No, as tempting as it was to jump ship, it was something they could not do.

They lowered the anchor and turned on the navigation lights. It wasn't zombies that they were worried about now, but other ships. Hopefully there weren't any ferries or cargo ships, or worse, pirates and police, who would board them in the middle of the night. All they could do was accept their fate and when it came time to sleep, just lock the door and hope for the best.

Sebastian prepared a lovely meal in the hope of cheering Danielle up. He even threw a line over the edge and caught a few fish. These went into the refrigerator to become tomorrow's breakfast. She had to admit to herself it was pleasant. And after France, it was heartening to at least see civilization. There were regular car headlights on shore, the navigation lights of a few boats, and the glow of towns on the horizon. The state of the country seemed more like they had seen in Algeria. A society that was functioning, but only just.

They had no visitors during the night, and even if they did, they wouldn't have noticed. It seemed that the gentle rocking of the boat lulled them into a deep sleep that lasted all night. They ate the fish for breakfast before weighing anchor. They could have motored and ate at the same time, but what was the rush? As soon as Danielle felt unwelcome in her homeland, she lost a lot of enthusiasm. To use a nautical term, it really took the wind out of her sails.

They looked at the fuel gauge and it had barely moved. She gave it a tap just to check it wasn't stuck, but it still read just a couple of bars short of full.

"Where to?" Sebastian asked.

"Just keep following the coast. I'm going to have a shower and then we can have a look at the charts and make up a new plan."

She disappeared below for a long time. So long in fact that Sebastian even called down after her. It's not like she could have gone very far on a boat. When she came back up, she was in a brighter mood. Maybe she just needed some time alone to process things and gain some clarity.

"Are you OK?" he asked.

"Yes, I'm feeling better now. So, this is the plan," she said. "We'll just keep following the coast around."

"Alright. So how far? Like as far as Dover? I thought we wanted to avoid Dover and the Channel Tunnel," he said.

"No, we keep going after that, and we turn and head North. We go far enough North to be above the zombie line."

"Oh, I see. You realize that's going to take a few days, don't you?"

"Yes, I know," she said.

"Well alright then," he said, "and away we go."

He pushed the throttle forward and increased the speed by an extra coupe of knots and would hold that whilst the sea was calm.

They stayed a couple of kilometers offshore to avoid any entanglements. The last thing they wanted was the navy coming out to shoo them off. After a full day they had arrive off England's Eastern most point, Lowestoft on the Suffolk coast. This would put them just about on the border between zombie England, and for want of a better word, free England. Any entry above this point would be a different experience. Sure, they may have to go into quarantine, but at least the population wouldn't be traumatized, and the government and administrative system were likely functioning properly.

They dropped anchor 3km offshore to avoid the boat traffic they could see closer to the shore. The city lights shone, and they could see many cars were driving about like ants. Every now and then there would be an aircraft taking off. Most of the time it was a helicopter, but every now and then it was a jet. However, none of the flights went over the sea to the Continent, instead they were either domestic or headed North and Northeast. They switched on the navigation lights, enjoyed a sunset dinner, and then did a spot of fishing.

The following morning, they were underway at dawn; Danielle said they had a big day ahead of them. When Sebastian asked where they were going, she just smiled and said, "I'm going to surprise you."

"It will be England though?" he asked.

"Oh yes, definitely. And we will be there by evening."

"Well OK then," he said, then added, "although I've finally got my sea legs, I'm still looking very much forward to standing on solid ground again."

The first half of the day was pleasant, and they made good headway, however, on the horizon it was becoming dark grey.

"I think we've got some weather coming," Sebastian said.

They turned on the radio and were able to get a shipping forecast. It warned of an approaching weather system that would bring low cloud and fog.

"This may work to our advantage," Danelle remarked. "Sure, we won't be able to see very well, but that also means that others won't be able to see us. I'm hoping we will be able to sneak in, hidden in the fog."

By the afternoon the weather really close in around them. The last reference point they saw with any clarity was the New Flamborough lighthouse at Humberside.

Danielle was good at math and took well to the charts and calculations that they required. She knew their speed, their heading, and she kept an eye on the clock. It was getting near dark and Sebastian said, "Shouldn't we be looking for a sheltered bay to drop anchor for the night?"

"No, keep going," she said. "Stay on this heading and at this speed. In around another 50km we will come up on the South Gare Lighthouse. But we need to stay wide because there are some wind turbines in the water. We should be able to see their warning lights, even through the fog."

They kept a true course until they could see the lighthouse. By now it was completely dark and foggy on the water, and it would have been disorientating if not for the city of Middlesbrough glowing to their West.

After they had put the lighthouse to their back quarter, she said, "OK, turn hard to port through 90 degrees and then continue until you see a row of beacons. When you get level with the first one, slow down and follow them into the mouth of the River Tees."

Sebastian couldn't really see where he was going. All he could see were winking lights in the fog and was happy to be traveling at half speed. Gradually the land and the lights closed in around them until they had entered the mouth of the river. He reduced the speed further and then asked, "How deep is this river. We're not going to run aground, are we?"

Danielle said, "Not according to the charts. On

the high tide, which we are on right now, it is navigable all the way to Worsall, which is nearly 50km upriver. But we're not going that far. Just take it slow and stay in the center of the channel. I'll let you know if there are any sand banks or obstacles."

Slowly, hidden in the fog, they made their way up the River Tees with the city of Middlesbrough all about them. There were road and rail bridges over the river, with traffic on them, and people on paths walking beside the riverbank. No one paid any attention. Their boat blended right in as if it were supposed to be there. People probably thought they were a fishing boat returning to the docks. It was a stroke of genius on Danielle's part, and Sebastian said as much.

She graciously accepted the praise and then said, "The next town along the river is where I grew up. I've got lots of family and friends there, so we should be able to get some help, and get through to the appropriate authorities."

They took a sharp curve around Durham University, and then leaving the urban area behind, dark forest arose on either side of the river, and then it opened out to fields and farmland. Finally, the town of Yarm came up on their port side, and between the Princess Alexandra Auditorium, and the medieval arched Yarm Bridge, was a wharf where they could pull in and tie up.

In almost complete silence they glided in, put the buffers down the side of the hull, and then threw the ropes over the mooring bollards. With the boat secured, they locked it up and headed to High Street on foot. They were back in civilization now, so they couldn't just steal a car, or break into a house and take whatever they needed. They had to follow the civil codes they had so dutifully been brought up with.

After a short walk they stood on the side of a busy road feeling very much out of place. People were walking past them and going about their business, not paying any attention to the two of them. Everyone was wearing a mask, including themselves, but that was pretty much the only sign of the pandemic destroying the rest of the world.

Danielle asked Sebastian, "What day is it?"

Sebastian looked at his watch and said, "It's Friday, 9PM to be precises."

She looked about and then said, "Follow me."

She walked toward an old, whitewashed pub called The Ketton Ox. People were outside in the balmy summer evening, even though it was cool and foggy. They sat on patio furniture arranged outside of the pub, drinking beer, and enjoying hot chips and other finger food. She opened the door and had to weave her way through the crowd. The public and the authorities must have had absolute faith in their border controls and quarantine; yet it was misplaced seeming the two of them had just sneaked in from Africa. If the population had only seen and experienced the horrors that Danielle and Sebastian had, then they would not be so complacent, especially being in such close quarters, and breathing such dangerous air.

Over the noise, Danielle asked Sebastian, "Yar wanna pint o'lager?" Her accent had immediately come home strong.

"Do I want a what?" He asked with a dumb expression on his face.

"A lager. You know, a beer," she said.

"A brewski. Oh sure, I'd love one. But I don't have any money. Do you?"

"Yeah, I've got some money," and she went over to the bar and ordered a couple of pints.

Whilst she stood amongst the crowd there was a loud scream. It made Sebastian jump, and he instinctively grabbed for his gun. Of course he didn't have it on him, it was safely locked away back at the boat. A woman came running over to Danielle and threw her arms around her.

"Ahh!" the woman yelled out. "Where have you been? I've missed you so much."

They made small talk and then the three of them when outside with their beers and sat at a table.

Danielle introduced Sebastian as her husband and the girl went back to screaming and hugging, both of them this time. She probably had had more than enough to drink and would need a taxi to get home later.

Danielle explained where she had been for the past twelve months, including her time with MSF, and her mission in Algeria. She left out a lot of the information relating to the past few weeks. There was no need to get into that at the moment, or with this particular person. She asked the woman about several people, including if they were still in town, and where they lived, so she could build up a list of potential contacts and option.

After about 30 minutes Danielle told her old friend that her and Sebastian had to go. She was about to hail a taxi when the girl pulled out her keys and said, "No, you can take my car, I'll take a taxi home. Just leave it at your parents' house and I'll pick it up tomorrow."

It was a generous offer. The woman wasn't sober enough to be driving anyway, so they accepted.

As they got into the car Sebastian said, "So does this mean I'm now going to meet your parents?"

"Yes, I suppose it does. And my little brother if he is still staying there."

"I wish I was better prepared," Sebastian said as he looked at his clothes and then brushed his fingers through his hair. "It would have been nice to have had a shower and changed my clothes."

She laughed and said, "If you do that, they will never believe my story. No, you'll be fine. They'll be fine. Everyone will be just fine, and pleased to see me, I mean us."

It wasn't a very big town, but there were lots packed into it, with its narrow roads and double story terrace houses. Sebastian was completely lost by the time she pulled up out front of one particular house. He said, "I don't know how you can find your way around in here, or remember which house is yours. They all look the same to me."

"Yeah... well, we say that about you Canadians. You all look the same to us," she said with a laugh and then gave him a kiss on the cheek.

CHAPTER 28

The lights were on, and the curtains were drawn. She knocked on the front door and when her mother opened it, she was ecstatic to see her, followed quickly by her father. It had been a year since Danielle had seen them.

Inside the house was modest and tidy, like all of their neighbors. When she introduced Sebastian, she did not hold back, saying this is my husband and we were married last week. It was best just to blurt it all out and get it on the table as quickly and directly as possible.

They showed no reservations towards him, trusting their daughter's judgment. They were a bit taken back when he spoke with his Canadian accent, but then again, with media being such a homogenizing influence on culture, then it wasn't long before they didn't really notice.

After the initial shock and then pleasantries, her father said, "We had a visit from some people a couple of days back, they were looking for you and left a card on the off chance that you showed up."

"Oh, really," Danielle said as she looked at Sebastian.

"How could they have possibly known that?"

she said with confusion.

"It seems that your friends in Copenhagen alerted the authorities there, and they in turn contacted those in the UK."

Danielle grabbed Sebastian's hand and squeezed it with joy. Excitedly she said, "They made it, Sophie and Andrea made it."

She then went on to explain that these were their travelling companions and then recalled some of the experiences that they had shared.

Her father passed her the card from a Professor Smith at the University of Birmingham, Institute of Microbiology and Infection. She immediately called the number, but it went straight to voice message. Danielle then explained to her parent how Sebastian and she had travelled from the central Sahara with a cure for R24, and that was probably why people had come looking for them. No doubt there was already research being done on Sophie and Andrea's samples in Copenhagen, but still they had to get their samples, and her knowledge, down to Birmingham as soon as possible.

It was hard to believe how normal life was back at home. How people could still leave their jobs at 5PM and then go down the pub to socialize. Although, granted it was probably not the same below the zombie line in the UK. Her parents explained how the authorities had put in a hard border right across the lower belt of the country.

They said that there were still zombies in London and its surrounds. But they were actively being hunted down and shot, with the police and army, in some places going from building to building and clearing them out, as they would terrorists.

Her parents were amazed when she described how they had arrived by boat, and about being able to make it all the way up the River Tees to Yarm. They said there had been a concerted effort by the authorities to stop all boats, even to the point of firing upon them. They suggested that it may have been the fog, and a lot of luck, which allowed them to get through. Danielle and Sebastien would never realize how close they came to being detected, turned away, or sunk. On some of those long dark nights, patrols came within just hundreds of meters of them whilst they slept.

In typical English fashion her parents commented that it was such a long way to travel to Birmingham, being 270km away. Danielle and Sebastian almost burst out laughing. They had covered such vast distances, and in such dangerous conditions, over the past few weeks. Two hundred and seventy kilometers on a freeway, in a modern car, no zombies, or barricades, or bandits, it now seemed like a trip to the corner store.

"We will drive down there," Danielle said.

"What now?" her mother said with a shocked

expression. "Surely not. At the very least it can wait 'till morning."

Sebastian read the room and said, "Yes of course, in the morning, in the daylight, after we've had a good nights' sleep."

Danielle hadn't calmed down yet. She was still in fight or flight at her core. She didn't want to wait, but in this instance, she took Sebastian's lead and trusted his judgement. Still, they didn't want to leave the valuable materials on the boat, so with the help of her parent, they returned to the wharf and unloaded the boat. They took everything back to her parents' house, and fortunately there was a spare room for themselves and the luggage. After tea and cake, and then a nice hot shower, they retired to bed.

They left early the following morning for the three-hour drive to Birmingham. Once again it was on freeways, but this time there was traffic. It seemed like they had gone back in time. Also, after so much time spent in the desert, the sheer greenness of the countryside, with trees everywhere, opened their eyes with renewed fascination.

They had to travel though the center of the city to reach the University which was located on the far Southwestern side. According to all of the warning signs they were seeing, it wasn't very far from the barricade that kept the North safe. It was like a modern-day Hadrian's Wall, starting at the River Severn near Gloucester. Then in a straight-line it went across the country, through Oxford and Chelmsford, and then back to the ocean at the River Blackwater at Heybridge. This meant that Wales, the Irelands, and Scottland, were all part of the 'Free World'.

They parked at the University, and even put coins in the meter, before heading to reception to get directions. It was Saturday morning, but the campus was still busy. Students had assignments due, and researchers had deadlines to meet. Whether there was any purpose in continuing economics, law, or marketing degrees was debatable. How long would the old world continue to try and maintain the old systems? Perhaps the rich and powerful planned to profit from this. It wouldn't be anything new. Would it be possible that the UK and Denmark, and those few other far flung island nations, could continue as if nothing had happened? Were they maybe planning to sit out all the carnage and then sweep in when there was no one left to resist, and there would be a new grab for territories? Yes, that sounded like the human way, and certainly the British way.

They found the right building, but because it was the weekend, there was no one at the department desk. So, they just wandered the halls and followed the signs. Finally, they came across a door that was open and there was an elderly looking gentleman sitting at a desk. The name plate read Professor Brian Smith, so Danielle knocked on the door.

He looked up and said in a cheerful voice, "Come in. What can I do for you?"

They walked in and Danielle said, "Hello Professor Smith, my name is Dr Danielle Wilson." She hadn't yet decided if she was going to take Sebastian's surname. It wasn't something that they had discussed, and under the current circumstances, the world only knew her by her maiden name, or should that be referred to as her professional name?

"I've come here because someone contacted my parents and said that I should meet with you."

A broad smile came across his face, and he said, "So, you are *the* Dr Wilson, the one who has come from Africa?"

"Yes, that's right," she said.

"With the cure?" he said as his excitement grew.

"Yes," she said as Sebastian put the bag, with all of the valuable items, down on the professor's desk. He then proceeded to open it, and the professor peered down inside. It contained bottles of potion, specimens of plants, and zip lock bags with the black seeds. There was also the only remaining copy of the booklet that Danielle had written that contained all the information on how to find the ingredients, prepare the potion, and then how to treat the patients.

"And you must be Sebastian, her companion," he said as he offered his hand.

"Yes sir, husband actually," Sebastian said.

The professor dug into the bag and started to pull things out. As he did, he said, "We were informed that you may be arriving. Your colleagues arrived in Copenhagen a few days back. It seems that they had everything except for the instructions, and as you probably know, they did not have any of the technical information in their heads, like you presumably do."

He held up the booklet and said, "And these are the all-important instructions?"

Danielle nodded and said, "It is the only copy we have left. I gave out a few to some of the hospitals we stopped at along the way."

"Oh," the professor said, and ever so slightly he flinched, like he had a nervous tick, "and were they all in Africa?"

"Yes, there was Algiers..." she started to say, and then she felt Sebastian gently kick her foot under the table. She stopped and then said, "Yes, it was somewhere in Algiers. I'm not sure where. It was all a blur as you could imagine, with the zombies, and the breakdown in civil control. It was very frightening and confusing."

The professor responded, "Yes, from the stories your friends have recounted, it sounds like it has been a hell of a journey. They say they lost their instruction booklet when being chased by zombies. Lucky for everyone they escaped with their lives, and the potion."

"What happens now?" Danielle asked.

"We get these to the lab straight away and start to work out exactly what it's all about. How and why it works, and then how we can make it in industrial quantities. We will be putting every possible person and resource onto it."

She asked, "When you say we, who do you mean?"

He brushed it off and said, "The labs are very good at doing this, there is no need for you to be concerned. They'll have this to market... I mean available to the public, probably within a few months. Then we will be able to distribute it internationally. It's all worked out, so as I said no need to worry. You have done an excellent job, and it was the right decision coming to me."

'Decision', she thought. What decision? Did she have a choice? And he said 'market', and distribution. This didn't sound right. She was starting to suspect that he was with a pharmaceutical company rather than the government or the United Nations. It was not unusual for academics to wear two hats, or to receive substantial funding from the private sector, as they bought influence and access to otherwise privileged information.

He stood up and walked them back over to the door. It kind of felt odd. Like an anticlimax. Were they missing something here? Did they have unrealistic expectation? She was expecting that there would be teams of scientists and doctors wanting to interrogate her, them. But it seemed he was just going to show them the door and send them on their way.

Danielle stopped to seek clarification and asked, "So, when they produce the cure, and the vaccine, the information and supplies will be distributed free to everyone who needs them."

"Oh yes, of course, you have no need to concern yourself about that."

No, something wasn't right. It was too easy; he was too flippant. Nothing during this whole mission had been easy. Everything had been a life and death struggle. It had been her and the team against almost insurmountable odds. And now, she was expected to just hand over everything they had worked for to this affable professor and just walk away. She couldn't do it, and she sensed that Sebastian was feeling the same thing.

She looked at Sebastian and cocked her head back toward the bag, gesturing to scoop everything up and run.

He noticed it instantly and quickly started putting the items back into the bag.

The professor tried to stop him, grabbing at his arms, but Sebastian was too strong. The professor began shouting, "What are you doing? These are no longer yours to take. You gave them to me. This is theft and I will call security."

Danielle went over to his phone and pulled it from the wall, and then she grabbed the mobile phone from his desk and put it in her pocket. She would drop it into a flowerpot or bush on her way out. She said, "You won't be telling anyone anything."

She was not the same person she was two months ago. Neither of them was. They were tougher and wilier. They trusted the world less, and each other more; and most of all, they followed their gut instincts.

They rushed out the door, and the professor followed behind them shouting for security. If they were anywhere other than North England, they would have bound and gagged him, at the very least. It seemed that he, or the company he was sponsored by, had gotten wind of the cure. They had left the card at her parent's house in the off chance that he could intercept her and then steal the secrets of the cure.

Yes, probably he and the company would have made it available to the world, but they would have also taken the credit, and probably a very sizeable cut of the profits that he, the company, and its backers or enablers, intended to make. They had almost delivered the golden goose to the modern-day equivalent of the East India

Company.

Danielle and Sebastian ran through the halls and out onto the campus grounds, wary that at any minute security would be alerted and block their escape. Fortunately, they made it to the car without being intercepted and then went out onto the public streets; but where to go, and who to trust? Danielle felt as if she was back in a foreign country. Everything was different now, perhaps everyone would try to take advantage of the changed situation and take advantage of her. Or was this how it has always been, except in the past she, specifically, wasn't important enough and didn't have anything valuable enough worth stealing. Was this like the curse of oil, or the poison chalice.

They stopped the car down a side road so they could think and plan. Sebastian asked, "Where should we go?"

"I just don't know anymore," she replied. "I'm just scared that the drug companies have got their tentacles into everything."

"Including the politicians?" Sebastian asked.

"Especially the politicians," she said.

"OK..." then he thought for a moment and said, "Is there anyone you know from your past. Someone that you can really trust?"

She sat there with her mother's phone. She'd broken her own sometime during the journey, thus losing all of her contacts. She said, "There was an old professor I had; he had hooked me up with MSF. He is also connected with WHO. The last time I talked to him he was at the University of Edinburgh in Scotland. He had impeccable morals and used to teach about the dangers of the pharmaceutical and medical insurance industries. If anyone was incorruptible, then it would be him."

Scrolling through the Internet she found a contact number. She called and someone answered. It was a research assistant who collaborated with Professor Alec Stewart, the person she was chasing.

"Hello is Professor Stewart available?" she asked.

"Noo I'ma sewry, he's a noo h're, but eh be back dis ah'fernoon. Cana eh take'a message, ana say whooz calling," she said in a very thick Scottish accent.

"Ahh..." Danielle hesitated, "it's an old friend. Do you know if he has his phone on him. Perhaps I could give him a call?"

"I doona thunk eh be unswrin. Eh be oot wolk'n da Byrecleuck ne'a Bell Burn."

"Oh...," she said, but had no idea where that was. However, she did recall that he was an avid naturalist and enjoyed doing walks in the wilderness.

"So, this afternoon you say. He would be back in his office?" she enquired.

"Aye, afer four o'cloock."

"I will come to see him. Please tell him that Danielle is on her way, and to expect me around 5:30PM at the University."

"Noo, eh be a ome bar thern," she said. "Di ya noo is ome," she said.

"Oh yes, I do know his home. Out at Rosslyn?"

"Aye,"

"OK, I will see him there, please pass on the message."

"Aye, rit ya'r, byee then." She said and then hung up the phone.

The phone was on speaker, and Sebastian looked at her with a shocked face and then said in amazement, "And you understood all of that?"

"Understood what, the lady? Sure. You think that was difficult, you want to try understanding some of the Gaelic languages, or even some of the regional English dialects."

"I'm learning new things every day," he said. "I though you Brits just spoke one English," he said.

She just laughed and said, "Yeah, we do, most of the time."

It would be a five-hour journey, back up North via the Western side of the country. They would have a freeway all the way to Beattock, 75km over the Scottish border. Then they would travel a B-road through the hills and countryside for another hour to Rosslyn, a semi-rural town on the outskirts of greater Edinburgh.

They wasted no time departing and making good time on the freeway. Normally under such conditions they would see army movements and police, but apparently every resource had been relocated to the zombie barricade and beyond. There was also less commercial traffic on the roads. With basically all of the foreign markets closed, business only operated to supply the local markets. This also meant that there were no imports. No exotic fruit and vegetables, no electronics or raw materials. All that was available was what was produced locally. And in what was an increasingly globalized world, that meant that they would soon run out of the many cheap manufactured goods and raw materials that had arrived from overseas. If the population thought that leaving the EU was a blow, then this was many orders of magnitude worse.

After swapping over at a gas station Danielle now drove. Finally, they arrived in the pretty little town of Rosslyn. It wasn't a big town but there were still lots of narrow streets and lanes. She was winding her way through trying to find something that she recognized.

"Are we lost?" Sebastian asked.

"No, not lost. It's just that the last time I came out here it was daytime, and that was over a year ago. It all looks so different in the dark. I know it is down one of these lanes on the edge of town. His cottage looks out across the fields."

She jammed on the brakes and said, "That's it. I'm sure that is it. I remember the old stone fence and the garden. He loves his gardening."

She pulled the car to the side, even though it still almost blocked the narrow lane. Sebastian went to grab the bag, but she said, "No leave that here for now. Let's just make sure everything is OK before we show it to him. It is possible that even he has been compromised."

She wondered whether she was becoming too paranoid. Was it possible that the events of the last few weeks had scared her, and now she couldn't think straight? She turned to Sebastian and asked, "I'm not overreacting, am I?"

"What? No, definitely not. If anything, I think you are too trusting. But then again what else can we do? At some point we are going to have to trust someone."

They stood at the front door, in the dark, and she rang the doorbell. They could hear noise inside and then an elderly gentleman, wearing small round spectacles, opened the door.

"Hello," he said, straining his eyes to see into the dark, and then he thought to turn on the light.

"Hello, Professor Stewart. It's Danielle Wilson. I left a message with your assistant today saying that I would be calling in."

"Ah yes, come in please, I've been expecting you," he said as he turned and hobbled back into the lounge room."

Danielle asked, "Have you hurt yourself Professor?"

"Oh, I'm OK. Just overdid it when I was out walking today. I'm not as young and spritely as I once was. Just a bit of a gammy hip and knee. Probably all connected to something else that I will need to have looked at one day," he said as he lowered himself down into a recliner with a bit of a wince and groan.

Sebastian introduced himself, and as he shook his hand, he thought that if the Professor had a beard and a pointed hat, then he would be the spitting image of a fairytale wizard.

The Professor said, "After my assistant mentioned you, I thought I would make some enquiries. Apparently, there are some people looking for you, but they are not the police. Apparently, something to do with assaulting someone down in Birmingham and stealing something valuable from his office."

Danielle immediately protested, "That's not what happened! We didn't assault anyone, or steal anything…"

The professor put his hand up, cutting her off and said, "It's OK, I believe you. It's those damn drug companies, and their big money friends. It's turned into the Wild West, a free for all since the pandemic. I'm not sure if the government is even in control anymore; but then were they ever? I know that chap Smith. He is a bit of a rotter if you ask me. Would sell his grandmother if there was a dollar in it for him.

"However, my contacts also tell me that there was a general alert to the authorities to look out for the both of you. That included the police, navy, and everyone else. I'm surprised you hadn't been picked up already. You must have really been travelling under the radar. Anyway, it is not because you were in trouble, but because you had something valuable that you brought back from Africa. A cure for R24 I am told. Is this true?"

"Yes, yes, we have everything. The potion, the plants, and a whole preparation and treatment plan. We tried it on patients, and it has worked, both as a vaccine and as a cure to turn zombies back to human. Well at least those that had only recently turned. Of course, there is so much more to learn, and we have no idea if there are any side effects. But at least it is a start."

"Excellent. I always knew you would do well. You were an excellent student, and you have a good heart. You didn't sell your soul to the devil. Good on you."

Danielle blushed. It was probably the first time that Sebastian had seen her so humble. Then she asked the professor, "So, what should we do? I want to get the samples and information to the right people. Can you help us?"

"Oh yes, and we can do that right now; we

must do it now. There are offices of the World Health Organization, and the United Nations, which were recently set up in Edinburgh, just after the pandemic started. We should go there immediately. They will then disseminate the information to every functioning hospital and university in their network. They will make sure that no individual or company can monopolize, restrict, or profit from your discovery. Is that what you had in mind?"

"Yes, that is exactly what I was wanting. But I just want to correct you, it wasn't me. I didn't discover anything. It was an ancient recipe from the Sahara that got revealed to me by an old woman," she said with a sigh of relief.

He smiled and said, "That may be the case, but it was you that then took that potion, applied it, and did all of the treatment research. You must take credit for how it was applied and was able to save lives. Without you, it would still be hidden in the desert and the world would be none the wiser."

"Thank you," she said, and then squeezed Sebastian's hand.

"Well then, we had better get to it," he said as he climbed back up out of his chair and put on a tartan cap and a scarf. Then he said, "I presume you will be driving?"

During the drive to Edinburgh the professor made some phone calls, giving advanced notice that he was coming, and who was with him. When they arrived, it was more like Danielle had expected. They were escorted into the building by police, and once inside they were introduced to lots of people. Many were the top in their fields, and there were even some Nobel laureates. When the bag carrying the potion and specimens was placed on a large table in a conference room, the crowd immediately pulled everything out, and the cogs began to turn in the minds of the world's best scientist. It would take time to treat humanity, but now Danielle was sure that it would happen, and happen in an ethical and civilized way.

In the following days, a military aeroplane was organized to collect Rudy, and the other patients including the teenage girl who had made a full recovery, from Djanet. They would be flown to Edinburgh to be poked and prodded, and then it was Rudy's wish that he be resettled in Denmark. Samia travelled with him, and she would also follow him to Denmark. They would remain inseparable for the rest of their lives.

Danielle and Sebastian kept the boat. After a re-fit, the following summer they used it to travel from England to Denmark where they were reunited with Sophie and Andrea. Sophie had already had their first child, and another one would be on the way soon. Sophie was uniquely

Sophie, humanity's mother, and Andrea loved her for that.

They also heard from Mishka. She had become quite the baroness, assisting Mateo with his burgeoning coffee empire, and with an heir. Danielle and Sebastian planned to visit Andalusia again one day, and to not only see Mishka, Mateo and their child, but also the old Spanish man, his family, and the villa where they spent their honeymoon. Zombies were now extremely rare in Europe; thus, a driving holiday was not out of the question. And it was not like traffic was going to be a problem.

When Sebastian wasn't assisting Danielle in her medical clinic, he painted in oils the Tadrart Rouge, the Tuareg, and the Spanish countryside, from the thousands of photographs that he had taken. He also published a 'best-selling' coffee table book that documented their miraculous journey from the central Sahara to Scotland.

The book was considered the official record of how the pandemic was stopped and humanity was saved. Danielle featured heavily in the book, and there were many photos that he had taken candidly. He had been far more active than Dannielle had realized. Even before they were together, he photographed her. It wasn't creepy, it was just that he saw something special in her that he wanted to share with the world. There were several poignant photos where she looked toward the distant desert horizon, the Mediterranean Sea, and when she alone cried at Bernie's funeral, and then placed the first stone upon her grave. In the years to come Bernie would not be forgotten, but instead her grave would become a place of pilgrimage.

Danielle was awarded the Nobel Prize for medicine, and for services to humanity. She was also named Time's Person of the Year, albeit from the magazine's UK office. Yet despite the fame, she remained humble and worked regular hours in her clinic, and she did enjoy the cold wet grey domestic life. This was how it would be. At least until the next adventure.

The End

ABOUT THE AUTHOR

Mike graduated in Environmental and Political Science, then worked for government and industry writing on climate change, food, and energy security. His background is reflected in the 'hard' science of 'Deep Sahara' and the 'Dark Earth' Sci-Fi novel series. Even in the darkest of times Mike's stories offer humanity a glimmer of hope by exploring alternative societies and futures.